The Brass Bottle by F. Anstey

F. Anstey was the pseudonym of Thomas Anstey Guthrie who was born in Kensington, London on August 8th, 1856, to Augusta Amherst Austen, an organist and composer, and Thomas Anstey Guthrie., a prosperous military tailor

Anstey was educated at King's College School and then at Trinity Hall, Cambridge. Although his education was first rate Anstey could only manage a third-class degree; A Gentlemen's degree as it was euphemistically known.

In 1880 he was called to the bar. However this career path rapidly fell away in his desire to become an author. The successful publication of Vice Versa, in 1882, with the premise of a substitution of a father for his schoolboy son, made his name and reputation as a refreshing and original humorist.

The following year he published a rather more serious work, The Giant's Robe. Interestingly the story is about a plagiarist and Anstey was, ironically, accused of plagiarism in writing the work. Despite good reviews both he and his public knew that his writing career was to be that of a humorist.

In the following years he published prolifically beginning with; The Black Poodle (1884), The Tinted Venus (1885), A Fallen Idol (1886), and Baboo Jabberjee B.A. (1897).

Anstey worked not only as a novelist and short story writer but was also a valued member of the staff at the humorous Punch magazine, in which his voces populi and his parodies of a reciter's stock-piece (Burglar Bill) represent perhaps his best work.

In 1901, his successful farce, The Man from Blankleys, based on a story that originally appeared in Punch, was first produced on stage at the Prince of Wales Theatre, in London.

Anstey had become a writer, and a successful one at that, of many talents.

Many more of his stories were made into plays and films over the years. Others were simply taken for the premise alone, usually with no credit to the original author.

By the end of the First World War Anstey's original publications had slowed to a crawl and he seemed rather more interested in translating and publishing some works of Moliere.

Thomas Anstey Guthrie died of pneumonia on March 10th, 1934 in London.

His self-deprecating autobiography, A Long Retrospect, was published in 1936.

Index of Contents

CHAPTER I

HORACE VENTIMORE RECEIVES A COMMISSION

"This day six weeks—just six weeks ago!" Horace Ventimore said, half aloud, to himself, and pulled out his watch. "Half-past twelve—what was I doing at half-past twelve?"

As he sat at the window of his office in Great Cloister Street, Westminster, he made his thoughts travel back to a certain glorious morning in August which now seemed so remote and irrecoverable. At this precise time he was waiting on the balcony of the Hôtel de la Plage—the sole hostelry of St. Luc-en-Port, the tiny Normandy watering-place upon which, by some happy inspiration, he had lighted during a solitary cycling tour—waiting until She should appear.

He could see the whole scene: the tiny cove, with the violet shadow of the cliff sleeping on the green water; the swell of the waves lazily lapping against the diving-board from which he had plunged half an hour before; he remembered the long swim out to the buoy; the exhilarated anticipation with which he had dressed and climbed the steep path to the hotel terrace.

For was he not to pass the whole remainder of that blissful day in Sylvia Futvoye's society? Were they not to cycle together (there were, of course, others of the party—but they did not count), to cycle over to Veulettes, to picnic there under the cliff, and ride back—always together—in the sweet-scented dusk, over the slopes, between the poplars or the cornfields glowing golden against a sky of warm purple?

Now he saw himself going round to the gravelled courtyard in front of the hotel with a sudden dread of missing her. There was nothing there but the little low cart, with its canvas tilt which was to convey Professor Futvoye and his wife to the place of rendezvous.

There was Sylvia at last, distractingly fair and fresh in her cool pink blouse and cream-coloured skirt; how gracious and friendly and generally delightful she had been throughout that unforgettable day, which was supreme amongst others only a little less perfect, and all now fled for ever!

They had had drawbacks, it was true. Old Futvoye was perhaps the least bit of a bore at times, with his interminable disquisitions on Egyptian art and ancient Oriental character-writing, in which he seemed convinced that Horace must feel a perfervid interest, as, indeed, he thought it politic to affect. The Professor was a most learned archeologist, and positively bulged with information on his favourite subjects; but it is just possible that Horace might have been less curious concerning the distinction between Cuneiform and Aramean or Kufic and Arabic inscriptions if his informant had happened to be the father of anybody else. However, such insincerities as these are but so many evidences of sincerity.

So with self-tormenting ingenuity Horace conjured up various pictures from that Norman holiday of his: the little half-timbered cottages with their faded blue shutters and the rushes growing out of their thatch roofs; the spires of village churches gleaming above the bronze-green beeches; the bold headlands, their ochre and yellow cliffs contrasting grimly with the soft ridges of the turf above them; the tethered black-and-white cattle grazing peacefully against a background of lapis lazuli and malachite sea, and in every scene the sensation of Sylvia's near presence, the sound of her voice in his ears. And now?... He looked up from the papers and tracing-cloth on his desk, and round the small panelled room which served him as an office, at the framed plans and photographs, the set squares and T squares on the walls, and felt a dull resentment against his surroundings. From his window he commanded a cheerful view of a tall, mouldering wall, once part of the Abbey boundaries, surmounted by chevaux-de-frise, above whose rust-attenuated spikes some plane trees stretched their yellowing branches.

"She would have come to care for me," Horace's thoughts ran on, disjointedly. "I could have sworn that that last day of all—and her people didn't seem to object to me. Her mother asked me cordially enough to call on them when they were back in town. When I did—"

When he had called, there had been a difference—not an unusual sequel to an acquaintanceship begun in a Continental watering-place. It was difficult to define, but unmistakable—a certain formality and constraint on Mrs. Futvoye's part, and even on Sylvia's, which seemed intended to warn him that it is not every friendship that survives the Channel passage. So he had gone away sore at heart, but fully recognising that any advances in future must come from their side. They might ask him to dinner, or at least to call again; but more than a month had passed, and they had made no sign. No, it was all over; he must consider himself dropped.

"After all," he told himself, with a short and anything but mirthful laugh, "it's natural enough. Mrs. Futvoye has probably been making inquiries about my professional prospects. It's better as it is. What earthly chance have I got of marrying unless I can get work of my own? It's all I can do to keep myself decently. I've no right to dream of asking any one—to say nothing of Sylvia—to marry me. I should only be rushing into temptation if I saw any more of her. She's not for a poor beggar like me, who was born unlucky. Well, whining won't do any good—let's have a look at Beevor's latest performance."

He spread out a large coloured plan, in a corner of which appeared the name of "William Beevor, Architect," and began to study it in a spirit of anything but appreciation.

"Beevor gets on," he said to himself. "Heaven knows that I don't grudge him his success. He's a good fellow—though he does build architectural atrocities, and seem to like 'em. Who am I to give myself airs? He's successful—I'm not. Yet if I only had his opportunities, what wouldn't I make of them!"

Let it be said here that this was not the ordinary self-delusion of an incompetent. Ventimore really had talent above the average, with ideals and ambitions which might under better conditions have attained recognition and fulfilment before this.

But he was not quite energetic enough, besides being too proud, to push himself into notice, and hitherto he had met with persistent ill-luck.

So Horace had no other occupation now but to give Beevor, whose offices and clerk he shared, such slight assistance as he might require, and it was by no means cheering to feel that every year of this enforced semi-idleness left him further handicapped in the race for wealth and fame, for he had already passed his twenty-eighth birthday.

If Miss Sylvia Futvoye had indeed felt attracted towards him at one time it was not altogether incomprehensible. Horace Ventimore was not a model of manly beauty—models of manly beauty are rare out of novels, and seldom interesting in them; but his clear-cut, clean-shaven face possessed a certain distinction, and if there were faint satirical lines about the mouth, they were redeemed by the expression of the grey-blue eyes, which were remarkably frank and pleasant. He was well made, and tall enough to escape all danger of being described as short; fair-haired and pale, without being unhealthily pallid, in complexion, and he gave the impression of being a man who took life as it came, and whose sense of humour would serve as a lining for most clouds that might darken his horizon.

There was a rap at the door which communicated with Beevor's office, and Beevor himself, a florid, thick-set man, with small side-whiskers, burst in.

"I say, Ventimore, you didn't run off with the plans for that house I'm building at Larchmere, did you? Because—ah, I see you're looking over them. Sorry to deprive you, but—"

"Thanks, old fellow, take them, by all means. I've seen all I wanted to see."

"Well, I'm just off to Larchmere now. Want to be there to check the quantities, and there's my other house at Fittlesdon. I must go on afterwards and set it out, so I shall probably be away some days. I'm taking Harrison down, too. You won't be wanting him, eh?"

Ventimore laughed. "I can manage to do nothing without a clerk to help me. Your necessity is greater than mine. Here are the plans."

"I'm rather pleased with 'em myself, you know," said Beevor; "that roof ought to look well, eh? Good idea of mine lightening the slate with that ornamental tile-work along the top. You saw I put in one of your windows with just a trifling addition. I was almost inclined to keep both gables alike, as you suggested, but it struck me a little variety—one red brick and the other 'parged'—would be more out-of-the-way."

"Oh, much," agreed Ventimore, knowing that to disagree was useless.

"Not, mind you," continued Beevor, "that I believe in going in for too much originality in domestic architecture. The average client no more wants an original house than he wants an original hat; he wants something he won't feel a fool in. I've often thought, old man, that perhaps the reason why you haven't got on—you don't mind my speaking candidly, do you?"

"Not a bit," said Ventimore, cheerfully. "Candour's the cement of friendship. Dab it on."

"Well, I was only going to say that you do yourself no good by all those confoundedly unconventional ideas of yours. If you had your chance to-morrow, it's my belief you'd throw it away by insisting on some fantastic fad or other."

"These speculations are a trifle premature, considering that there doesn't seem the remotest prospect of my ever getting a chance at all."

"I got mine before I'd set up six months," said Beevor. "The great thing, however," he went on, with a flavour of personal application, "is to know how to use it when it does come. Well, I must be off if I mean to catch that one o'clock from Waterloo. You'll see to anything that may come in for me while I'm away, won't you, and let me know? Oh, by the way, the quantity surveyor has just sent in the quantities for that schoolroom at Woodford—do you mind running through them and seeing they're right? And there's the specification for the new wing at Tusculum Lodge—you might draft that some time when you've nothing else to do. You'll find all the papers on my desk. Thanks awfully, old chap."

And Beevor hurried back to his own room, where for the next few minutes he could be heard bustling Harrison, the clerk, to make haste; then a hansom was whistled for, there were footsteps down the old stairs, the sounds of a departing vehicle on the uneven stones, and after that silence and solitude.

It was not in Nature to avoid feeling a little envious. Beevor had work to do in the world: even if it chiefly consisted in profaning sylvan retreats by smug or pretentious villas, it was still work which entitled him to consideration and respect in the eyes of all right-minded persons.

And nobody believed in Horace; as yet he had never known the satisfaction of seeing the work of his brain realised in stone and brick and mortar; no building stood anywhere to bear testimony to his existence and capability long after he himself should have passed away.

It was not a profitable train of thought, and, to escape from it, he went into Beevor's room and fetched the documents he had mentioned—at least they would keep him occupied until it was time to go to his club and lunch. He had no sooner settled down to his calculations, however, when he heard a shuffling step on the landing, followed by a knock at Beevor's office-door. "More work for Beevor," he thought; "what luck the fellow has! I'd better go in and explain that he's just left town on business."

But on entering the adjoining room he heard the knocking repeated—this time at his own door; and hastening back to put an end to this somewhat undignified form of hide-and-seek, he discovered that this visitor at least was legitimately his, and was, in fact, no other than Professor Anthony Futvoye himself.

The Professor was standing in the doorway peering short-sightedly through his convex glasses, his head protruded from his loosely-fitting great-coat with an irresistible suggestion of an inquiring tortoise. To Horace his appearance was more welcome than that of the wealthiest client—for why should Sylvia's father take the trouble to pay him this visit unless he still wished to continue the acquaintanceship? It might even be that he was the bearer of some message or invitation.

So, although to an impartial eye the Professor might not seem the kind of elderly gentleman whose society would produce any wild degree of exhilaration, Horace was unfeignedly delighted to see him.

"Extremely kind of you to come and see me like this, sir," he said warmly, after establishing him in the solitary armchair reserved for hypothetical clients.

"Not at all. I'm afraid your visit to Cottesmore Gardens some time ago was somewhat of a disappointment."

"A disappointment?" echoed Horace, at a loss to know what was coming next.

"I refer to the fact—which possibly, however, escaped your notice"—explained the Professor, scratching his scanty patch of grizzled whisker with a touch of irascibility, "that I myself was not at home on that occasion."

"Indeed, I was greatly disappointed," said Horace, "though of course I know how much you are engaged. It's all the more good of you to spare time to drop in for a chat just now."

"I've not come to chat, Mr. Ventimore. I never chat. I wanted to see you about a matter which I thought you might be so obliging as to— But I observe you are busy—probably too busy to attend to such a small affair."

It was clear enough now; the Professor was going to build, and had decided—could it be at Sylvia's suggestion?—to entrust the work to him! But he contrived to subdue any self-betraying eagerness, and reply (as he could with perfect truth) that he had nothing on hand just then which he could not lay aside, and that if the Professor would let him know what he required, he would take it up at once.

"So much the better," said the Professor; "so much the better. Both my wife and daughter declared that it was making far too great a demand upon your good nature; but, as I told them, 'I am much mistaken,' I said, 'if Mr. Ventimore's practice is so extensive that he cannot leave it for one afternoon—'"

Evidently it was not a house. Could he be needed to escort them somewhere that afternoon? Even that was more than he had hoped for a few minutes since. He hastened to repeat that he was perfectly free that afternoon.

"In that case," said the Professor, beginning to fumble in all his pockets—was he searching for a note in Sylvia's handwriting?—"in that case, you will be conferring a real favour on me if you can make it convenient to attend a sale at Hammond's Auction Rooms in Covent Garden, and just bid for one or two articles on my behalf."

Whatever disappointment Ventimore felt, it may be said to his credit that he allowed no sign of it to appear. "Of course I'll go, with pleasure," he said, "if I can be of any use."

"I knew I shouldn't come to you in vain," said the Professor. "I remembered your wonderful good nature, sir, in accompanying my wife and daughter on all sorts of expeditions in the blazing hot weather we had at St. Luc—when you might have remained quietly at the hotel with me. Not that I should trouble you now, only I have to lunch at the Oriental Club, and I've an appointment afterwards to examine and report on a recently-discovered inscribed cylinder for the Museum, which will fully occupy the rest of the afternoon, so that it's physically impossible for me to go to Hammond's myself, and I strongly object to employing a broker when I can avoid it. Where did I put that catalogue?... Ah, here it is. This was sent to me by the executors of my old friend, General Collingham, who died the other day. I met him at Nakada when I was out excavating some years ago. He was something of a collector in his way, though he knew very little about it, and, of course, was taken in right and left. Most of his things are downright rubbish, but there are just a few lots that are worth securing, at a reasonable figure, by some one who knew what he was about."

"But, my dear Professor," remonstrated Horace, not relishing this responsibility, "I'm afraid I'm as likely as not to pick up some of the rubbish. I've no special knowledge of Oriental curios."

"At St. Luc," said the Professor, "you impressed me as having, for an amateur, an exceptionally accurate and comprehensive acquaintance with Egyptian and Arabian art from the earliest period." (If this were so, Horace could only feel with shame what a fearful humbug he must have been.) "However, I've no wish to lay too heavy a burden on you, and, as you will see from this catalogue, I have ticked off the lots in which I am chiefly interested, and made a note of the limit to which I am prepared to bid, so you'll have no difficulty."

"Very well," said Horace; "I'll go straight to Covent Garden, and slip out and get some lunch later on."

"Well, perhaps, if you don't mind. The lots I have marked seem to come on at rather frequent intervals, but don't let that consideration deter you from getting your lunch, and if you should miss anything by not being on the spot, why, it's of no consequence, though I don't say it mightn't be a pity. In any case, you won't forget to mark what each lot fetches, and perhaps you wouldn't mind dropping me a line when you return the catalogue—or stay, could you look in some time after dinner this evening, and let me know how you got on?—that would be better."

Horace thought it would be decidedly better, and undertook to call and render an account of his stewardship that evening. There remained the question of a deposit, should one or more of the lots be knocked down to him; and, as he was obliged to own that he had not so much as ten pounds about him at that particular moment, the Professor extracted a note for that amount from his case, and handed it to him with the air of a benevolent person relieving a deserving object. "Don't exceed my limits," he said, "for I can't afford more just now; and mind you give Hammond your own name, not mine. If the dealers get to know I'm after the things, they'll run you up. And now, I don't think I need detain you any longer, especially as time is running on. I'm sure I can trust you to do the best you can for me. Till this evening, then."

A few minutes later Horace was driving up to Covent Garden behind the best-looking horse he could pick out.

The Professor might have required from him rather more than was strictly justified by their acquaintanceship, and taken his acquiescence too much as a matter of course—but what of that? After all, he was Sylvia's parent.

"Even with my luck," he was thinking, "I ought to succeed in getting at least one or two of the lots he's marked; and if I can only please him, something may come of it."

And in this sanguine mood Horace entered Messrs. Hammond's well-known auction rooms.

CHAPTER II

A CHEAP LOT

In spite of the fact that it was the luncheon hour when Ventimore reached Hammond's Auction Rooms, he found the big, skylighted gallery where the sale of the furniture and effects of the late General Collingham was proceeding crowded to a degree which showed that the deceased officer had some reputation as a connoisseur.

The narrow green baize tables below the auctioneer's rostrum were occupied by professional dealers, one or two of them women, who sat, paper and pencil in hand, with much the same air of apparent apathy and real vigilance that may be noticed in the Casino at Monte Carlo. Around them stood a decorous and businesslike crowd, mostly dealers, of various types. On a magisterial-looking bench sat the auctioneer, conducting the sale with a judicial impartiality and dignity which forbade him, even in his most laudatory comments, the faintest accent of enthusiasm.

The October sunshine, striking through the glazed roof, re-gilded the tarnished gas-stars, and suffused the dusty atmosphere with palest gold. But somehow the utter absence of excitement in the crowd, the calm, methodical tone of the auctioneer, and the occasional mournful cry of "Lot here, gentlemen!" from the porter when any article was too large to move, all served to depress Ventimore's usually mercurial spirits.

For all Horace knew, the collection as a whole might be of little value, but it very soon became clear that others besides Professor Futvoye had singled out such gems as there were, also that the Professor had considerably under-rated the prices they were likely to fetch.

Ventimore made his bids with all possible discretion, but time after time he found the competition for some perforated mosque lantern, engraved ewer, or ancient porcelain tile so great that his limit was soon reached, and his sole consolation was that the article eventually changed hands for sums which were very nearly double the Professor's estimate.

Several dealers and brokers, despairing of a bargain that day, left, murmuring profanities; most of those who remained ceased to take a serious interest in the proceedings, and consoled themselves with cheap witticisms at every favourable occasion.

The sale dragged slowly on, and, what with continual disappointment and want of food, Horace began to feel so weary that he was glad, as the crowd thinned, to get a seat at one of the green baize tables, by which time the skylights had already changed from livid grey to slate colour in the deepening dusk.

A couple of meek Burmese Buddhas had just been put up, and bore the indignity of being knocked down for nine-and-sixpence the pair with dreamy, inscrutable simpers; Horace only waited for the final lot marked by the Professor—an old Persian copper bowl, inlaid with silver and engraved round the rim with an inscription from Hafiz.

The limit to which he was authorised to go was two pounds ten; but, so desperately anxious was Ventimore not to return empty-handed, that he had made up his mind to bid an extra sovereign if necessary, and say nothing about it.

However, the bowl was put up, and the bidding soon rose to three pounds ten, four pounds, four pounds ten, five pounds, five guineas, for which last sum it was acquired by a bearded man on Horace's right, who immediately began to regard his purchase with a more indulgent eye.

Ventimore had done his best, and failed; there was no reason now why he should stay a moment longer—and yet he sat on, from sheer fatigue and disinclination to move.

"Now we come to Lot 254, gentlemen," he heard the auctioneer saying, mechanically; "a capital Egyptian mummy-case in fine con— No, I beg pardon, I'm wrong. This is an article which by some mistake has been omitted from the catalogue, though it ought to have been in it. Everything on sale to-day, gentlemen, belonged to the late General Collingham. We'll call this No. 253a. Antique brass bottle. Very curious."

One of the porters carried the bottle in between the tables, and set it down before the dealers at the farther end with a tired nonchalance.

It was an old, squat, pot-bellied vessel, about two feet high, with a long thick neck, the mouth of which was closed by a sort of metal stopper or cap; there was no visible decoration on its sides, which were rough and pitted by some incrustation that had formed on them, and been partially scraped off. As a piece of bric-à-brac it certainly possessed few attractions, and there was a marked tendency to "guy" it among the more frivolous brethren.

"What do you call this, sir?" inquired one of the auctioneer, with the manner of a cheeky boy trying to get a rise out of his form-master. "Is it as 'unique' as the others?"

"You're as well able to judge as I am," was the guarded reply. "Any one can see for himself it's not modern rubbish."

"Make a pretty little ornament for the mantelpiece!" remarked a wag.

"Is the top made to unscrew, or what, sir?" asked a third. "Seems fixed on pretty tight."

"I can't say. Probably it has not been removed for some time."

"It's a goodish weight," said the chief humorist, after handling it. "What's inside of it, sir—sardines?"

"I don't represent it as having anything inside it," said the auctioneer. "If you want to know my opinion, I think there's money in it."

"'Ow much?"

"Don't misunderstand me, gentlemen. When I say I consider there's money in it, I'm not alluding to its contents. I've no reason to believe that it contains anything. I'm merely suggesting the thing itself may be worth more than it looks."

"Ah, it might be that without 'urting itself!"

"Well, well, don't let us waste time. Look upon it as a pure speculation, and make me an offer for it, some of you. Come."

"Tuppence-'ap'ny!" cried the comic man, affecting to brace himself for a mighty effort.

"Pray be serious, gentlemen. We want to get on, you know. Anything to make a start. Five shillings? It's not the value of the metal, but I'll take the bid. Six. Look at it well. It's not an article you come across every day of your lives."

The bottle was still being passed round with disrespectful raps and slaps, and it had now come to Ventimore's right-hand neighbour, who scrutinised it carefully, but made no bid.

"That's all right, you know," he whispered in Horace's ear. "That's good stuff, that is. If I was you, I'd 'ave that."

"Seven shillings—eight—nine bid for it over there in the corner," said the auctioneer.

"If you think it's so good, why don't you have it yourself?" Horace asked his neighbour.

"Me? Oh, well, it ain't exactly in my line, and getting this last lot pretty near cleaned me out. I've done for to-day, I 'ave. All the same, it is a curiosity; dunno as I've seen a brass vawse just that shape before, and it's genuine old, though all these fellers are too ignorant to know the value of it. So I don't mind giving you the tip."

Horace rose, the better to examine the top. As far as he could make out in the flickering light of one of the gas-stars, which the auctioneer had just ordered to be lit, there were half-erased scratches and triangular marks on the cap that might possibly be an inscription. If so, might there not be the means here of regaining the Professor's favour, which he felt that, as it was, he should probably forfeit, justly or not, by his ill-success?

He could hardly spend the Professor's money on it, since it was not in the catalogue, and he had no authority to bid for it, but he had a few shillings of his own to spare. Why not bid for it on his own account as long as he could afford to do so? If he were outbid, as usual, it would not particularly matter.

"Thirteen shillings," the auctioneer was saying, in his dispassionate tones. Horace caught his eye, and slightly raised his catalogue, while another man nodded at the same time. "Fourteen in two places." Horace raised his catalogue again. "I won't go beyond fifteen," he thought.

"Fifteen. It's against you, sir. Any advance on fifteen? Sixteen—this very quaint old Oriental bottle going for only sixteen shillings.

"After all," thought Horace, "I don't mind anything under a pound for it." And he bid seventeen shillings. "Eighteen," cried his rival, a short, cheery, cherub-faced little dealer, whose neighbours adjured him to "sit quiet like a good little boy and not waste his pocket-money."

"Nineteen!" said Horace. "Pound!" answered the cherubic man.

"A pound only bid for this grand brass vessel," said the auctioneer, indifferently. "All done at a pound?"

Horace thought another shilling or two would not ruin him, and nodded.

"A guinea. For the last time. You'll lose it, sir," said the auctioneer to the little man.

"Go on, Tommy. Don't you be beat. Spring another bob on it, Tommy," his friends advised him ironically; but Tommy shook his head, with the air of a man who knows when to draw the line. "One guinea—and that's not half its value! Gentleman on my left," said the auctioneer, more in sorrow than in anger—and the brass bottle became Ventimore's property.

He paid for it, and, since he could hardly walk home nursing a large metal bottle without attracting an inconvenient amount of attention, directed that it should be sent to his lodgings at Vincent Square.

But when he was out in the fresh air, walking westward to his club, he found himself wondering more and more what could have possessed him to throw away a guinea—when he had few enough for legitimate expenses—on an article of such exceedingly problematical value.

CHAPTER III

AN UNEXPECTED OPENING

Ventimore made his way to Cottesmore Gardens that evening in a highly inconsistent, not to say chaotic, state of mind. The thought that he would presently see Sylvia again made his blood course quicker, while he was fully determined to say no more to her than civility demanded.

At one moment he was blessing Professor Futvoye for his happy thought in making use of him; at another he was bitterly recognising that it would have been better for his peace of mind if he had been left alone. Sylvia and her mother had no desire to see more of him; if they had, they would have asked him to come before this. No doubt they would tolerate him now for the Professor's sake; but who would not rather be ignored than tolerated?

The more often he saw Sylvia the more she would make his heart ache with vain longing—whereas he was getting almost reconciled to her indifference; he would very soon be cured if he didn't see her.

Why should he see her? He need not go in at all. He had merely to leave the catalogue with his compliments, and the Professor would learn all he wanted to know.

On second thoughts he must go in—if only to return the bank-note. But he would ask to see the Professor in private. Most probably he would not be invited to join his wife and daughter, but if he were, he could make some excuse. They might think it a little odd—a little discourteous, perhaps; but they would be too relieved to care much about that.

When he got to Cottesmore Gardens, and was actually at the door of the Futvoyes' house, one of the neatest and demurest in that retired and irreproachable quarter, he began to feel a craven hope that the Professor might be out, in which case he need only leave the catalogue and write a letter when he got home, reporting his non-success at the sale, and returning the note.

And, as it happened, the Professor was out, and Horace was not so glad as he thought he should be. The maid told him that the ladies were in the drawing-room, and seemed to take it for granted that he was coming in, so he had himself announced. He would not stay long—just long enough to explain his business there, and make it clear that he had no wish to force his acquaintance upon them. He found Mrs. Futvoye in the farther part of the pretty double drawing-room, writing letters, and Sylvia, more dazzlingly fair than ever in some sort of gauzy black frock with a heliotrope sash and a bunch of Parma violets on her breast, was comfortably established with a book in the front room, and seemed surprised, if not resentful, at having to disturb herself.

"I must apologise," he began, with an involuntary stiffness, "for calling at this very unceremonious time; but the fact is, the Professor—"

"I know all about it," interrupted Mrs. Futvoye, brusquely, while her shrewd, light-grey eyes took him in with a cool stare that was humorously observant without being aggressive. "We heard how shamefully my husband abused your good-nature. Really, it was too bad of him to ask a busy man like you to put aside his work and go and spend a whole day at that stupid auction!"

"Oh, I'd nothing particular to do. I can't call myself a busy man—unfortunately," said Horace, with that frankness which scorns to conceal what other people know perfectly well already.

"Ah, well, it's very nice of you to make light of it; but he ought not to have done it—after so short an acquaintance, too. And to make it worse, he has had to go out unexpectedly this evening, but he'll be back before very long if you don't mind waiting."

"There's really no need to wait," said Horace, "because this catalogue will tell him everything, and, as the particular things he wanted went for much more than he thought, I wasn't able to get any of them."

"I'm sure I'm very glad of it," said Mrs. Futvoye, "for his study is crammed with odds and ends as it is, and I don't want the whole house to look like a museum or an antiquity shop. I'd all the trouble in the world to persuade him that a great gaudy gilded mummy-case was not quite the thing for a drawing-room. But, please sit down, Mr. Ventimore."

"Thanks," stammered Horace, "but—but I mustn't stay. If you will tell the Professor how sorry I was to miss him, and—and give him back this note which he left with me to cover any deposit, I—I won't interrupt you any longer."

He was, as a rule, imperturbable in most social emergencies, but just now he was seized with a wild desire to escape, which, to his infinite mortification, made him behave like a shy schoolboy.

"Nonsense!" said Mrs. Futvoye; "I am sure my husband would be most annoyed if we didn't keep you till he came."

"I really ought to go," he declared, wistfully enough.

"We mustn't tease Mr. Ventimore to stay, mother, when he so evidently wants to go," said Sylvia, cruelly.

"Well, I won't detain you—at least, not long. I wonder if you would mind posting a letter for me as you pass the pillar-box? I've almost finished it, and it ought to go to-night, and my maid Jessie has such a bad cold I really don't like sending her out with it."

It would have been impossible to refuse to stay after that—even if he had wished. It would only be for a few minutes. Sylvia might spare him that much of her time. He should not trouble her again. So Mrs. Futvoye went back to her bureau, and Sylvia and he were practically alone.

She had taken a seat not far from his, and made a few constrained remarks, obviously out of sheer civility. He returned mechanical replies, with a dreary wonder whether this could really be the girl who had talked to him with such charming friendliness and confidence only a few weeks ago in Normandy.

And the worst of it was, she was looking more bewitching than ever; her slim arms gleaming through the black lace of her sleeves, and the gold threads in her soft masses of chestnut hair sparkling in the light of the shaded lamp behind her. The slight contraction of her eyebrows and the mutinous downward curve of her mouth seemed expressive of boredom.

"What a dreadfully long time mamma is over that letter!" she said at last. "I think I'd better go and hurry her up."

"Please don't—unless you are particularly anxious to get rid of me."

"I thought you seemed particularly anxious to escape," she said coldly. "And, as a family, we have certainly taken up quite enough of your time for one day."

"That is not the way you used to talk at St. Luc!" he said.

"At St. Luc? Perhaps not. But in London everything is so different, you see."

"Very different."

"When one meets people abroad who—who seem at all inclined to be sociable," she continued, "one is so apt to think them pleasanter than they really are. Then one meets them again, and—and wonders what one ever saw to like in them. And it's no use pretending one feels the same, because they generally understand sooner or later. Don't you find that?"

"I do, indeed," he said, wincing, "though I don't know what I've done to deserve that you should tell me so!"

"Oh, I was not blaming you. You have been most angelic. I can't think how papa could have expected you to take all that trouble for him—still, you did, though you must have simply hated it."

"But, good heavens! don't you know I should be only too delighted to be of the least service to him—or to any of you?"

"You looked anything but delighted when you came in just now; you looked as if your one idea was to get it over as soon as you could. You know perfectly well you're longing now for mother to finish her letter and set you free. Do you really think I can't see that?"

"If all that is true, or partly true," said Horace, "can't you guess why?"

"I guessed how it was when you called here first that afternoon. Mamma had asked you to, and you thought you might as well be civil; perhaps you really did think it would be pleasant to see us again—but it wasn't the same thing. Oh, I saw it in your face directly—you became conventional and distant and horrid, and it made me horrid too; and you went away determined that you wouldn't see any more of us than you could help. That's why I was so furious when I heard that papa had been to see you, and with such an object."

All this was so near the truth, and yet missed it with such perverse ingenuity, that Horace felt bound to put himself right.

"Perhaps I ought to leave things as they are," he said, "but I can't. It's no earthly use, I know; but may I tell you why it really was painful to me to meet you again? I thought you were changed, that you wished to forget, and wished me to forget—only I can't—that we had been friends for a short time. And though I never blamed you—it was natural enough—it hit me pretty hard—so hard that I didn't feel anxious to repeat the experience."

"Did it hit you hard?" said Sylvia, softly. "Perhaps I minded too, just a very little. However," she added, with a sudden smile, that made two enchanting dimples in her cheeks, "it only shows how much more sensible it is to have things out. Now perhaps you won't persist in keeping away from us?"

"I believe," said Horace, gloomily, still determined not to let any direct avowal pass his lips, "it would be best that I should keep away."

Her half-closed eyes shone through their long lashes; the violets on her breast rose and fell. "I don't think I understand," she said, in a tone that was both hurt and offended.

There is a pleasure in yielding to some temptations that more than compensates for the pain of any previous resistance. Come what might, he was not going to be misunderstood any longer.

"If I must tell you," he said, "I've fallen desperately, hopelessly, in love with you. Now you know the reason."

"It doesn't seem a very good reason for wanting to go away and never see me again. Does it?"

"Not when I've no right to speak to you of love?"

"But you've done that!"

"I know," he said penitently; "I couldn't help it. But I never meant to. It slipped out. I quite understand how hopeless it is."

"Of course, if you are so sure as all that, you are quite right not to try."

"Sylvia! You can't mean that—that you do care, after all?"

"Didn't you really see?" she said, with a low, happy laugh. "How stupid of you! And how dear!"

He caught her hand, which she allowed to rest contentedly in his. "Oh, Sylvia! Then you do—you do! But, my God, what a selfish brute I am! For we can't marry. It may be years before I can ask you to come to me. You father and mother wouldn't hear of your being engaged to me."

"Need they hear of it just yet, Horace?"

"Yes, they must. I should feel a cur if I didn't tell your mother, at all events."

"Then you shan't feel a cur, for we'll go and tell her together." And Sylvia rose and went into the farther room, and put her arms round her mother's neck. "Mother darling," she said, in a half whisper, "it's really all your fault for writing such very long letters, but—but—we don't exactly know how we came to do it—but Horace and I have got engaged somehow. You aren't very angry, are you?"

"I think you're both extremely foolish," said Mrs. Futvoye, as she extricated herself from Sylvia's arms and turned to face Horace. "From all I hear, Mr. Ventimore, you're not in a position to marry at present."

"Unfortunately, no" said Horace; "I'm making nothing as yet. But my chance must come some day. I don't ask you to give me Sylvia till then."

"And you know you like Horace, mother!" pleaded Sylvia. "And I'm ready to wait for him, any time. Nothing will induce me to give him up, and I shall never, never care for anybody else. So you see you may just as well give us your consent!"

"I'm afraid I've been to blame," said Mrs. Futvoye. "I ought to have foreseen this at St. Luc. Sylvia is our only child, Mr. Ventimore, and I would far rather see her happily married than making what is called a 'grand match.' Still, this really does seem rather hopeless. I am quite sure her father would never approve of it. Indeed, it must not be mentioned to him—he would only be irritated."

"So long as you are not against us," said Horace, "you won't forbid me to see her?"

"I believe I ought to," said Mrs. Futvoye; "but I don't object to your coming here occasionally, as an ordinary visitor. Only understand this—until you can prove to my husband's satisfaction that you are able to support Sylvia in the manner she has been accustomed to, there must be no formal engagement. I think I am entitled to ask that of you."

She was so clearly within her rights, and so much more indulgent than Horace had expected—for he had always considered her an unsentimental and rather worldly woman—that he accepted her conditions almost gratefully. After all, it was enough for him that Sylvia returned his love, and that he should be allowed to see her from time to time.

"It's rather a pity," said Sylvia, meditatively, a little later, when her mother had gone back to her letter-writing, and she and Horace were discussing the future; "it's rather a pity that you didn't manage to get something at that sale. It might have helped you with papa."

"Well, I did get something on my own account," he said, "though I don't know whether it is likely to do me any good with your father." And he told her how he had come to acquire the brass bottle.

"And you actually gave a guinea for it?" said Sylvia, "when you could probably get exactly the same thing, only better, at Liberty's for about seven-and-sixpence! Nothing of that sort has any charms for papa, unless it's dirty and dingy and centuries old."

"This looks all that. I only bought it because, though it wasn't down on the catalogue, I had a fancy that it might interest the Professor."

"Oh!" cried Sylvia, clasping her pretty hands, "if only it does, Horace! If it turns out to be tremendously rare and valuable! I do believe dad would be so delighted that he'd consent to anything. Ah, that's his step outside ... he's letting himself in. Now mind you don't forget to tell him about that bottle."

The Professor did not seem in the sweetest of humours as he entered the drawing-room. "Sorry I was obliged to be from home, and there was nobody but my wife and daughter here to entertain you. But I am glad you stayed—yes, I'm rather glad you stayed."

"So am I, sir," said Horace, and proceeded to give his account of the sale, which did not serve to improve the Professor's temper. He thrust out his under lip at certain items in the catalogue. "I wish I'd gone myself," he said; "that bowl, a really fine example of sixteenth-century Persian work, going for only five guineas! I'd willingly have given ten for it. There, there, I thought I could have depended on you to use your judgment better than that!"

"If you remember, sir, you strictly limited me to the sums you marked."

"Nothing of the sort," said the Professor, testily; "my marginal notes were merely intended as indications, no more. You might have known that if you had secured one of the things at any price I should have approved."

Horace had no grounds for knowing anything of the kind, and much reason for believing the contrary, but he saw no use in arguing the matter further, and merely said he was sorry to have misunderstood.

"No doubt the fault was mine," said the Professor, in a tone that implied the opposite. "Still, making every allowance for inexperience in these matters, I should have thought it impossible for any one to spend a whole day bidding at a place like Hammond's without even securing a single article."

"But, dad," put in Sylvia, "Mr. Ventimore did get one thing—on his own account. It's a brass bottle, not down in the catalogue, but he thinks it may be worth something perhaps. And he'd very much like to have your opinion."

"Tchah!" said the Professor. "Some modern bazaar work, most probably. He'd better have kept his money. What was this bottle of yours like, now, eh?"

Horace described it.

"H'm. Seems to be what the Arabs call a 'kum-kum,' probably used as a sprinkler, or to hold rose-water. Hundreds of 'em about," commented the Professor, crustily.

"It had a lid, riveted or soldered on," said Horace; "the general shape was something like this ..." And he made a rapid sketch from memory, which the Professor took reluctantly, and then adjusted his glasses with some increase of interest.

"Ha—the form is antique, certainly. And the top hermetically fastened, eh? That looks as if it might contain something."

"You don't think it has a genie inside, like the sealed jar the fisherman found in the 'Arabian Nights'?" cried Sylvia. "What fun if it had!"

"By genie, I presume you mean a Jinnee, which is the more correct and scholarly term," said the Professor. "Female, Jinneeyeh, and plural Jinn. No, I do not contemplate that as a probable contingency. But it is not quite impossible that a vessel closed as Mr. Ventimore describes may have been designed as a receptacle for papyri or other records of archæological interest, which may be still in preservation. I should recommend you, sir, to use the greatest precaution in removing the lid—don't expose the documents, if any, too suddenly to the outer air, and it would be better if you did not handle them yourself. I shall be rather curious to hear whether it really does contain anything, and if so, what."

"I will open it as carefully as possible," said Horace, "and whatever it may contain, you may rely upon my letting you know at once."

He left shortly afterwards, encouraged by the radiant trust in Sylvia's eyes, and thrilled by the secret pressure of her hand at parting.

He had been amply repaid for all the hours he had spent in the close sale-room. His luck had turned at last: he was going to succeed; he felt it in the air, as if he were already fanned by Fortune's pinions.

Still thinking of Sylvia, he let himself into the semi-detached, old-fashioned house on the north side of Vincent Square, where he had lodged for some years. It was nearly twelve o'clock, and his landlady, Mrs. Rapkin, and her husband had already gone to bed.

Ventimore went up to his sitting-room, a comfortable apartment with two long windows opening on to a trellised verandah and balcony—a room which, as he had furnished and decorated it himself to suit his own tastes, had none of the depressing ugliness of typical lodgings.

It was quite dark, for the season was too mild for a fire, and he had to grope for the matches before he could light his lamp. After he had done so and turned up the wicks, the first object he saw was the bulbous, long-necked jar which he had bought that afternoon, and which now stood on the stained boards near the mantelpiece. It had been delivered with unusual promptitude!

Somehow he felt a sort of repulsion at the sight of it. "It's a beastlier-looking object than I thought," he said to himself disgustedly. "A chimney-pot would be about as decorative and appropriate in my room. What a thundering ass I was to waste a guinea on it! I wonder if there really is anything inside it. It is so infernally ugly that it ought to be useful. The Professor seemed to fancy it might hold documents, and he ought to know. Anyway, I'll find out before I turn in."

He grasped it by its long, thick neck, and tried to twist the cap off; but it remained firm, which was not surprising, seeing that it was thickly coated with a lava-like crust.

"I must get some of that off first, and then try again," he decided; and after foraging downstairs, he returned with a hammer and chisel, with which he chipped away the crust till the line of the cap was revealed, and an uncouth metal knob that seemed to be a catch.

This he tapped sharply for some time, and again attempted to wrench off the lid. Then he gripped the vessel between his knees and put forth all his strength, while the bottle seemed to rock and heave under him in sympathy. The cap was beginning to give way, very slightly; one last wrench—and it came off in his hand with such suddenness that he was flung violently backwards, and hit the back of his head smartly against an angle of the wainscot.

He had a vague impression of the bottle lying on its side, with dense volumes of hissing, black smoke pouring out of its mouth and towering up in a gigantic column to the ceiling; he was conscious, too, of a pungent and peculiarly overpowering perfume. "I've got hold of some sort of infernal machine," he thought, "and I shall be all over the square in less than a second!" And, just as he arrived at this cheerful conclusion, he lost consciousness altogether.

He could not have been unconscious for more than a few seconds, for when he opened his eyes the room was still thick with smoke, through which he dimly discerned the figure of a stranger, who seemed of abnormal and almost colossal height. But this must have been an optical illusion caused by the magnifying effects of the smoke; for, as it cleared, his visitor proved to be of no more than ordinary stature. He was elderly, and, indeed, venerable of appearance, and wore an Eastern robe and head-dress of a dark-green hue. He stood there with uplifted hands, uttering something in a loud tone and a language unknown to Horace.

Ventimore, being still somewhat dazed, felt no surprise at seeing him. Mrs. Rapkin must have let her second floor at last—to some Oriental. He would have preferred an Englishman as a fellow-lodger, but this foreigner must have noticed the smoke and rushed in to offer assistance, which was both neighbourly and plucky of him.

"Awfully good of you to come in, sir," he said, as he scrambled to his feet. "I don't know what's happened exactly, but there's no harm done. I'm only a trifle shaken, that's all. By the way, I suppose you can speak English?"

"Assuredly I can speak so as to be understood by all whom I address," answered the stranger.

"Dost thou not understand my speech?"

"Perfectly, now," said Horace. "But you made a remark just now which I didn't follow—would you mind repeating it?"

"I said: 'Repentance, O Prophet of God! I will not return to the like conduct ever.'"

"Ah," said Horace. "I dare say you were rather startled. So was I when I opened that bottle."

"Tell me—was it indeed thy hand that removed the seal, O young man of kindness and good works?"

"I certainly did open it," said Ventimore, "though I don't know where the kindness comes in—for I've no notion what was inside the thing."

"I was inside it," said the stranger, calmly.

CHAPTER IV

AT LARGE

"So you were inside that bottle, were you?" said Horace, blandly. "How singular!" He began to realise that he had to deal with an Oriental lunatic, and must humour him to some extent. Fortunately he did not seem at all dangerous, though undeniably eccentric-looking. His hair fell in disorderly profusion from under his high turban about his cheeks, which were of a uniform pale rhubarb tint; his grey beard streamed out in three thin strands, and his long, narrow eyes, opal in hue, and set rather wide apart and at a slight angle, had a curious expression, part slyness and part childlike simplicity.

"Dost thou doubt that I speak truth? I tell thee that I have been confined in that accursed vessel for countless centuries—how long, I know not, for it is beyond calculation."

"I should hardly have thought from your appearance, sir, that you had been so many years in bottle as all that," said Horace, politely, "but it's certainly time you had a change. May I, if it isn't indiscreet, ask how you came into such a very uncomfortable position? But probably you have forgotten by this time."

"Forgotten!" said the other, with a sombre red glow in his opal eyes. "Wisely was it written: 'Let him that desireth oblivion confer benefits—but the memory of an injury endureth for ever.' I forget neither benefits nor injuries."

"An old gentleman with a grievance," thought Ventimore. "And mad into the bargain. Nice person to have staying in the same house with one!"

"Know, O best of mankind," continued the stranger, "that he who now addresses thee is Fakrash-el-Aamash, one of the Green Jinn. And I dwelt in the Palace of the Mountain of the Clouds above the City of Babel in the Garden of Irem, which thou doubtless knowest by repute?"

"I fancy I have heard of it," said Horace, as if it were an address in the Court Directory. "Delightful neighbourhood."

"I had a kinswoman, Bedeea-el-Jemal, who possessed incomparable beauty and manifold accomplishments. And seeing that, though a Jinneeyeh, she was of the believing Jinn, I despatched messengers to Suleyman the Great, the son of Daood, offering him her hand in marriage. But a certain Jarjarees, the son of Rejmoos, the son of Iblees—may he be for ever accursed!—looked with favour upon the maiden, and, going secretly unto Suleyman, persuaded him that I was preparing a crafty snare for the King's undoing."

"And, of course, you never thought of such a thing?" said Ventimore.

"By a venomous tongue the fairest motives may be rendered foul," was the somewhat evasive reply. "Thus it came to pass that Suleyman—on whom be peace!—listened unto the voice of Jarjarees and refused to receive the maiden. Moreover, he commanded that I should be seized and imprisoned in a bottle of brass and cast into the Sea of El-Karkar, there to abide the Day of Doom."

"Too bad—really too bad!" murmured Horace, in a tone that he could only hope was sufficiently sympathetic.

"But now, by thy means, O thou of noble ancestors and gentle disposition, my deliverance hath been accomplished; and if I were to serve thee for a thousand years, regarding nothing else, even thus could I not requite thee, and my so doing would be a small thing according to thy desserts!"

"Pray don't mention it," said Horace; "only too pleased if I've been of any use to you."

"In the sky it is written upon the pages of the air: 'He who doth kind actions shall experience the like.' Am I not an Efreet of the Jinn? Demand, therefore, and thou shalt receive."

"Poor old chap!" thought Horace, "he's very cracked indeed. He'll be wanting to give me a present of some sort soon—and of course I can't have that.... My dear Mr. Fakrash," he said aloud, "I've done nothing—nothing at all—and if I had, I couldn't possibly accept any reward for it."

"What are thy names, and what calling dost thou follow?"

"I ought to have introduced myself before—let me give you my card;" and Ventimore gave him one, which the other took and placed in his girdle. "That's my business address. I'm an architect, if you know what that is—a man who builds houses and churches—mosques, you know—in fact, anything, when he can get it to build."

"A useful calling indeed—and one to be rewarded with fine gold."

"In my case," Horace confessed, "the reward has been too fine to be perceived. In other words, I've never been rewarded, because I've never yet had the luck to get a client."

"And what is this client of whom thou speakest?"

"Oh, well, some well-to-do merchant who wants a house built for him and doesn't care how much he spends on it. There must be lots of them about—but they never seem to come in my direction."

"Grant me a period of delay, and, if it be possible, I will procure thee such a client."

Horace could not help thinking that any recommendation from such a quarter would hardly carry much weight; but, as the poor old man evidently imagined himself under an obligation, which he was anxious to discharge, it would have been unkind to throw cold water on his good intentions.

"My dear sir," he said lightly, "if you should come across that particular type of client, and can contrive to impress him with the belief that I'm just the architect he's looking out for—which, between ourselves, I am, though nobody's discovered it yet—if you can get him to come to me, you will do me the very greatest service I could ever hope for. But don't give yourself any trouble over it."

"It will be one of the easiest things that can be," said his visitor, "that is" (and here a shade of rather pathetic doubt crossed his face) "provided that anything of my former power yet remains unto me."

"Well, never mind, sir," said Horace; "if you can't, I shall take the will for the deed."

"First of all, it will be prudent to learn where Suleyman is, that I may humble myself before him and make my peace."

"Yes," said Horace, gently, "I would. I should make a point of that, sir. Not now, you know. He might be in bed. To-morrow morning."

"This is a strange place that I am in, and I know not yet in what direction I should seek him. But till I have found him, and justified myself in his sight, and had my revenge upon Jarjarees, mine enemy, I shall know no rest."

"Well, but go to bed now, like a sensible old chap," said Horace, soothingly, anxious to prevent this poor demented Asiatic from falling into the hands of the police. "Plenty of time to go and call on Suleyman to-morrow."

"I will search for him, even unto the uttermost ends of the earth!"

"That's right—you're sure to find him in one of them. Only, don't you see, it's no use starting to-night—the last trains have gone long ago." As he spoke, the night wind bore across the square the sound of Big Ben striking the quarters in Westminster Clock Tower, and then, after a pause, the solemn boom that announced the first of the small hours. "To-morrow," thought Ventimore, "I'll speak to Mrs. Rapkin, and get her to send for a doctor and have him put under proper care—the poor old boy really isn't fit to go about alone!"

"I will start now—at once," insisted the stranger "for there is no time to be lost."

"Oh, come!" said Horace, "after so many thousand years, a few hours more or less won't make any serious difference. And you can't go out now—they've shut up the house. Do let me take you upstairs to your room, sir."

"Not so, for I must leave thee for a season, O young man of kind conduct. But may thy days be fortunate, and the gate never cease to be repaired, and the nose of him that envieth thee be rubbed in the dust, for love for thee hath entered into my heart, and if it be permitted unto me, I will cover thee with the veils of my protection!"

As he finished this harangue the speaker seemed, to Ventimore's speechless amazement, to slip through the wall behind him. At all events, he had left the room somehow—and Horace found himself alone.

He rubbed the back of his head, which began to be painful. "He can't really have vanished through the wall," he said to himself. "That's too absurd. The fact is, I'm over-excited this evening—and no wonder, after all that's happened. The best thing I can do is to go to bed at once."

Which he accordingly proceeded to do.

CHAPTER V

CARTE BLANCHE

When Ventimore woke next morning his headache had gone, and with it the recollection of everything but the wondrous and delightful fact that Sylvia loved him and had promised to be his some day. Her mother, too, was on his side; why should he despair of anything after that? There was the Professor, to be sure—but even he might be brought to consent to an engagement, especially if it turned out that the brass bottle ... and here Horace began to recall an extraordinary dream in connection with that extremely speculative purchase of his. He had dreamed that he had forced the bottle open, and that it proved to contain, not manuscripts, but an elderly Jinnee who alleged that he had been imprisoned there by the order of King Solomon!

What, he wondered, could have put so grotesque a fancy into his head? and then he smiled as he traced it to Sylvia's playful suggestion that the bottle might contain a "genie," as did the famous jar in the "Arabian Nights," and to her father's pedantic correction of the word to "Jinnee." Upon that slight foundation his sleeping brain had built up all that elaborate fabric—a scene so vivid and a story so circumstantial and plausible that, in spite of its extravagance, he could hardly even now persuade himself that it was entirely imaginary. The psychology of dreams is a subject which has a fascinating mystery, even for the least serious student.

As he entered the sitting-room, where his breakfast awaited him, he looked round, half expecting to find the bottle lying with its lid off in the corner, as he had last seen it in his dream.

Of course, it was not there, and he felt an odd relief. The auction-room people had not delivered it yet, and so much the better, for he had still to ascertain if it had anything inside it; and who knew that it might not contain something more to his advantage than a maundering old Jinnee with a grievance several thousands of years old?

Breakfast over, he rang for his landlady, who presently appeared. Mrs. Rapkin was a superior type of her much-abused class. She was scrupulously clean and neat in her person; her sandy hair was so smooth and tightly knotted that it gave her head the colour and shape of a Barcelona nut; she had sharp, beady eyes, nostrils that seemed to smell battle afar off, a wide, thin mouth that apparently closed with a snap, and a dry, whity-brown complexion suggestive of bran.

But if somewhat grim of aspect, she was a good soul and devoted to Horace, in whom she took almost a maternal interest, while regretting that he was not what she called "serious-minded enough" to get on in the world. Rapkin had wooed and married her when they were both in service, and he still took occasional jobs as an outdoor butler, though Horace suspected that his more staple form of industry was the consumption of gin-and-water and remarkably full-flavoured cigars in the basement parlour.

"Shall you be dining in this evening, sir?" inquired Mrs. Rapkin.

"I don't know. Don't get anything in for me; I shall most probably dine at the club," said Horace; and Mrs. Rapkin, who had a confirmed belief that all clubs were hotbeds of vice and extravagance, sniffed disapproval. "By the way," he added, "if a kind of brass pot is sent here, it's all right. I bought it at a sale yesterday. Be careful how you handle it—it's rather old."

"There was a vawse come late last night, sir; I don't know if it's that, it's old-fashioned enough."

"Then will you bring it up at once, please? I want to see it."

Mrs. Rapkin retired, to reappear presently with the brass bottle. "I thought you'd have noticed it when you come in last night, sir," she explained, "for I stood it in the corner, and when I see it this morning it was layin' o' one side and looking that dirty and disrespectable I took it down to give it a good clean, which it wanted it."

It certainly looked rather the better for it, and the marks or scratches on the cap were more distinguishable, but Horace was somewhat disconcerted to find that part of his dream was true—the bottle had been there.

"I hope I've done nothing wrong," said Mrs. Rapkin, observing his expression; "I only used a little warm ale to it, which is a capital thing for brass-work, and gave it a scrub with 'Vitrolia' soap—but it would take more than that to get all the muck off of it."

"It is all right, so long as you didn't try to get the top off," said Horace.

"Why, the top was off it, sir. I thought you'd done it with the 'ammer and chisel when you got 'ome," said his landlady, staring. "I found them 'ere on the carpet."

Horace started. Then that part was true, too! "Oh, ah," he said, "I believe I did. I'd forgotten. That reminds me. Haven't you let the room above to—to an Oriental gentleman—a native, you know—wears a green turban?"

"That I most certainly 'ave not, Mr. Ventimore," said Mrs. Rapkin, with emphasis, "nor wouldn't. Not if his turbin was all the colours of the rainbow—for I don't 'old with such. Why, there was Rapkin's own sister-in-law let her parlour floor to a Horiental—a Parsee he was, or one o' them Hafrican tribes—and reason she 'ad to repent of it, for all his gold spectacles! Whatever made you fancy I should let to a blackamoor?"

"Oh, I thought I saw somebody about—er—answering that description, and I wondered if—"

"Never in this 'ouse, sir. Mrs. Steggars, next door but one, might let to such, for all I can say to the contrary, not being what you might call particular, and her rooms more suitable to savage notions—but I've enough on my hands, Mr. Ventimore, attending to you—not keeping a girl to do the waiting, as why should I while I'm well able to do it better myself?"

As soon as she relieved him of her presence, he examined the bottle: there was nothing whatever inside it, which disposed of all the hopes he had entertained from that quarter.

It was not difficult to account for the visionary Oriental as an hallucination probably inspired by the heavy fumes (for he now believed in the fumes) which had doubtless resulted from the rapid decomposition of some long-buried spices or similar substances suddenly exposed to the air.

If any further explanation were needed, the accidental blow to the back of his head, together with the latent suggestion from the "Arabian Nights," would amply provide it.

So, having settled these points to his entire satisfaction, he went to his office in Great Cloister Street, which he now had entirely to himself, and was soon engaged in drafting the specification for Beevor on which he had been working when so fortunately interrupted the day before by the Professor.

The work was more or less mechanical, and could bring him no credit and little thanks, but Horace had the happy faculty of doing thoroughly whatever he undertook, and as he sat there by his wide-open window he soon became entirely oblivious of all but the task before him.

So much so that, even when the light became obscured for a moment, as if by some large and opaque body in passing, he did not look up immediately, and, when he did, was surprised to find the only armchair occupied by a portly person, who seemed to be trying to recover his breath.

"I beg your pardon," said Ventimore; "I never heard you come in."

His visitor could only wave his head in courteous deprecation, under which there seemed a suspicion of bewildered embarrassment. He was a rosy-gilled, spotlessly clean, elderly gentleman, with white whiskers; his eyes, just then slightly protuberant, were shrewd, but genial; he had a wide, jolly mouth and a double chin. He was dressed like a man who is above disguising his prosperity; he wore a large, pear-shaped pearl in his crimson scarf, and had probably only lately discarded his summer white hat and white waistcoat.

"My dear sir," he began, in a rich, throaty voice, as soon as he could speak; "my dear sir, you must think this is a most unceremonious way of—ah!—dropping in on you—of invading your privacy."

"Not at all," said Horace, wondering whether he could possibly intend him to understand that he had come in by the window. "I'm afraid there was no one to show you in—my clerk is away just now."

"No matter, sir, no matter. I found my way up, as you perceive. The important, I may say the essential, fact is that I am here."

"Quite so," said Horace, "and may I ask what brought you?"

"What brought—" The stranger's eyes grew fish-like for the moment. "Allow me, I—I shall come to that—in good time. I am still a little—as you can see." He glanced round the room. "You are, I think, an architect, Mr. ah—Mr. um—?"

"Ventimore is my name," said Horace, "and I am an architect."

"Ventimore, to be sure!" he put his hand in his pocket and produced a card: "Yes, it's all quite correct: I see I have the name here. And an architect, Mr. Ventimore, so I—I am given to understand, of immense ability."

"I'm afraid I can't claim to be that," said Horace, "but I may call myself fairly competent."

"Competent? Why, of course you're competent. Do you suppose, sir, that I, a practical business man, should come to any one who was not competent?" he said, with exactly the air of a man trying to convince himself—against his own judgment—that he was acting with the utmost prudence.

"Am I to understand that some one has been good enough to recommend me to you?" inquired Horace.

"Certainly not, sir, certainly not. I need no recommendation but my own judgment. I—ah—have a tolerable acquaintance with all that is going on in the art world, and I have come to the conclusion, Mr.—eh—ah—Ventimore, I repeat, the deliberate and unassisted conclusion, that you are the one man living who can do what I want."

"Delighted to hear it," said Horace, genuinely gratified. "When did you see any of my designs?"

"Never mind, sir. I don't decide without very good grounds. It doesn't take me long to make up my mind, and when my mind is made up, I act, sir, I act. And, to come to the point, I have a small commission— unworthy, I am quite aware, of your—ah—distinguished talent—which I should like to put in your hands."

"Is he going to ask me to attend a sale for him?" thought Horace. "I'm hanged if I do."

"I'm rather busy at present," he said dubiously, "as you may see. I'm not sure whether—"

"I'll put the matter in a nutshell, sir—in a nutshell. My name is Wackerbath, Samuel Wackerbath— tolerably well known, if I may say so, in City circles." Horace, of course, concealed the fact that his visitor's name and fame were unfamiliar to him. "I've lately bought a few acres on the Hampshire border, near the house I'm living in just now; and I've been thinking—as I was saying to a friend only just now, as we were crossing Westminster Bridge—I've been thinking of building myself a little place there, just a humble, unpretentious home, where I could run down for the weekend and entertain a friend or two in a quiet way, and perhaps live some part of the year. Hitherto I've rented places as I wanted 'em— old family seats and ancestral mansions and so forth: very nice in their way, but I want to feel under a roof of my own. I want to surround myself with the simple comforts, the—ah—unassuming elegance of an English country home. And you're the man—I feel more convinced of it with every word you say— you're the man to do the job in style—ah—to execute the work as it should be done."

Here was the long-wished-for client at last! And it was satisfactory to feel that he had arrived in the most ordinary and commonplace course, for no one could look at Mr. Samuel Wackerbath and believe for a moment that he was capable of floating through an upper window; he was not in the least that kind of person.

"I shall be happy to do my best," said Horace, with a calmness that surprised himself. "Could you give me some idea of the amount you are prepared to spend?"

"Well, I'm no Croesus—though I won't say I'm a pauper precisely—and, as I remarked before, I prefer comfort to splendour. I don't think I should be justified in going beyond—well, say sixty thousand."

"Sixty thousand!" exclaimed Horace, who had expected about a tenth of that sum. "Oh, not more than sixty thousand? I see."

"I mean, on the house itself," explained Mr. Wackerbath; "there will be outbuildings, lodges, cottages, and so forth, and then some of the rooms I should want specially decorated. Altogether, before we are finished, it may work out at about a hundred thousand. I take it that, with such a margin, you could—ah—run me up something that in a modest way would take the shine out of—I mean to say eclipse—anything in the adjoining counties?"

"I certainly think," said Horace, "that for such a sum as that I can undertake that you shall have a home which will satisfy you." And he proceeded to put the usual questions as to site, soil, available building materials, the accommodation that would be required, and so on.

"You're young, sir," said Mr. Wackerbath, at the end of the interview, "but I perceive you are up to all the tricks of the—I should say, versed in the minutiæ of your profession. You would like to run down and look at the ground, eh? Well, that's only reasonable; and my wife and daughters will want to have their say in the matter—no getting on without pleasing the ladies, hey? Now, let me see. To-morrow's Sunday. Why not come down by the 8.45 a.m. to Lipsfield? I'll have a trap, or a brougham and pair, or something, waiting for you—take you over the ground myself, bring you back to lunch with us at Oriel Court, and talk the whole thing thoroughly over. Then we'll send you up to town in the evening, and you can start work the first thing on Monday. That suit you? Very well, then. We'll expect you to-morrow."

With this Mr. Wackerbath departed, leaving Horace, as may be imagined, absolutely overwhelmed by the suddenness and completeness of his good fortune. He was no longer one of the unemployed: he had work to do, and, better still, work that would interest him, give him all the scope and opportunity he could wish for. With a client who seemed tractable, and to whom money was clearly no object, he might carry out some of his most ambitious ideas.

Moreover, he would now be in a position to speak to Sylvia's father without fear of a repulse. His commission on £60,000 would be £3,000, and that on the decorations and other work at least as much again—probably more. In a year he could marry without imprudence; in two or three years he might be making a handsome income, for he felt confident that, with such a start, he would soon have as much work as he could undertake.

He was ashamed of himself for ever having lost heart. What were the last few years of weary waiting but probation and preparation for this splendid chance, which had come just when he really needed it, and in the most simple and natural manner?

He loyally completed the work he had promised to do for Beevor, who would have to dispense with his assistance in future, and then he felt too excited and restless to stay in the office, and, after lunching at his club as usual, he promised himself the pleasure of going to Cottesmore Gardens and telling Sylvia his good news.

It was still early, and he walked the whole way, as some vent for his high spirits, enjoying everything with a new zest—the dappled grey and salmon sky before him, the amber, russet, and yellow of the scanty foliage in Kensington Gardens, the pungent scent of fallen chestnuts and acorns and burning leaves, the blue-grey mist stealing between the distant tree-trunks, and then the cheery bustle and brilliancy of the High Street. Finally came the joy of finding Sylvia all alone, and witnessing her frank delight at what he had come to tell her, of feeling her hands on his shoulders, and holding her in his arms, as their lips met for the first time. If on that Saturday afternoon there was a happier man than Horace Ventimore, he would have done well to dissemble his felicity, for fear of incurring the jealousy of the high gods.

When Mrs. Futvoye returned, as she did only too soon, to find her daughter and Horace seated on the same sofa, she did not pretend to be gratified. "This is taking a most unfair advantage of what I was weak enough to say last night, Mr. Ventimore," she began. "I thought I could have trusted you!"

"I shouldn't have come so soon," he said, "if my position were what it was only yesterday. But it's changed since then, and I venture to hope that even the Professor won't object now to our being regularly engaged." And he told her of the sudden alteration in his prospects.

"Well," said Mrs. Futvoye, "you had better speak to my husband about it."

The Professor came in shortly afterwards, and Horace immediately requested a few minutes' conversation with him in the study, which was readily granted.

The study to which the Professor led the way was built out at the back of the house, and crowded with Oriental curios of every age and kind; the furniture had been made by Cairene cabinet-makers, and along the cornices of the book-cases were texts from the Koran, while every chair bore the Arabic for "Welcome" in a gilded firework on its leather back; the lamp was a perforated mosque lantern with long pendent glass tubes like hyacinth glasses; a mummy-case smiled from a corner with laboured bonhomie.

"Well," began the Professor, as soon as they were seated, "so I was not mistaken—there was something in the brass bottle after all, then? Let's have a look at it, whatever it is."

For the moment Horace had almost forgotten the bottle. "Oh!" he said, "I—I got it open; but there was nothing in it."

"Just as I anticipated, sir," said the Professor. "I told you there couldn't be anything in a bottle of that description; it was simply throwing money away to buy it."

"I dare say it was, but I wished to speak to you on a much more important matter;" and Horace briefly explained his object.

"Dear me," said the Professor, rubbing up his hair irritably, "dear me! I'd no idea of this—no idea at all. I was under the impression that you volunteered to act as escort to my wife and daughter at St. Luc purely out of good nature to relieve me from what—to a man of my habits in that extreme heat—would have been an arduous and distasteful duty."

"I was not wholly unselfish, I admit," said Horace. "I fell in love with your daughter, sir, the first day I met her—only I felt I had no right, as a poor man with no prospects, to speak to her or you at that time."

"A very creditable feeling—but I've yet to learn why you should have overcome it."

So, for the third time, Ventimore told the story of the sudden turn in his fortunes.

"I know this Mr. Samuel Wackerbath by name," said the Professor; "one of the chief partners in the firm of Akers and Coverdale, the great estate agents—a most influential man, if you can only succeed in satisfying him."

"Oh, I don't feel any misgivings about that, sir," said Horace. "I mean to build him a house that will be beyond his wildest expectations, and you see that in a year I shall have earned several thousands, and I need not say that I will make any settlement you think proper when I marry—"

"When you are in possession of those thousands," remarked the Professor, dryly, "it will be time enough to talk of marrying and making settlements. Meanwhile, if you and Sylvia choose to consider yourselves engaged, I won't object—only I must insist on having your promise that you won't persuade her to marry you without her mother's and my consent."

Ventimore gave this undertaking willingly enough, and they returned to the drawing-room. Mrs. Futvoye could hardly avoid asking Horace, in his new character of fiancé, to stay and dine, which it need not be said he was only too delighted to do.

"There is one thing, my dear—er—Horace," said the Professor, solemnly, after dinner, when the neat parlourmaid had left them at dessert, "one thing on which I think it my duty to caution you. If you are to justify the confidence we have shown in sanctioning your engagement to Sylvia, you must curb this propensity of yours to needless extravagance."

"Papa!" cried Sylvia. "What could have made you think Horace extravagant?"

"Really," said Horace, "I shouldn't have called myself particularly so."

"Nobody ever does call himself particularly extravagant," retorted the Professor; "but I observed at St. Luc that you habitually gave fifty centimes as a pourboire when twopence, or even a penny, would have been handsome. And no one with any regard for the value of money would have given a guinea for a worthless brass vessel on the bare chance that it might contain manuscripts, which (as any one could have foreseen) it did not."

"But it's not a bad sort of bottle, sir," pleaded Horace. "If you remember, you said yourself the shape was unusual. Why shouldn't it be worth all the money, and more?"

"To a collector, perhaps," said the Professor, with his wonted amiability, "which you are not. No, I can only call it a senseless and reprehensible waste of money."

"Well, the truth is," said Horace, "I bought it with some idea that it might interest you."

"Then you were mistaken, sir. It does not interest me. Why should I be interested in a metal jar which, for anything that appears to the contrary, may have been cast the other day at Birmingham?"

"But there is something," said Horace; "a seal or inscription of some sort engraved on the cap. Didn't I mention it?"

"You said nothing about an inscription before," replied the Professor, with rather more interest. "What is the character—Arabic? Persian? Kufic?"

"I really couldn't say—it's almost rubbed out—queer little triangular marks, something like birds' footprints."

"That sounds like Cuneiform," said the Professor, "which would seem to point to a Phoenician origin. And, as I am acquainted with no Oriental brass earlier than the ninth century of our era, I should regard your description as, à priori, distinctly unlikely. However, I should certainly like to have an opportunity of examining the bottle for myself some day."

"Whenever you please, Professor. When can you come?"

"Why, I'm so much occupied all day that I can't say for certain when I can get up to your office again."

"My own days will be fairly full now," said Horace; "and the thing's not at the office, but in my rooms at Vincent Square. Why shouldn't you all come and dine quietly there some evening next week, and then you could examine the inscription comfortably afterwards, you know, Professor, and find out what it really is? Do say you will." He was eager to have the privilege of entertaining Sylvia in his own rooms for the first time.

"No, no," said the Professor; "I see no reason why you should be troubled with the entire family. I may drop in alone some evening and take the luck of the pot, sir."

"Thank you, papa," put in Sylvia; "but I should like to come too, please, and hear what you think of Horace's bottle. And I'm dying to see his rooms. I believe they're fearfully luxurious."

"I trust," observed her father, "that they are far indeed from answering that description. If they did, I should consider it a most unsatisfactory indication of Horace's character."

"There's nothing magnificent about them, I assure you," said Horace. "Though it's true I've had them done up, and all that sort of thing, at my own expense—but quite simply. I couldn't afford to spend much on them. But do come and see them. I must have a little dinner, to celebrate my good fortune—it will be so jolly if you'll all three come."

"If we do come," stipulated the Professor, "it must be on the distinct understanding that you don't provide an elaborate banquet. Plain, simple, wholesome food, well cooked, such as we have had this evening, is all that is necessary. More would be ostentatious."

"My dear dad!" protested Sylvia, in distress at this somewhat dictatorial speech. "Surely you can leave all that to Horace!"

"Horace, my dear, understands that, in speaking as I did, I was simply treating him as a potential member of my family." Here Sylvia made a private little grimace. "No young man who contemplates marrying should allow himself to launch into extravagance on the strength of prospects which, for all he can tell," said the Professor, genially, "may prove fallacious. On the contrary, if his affection is sincere, he will incur as little expense as possible, put by every penny he can save, rather than subject the girl he professes to love to the ordeal of a long engagement. In other words, the truest lover is the best economist."

"I quite understand, sir," said Horace, good-temperedly; "it would be foolish of me to attempt any ambitious form of entertainment—especially as my landlady, though an excellent plain cook, is not exactly a cordon bleu. So you can come to my modest board without misgivings."

Before he left, a provisional date for the dinner was fixed for an evening towards the end of the next week, and Horace walked home, treading on air rather than hard paving-stones, and "striking the stars with his uplifted head."

The next day he went down to Lipsfield and made the acquaintance of the whole Wackerbath family, who were all enthusiastic about the proposed country house. The site was everything that the most exacting architect could desire, and he came back to town the same evening, having spent a pleasant day and learnt enough of his client's requirements, and—what was even more important—those of his client's wife and daughters, to enable him to begin work upon the sketch-plans the next morning.

He had not been long in his rooms at Vincent Square, and was still agreeably engaged in recalling the docility and ready appreciation with which the Wackerbaths had received his suggestions and rough sketches, their compliments and absolute confidence in his skill, when he had a shock which was as disagreeable as it was certainly unexpected.

For the wall before him parted like a film, and through it stepped, smiling benignantly, the green-robed figure of Fakrash-el-Aamash, the Jinnee.

CHAPTER VI

EMBARRAS DE RICHESSES

Ventimore had so thoroughly convinced himself that the released Jinnee was purely a creature of his own imagination, that he rubbed his eyes with a start, hoping that they had deceived him.

"Stroke thy head, O merciful and meritorious one," said his visitor, "and recover thy faculties to receive good tidings. For it is indeed I—Fakrash-el-Aamash—whom thou beholdest."

"I—I'm delighted to see you," said Horace, as cordially as he could. "Is there anything I can do for you?"

"Nay, for hast thou not done me the greatest of all services by setting me free? To escape out of a bottle is pleasant. And to thee I owe my deliverance."

It was all true, then: he had really let an imprisoned Genius or Jinnee, or whatever it was, out of that bottle! He knew he could not be dreaming now—he only wished he were. However, since it was done, his best course seemed to be to put a good face on it, and persuade this uncanny being somehow to go away and leave him in peace for the future.

"Oh, that's all right, my dear sir," he said, "don't think any more about it. I—I rather understood you to say that you were starting on a journey in search of Solomon?"

"I have been, and returned. For I visited sundry cities in his dominions, hoping that by chance I might hear news of him, but I refrained from asking directly lest thereby I should engender suspicion, and so Suleyman should learn of my escape before I could obtain an audience of him and implore justice."

"Oh, I shouldn't think that was likely," said Horace. "If I were you, I should go straight back and go on travelling till I did find Suleyman."

"Well was it said: 'Pass not any door without knocking, lest haply that which thou seekest should be behind it.'"

"Exactly," said Horace. "Do each city thoroughly, house by house, and don't neglect the smallest clue. 'If at first you don't succeed, try, try, try, again!' as one of our own poets teaches."

"'Try, try, try again,'" echoed the Jinnee, with an admiration that was almost fatuous. "Divinely gifted truly was he who composed such a verse!"

"He has a great reputation as a sage," said Horace, "and the maxim is considered one of his happiest efforts. Don't you think that, as the East is rather thickly populated, the less time you lose in following the poet's recommendation the better?"

"It may be as thou sayest. But know this, O my son, that wheresoever I may wander, I shall never cease to study how I may most fitly reward thee for thy kindness towards me. For nobly it was said: 'If I be possessed of wealth and be not liberal, may my head never be extended!'"

"My good sir," said Horace, "do please understand that if you were to offer me any reward for—for a very ordinary act of courtesy, I should be obliged to decline it."

"But didst thou not say that thou wast sorely in need of a client?"

"That was so at the time," said Horace; "but since I last had the pleasure of seeing you, I have met with one who is all I could possibly wish for."

"I am indeed rejoiced to hear it," returned the Jinnee, "for thou showest me that I have succeeded in performing the first service which thou hast demanded of me."

Horace staggered under this severe blow to his pride; for the moment he could only gasp: "You—you sent him to me?"

"I, and no other," said the Jinnee, beaming with satisfaction; "for while, unseen of men, I was circling in air, resolved to attend to thy affair before beginning my search for Suleyman (on whom be peace!), it chanced that I overheard a human being of prosperous appearance say aloud upon a bridge that he desired to erect for himself a palace if he could but find an architect. So, perceiving thee afar off seated at an open casement, I immediately transported him to the place and delivered him into thy hands."

"But he knew my name—he had my card in his pocket," said Horace.

"I furnished him with the paper containing thy names and abode, lest he should be ignorant of them."

"Well, look here, Mr. Fakrash," said the unfortunate Horace, "I know you meant well—but never do a thing like that again! If my brother-architects came to know of it I should be accused of most unprofessional behaviour. I'd no idea you would take that way of introducing a client to me, or I should have stopped it at once!"

"It was an error," said Fakrash. "No matter. I will undo this affair, and devise some other and better means of serving thee."

"No, no," he said, "for Heaven's sake, leave things alone—you'll only make them worse. Forgive me, my dear Mr. Fakrash, I'm afraid I must seem most ungrateful; but—but I was so taken by surprise. And really, I am extremely obliged to you. For, though the means you took were—were a little irregular, you have done me a very great service."

"It is naught," said the Jinnee, "compared to those I hope to render so great a benefactor."

"But, indeed, you mustn't think of trying to do any more for me," urged Horace, who felt the absolute necessity of expelling any scheme of further benevolence from the Jinnee's head once and for all. "You have done enough. Why, thanks to you, I am engaged to build a palace that will keep me hard at work and happy for ever so long."

"Are human beings, then, so enamoured of hard labour?" asked Fakrash, in wonder. "It is not thus with the Jinn."

"I love my work for its own sake," said Horace, "and then, when I have finished it, I shall have earned a very fair amount of money—which is particularly important to me just now."

"And why, my son, art thou so desirous of obtaining riches?"

"Because," said Horace, "unless a man is tolerably well off in these days he cannot hope to marry."

Fakrash smiled with indulgent compassion. "How excellent is the saying of one of old: 'He that adventureth upon matrimony is like unto one who thrusteth his hand into a sack containing many thousands of serpents and one eel. Yet, if Fate so decree, he may draw forth the eel.' And thou art comely, and of an age when it is natural to desire the love of a maiden. Therefore be of good heart and a cheerful eye, and it may be that, when I am more at leisure, I shall find thee a helpmate who shall rejoice thy soul."

"Please don't trouble to find me anything of the sort!" said Horace, hastily, with a mental vision of some helpless and scandalised stranger being shot into his dwelling like coals. "I assure you I would much rather win a wife for myself in the ordinary way—as, thanks to your kindness, I have every hope of doing before long."

"Is there already some damsel for whom thy heart pineth? If so, fear not to tell me her names and dwelling place, and I will assuredly obtain her for thee."

But Ventimore had seen enough of the Jinnee's Oriental methods to doubt his tact and discretion where Sylvia was concerned. "No, no; of course not. I spoke generally," he said. "It's exceedingly kind of you—but I do wish I could make you understand that I am overpaid as it is. You have put me in the way to make a name and fortune for myself. If I fail, it will be my own fault. And, at all events, I want nothing more from you. If you mean to find Suleyman (on whom be peace!) you must go and live in the East altogether—for he certainly isn't over here; you must give up your whole time to it, keep as quiet as possible, and don't be discouraged by any reports you may hear. Above all, never trouble your head about me or my affairs again!"

"O thou of wisdom and eloquence," said Fakrash, "this is most excellent advice. I will go, then; but may I drink the cup of perdition if I become unmindful of thy benevolence!"

And, raising his joined hands above his head as he spoke, he sank, feet foremost, through the carpet and was gone.

"Thank Heaven," thought Ventimore, "he's taken the hint at last. I don't think I'm likely to see any more of him. I feel an ungrateful brute for saying so, but I can't help it. I can not stand being under any obligation to a Jinnee who's been shut up in a beastly brass bottle ever since the days of Solomon, who probably had very good reasons for putting him there."

Horace next asked himself whether he was bound in honour to disclose the facts to Mr. Wackerbath, and give him the opportunity of withdrawing from the agreement if he thought fit.

On the whole, he saw no necessity for telling him anything; the only possible result would be to make his client suspect his sanity; and who would care to employ an insane architect? Then, if he retired from the undertaking without any explanations, what could he say to Sylvia? What would Sylvia's father say to him? There would certainly be an end to his engagement.

After all, he had not been to blame; the Wackerbaths were quite satisfied. He felt perfectly sure that he could justify their selection of him; he would wrong nobody by accepting the commission, while he would only offend them, injure himself irretrievably, and lose all hope of gaining Sylvia if he made any attempt to undeceive them.

And Fakrash was gone, never to return. So, on all these considerations, Horace decided that silence was his only possible policy, and, though some moralists may condemn his conduct as disingenuous and wanting in true moral courage, I venture to doubt whether any reader, however independent, straightforward, and indifferent to notoriety and ridicule, would have behaved otherwise in Ventimore's extremely delicate and difficult position.

Some days passed, every working hour of which was spent by Horace in the rapture of creation. To every man with the soul of an artist in him there comes at times—only too seldom in most cases—a revelation of latent power that he had not dared to hope for. And now with Ventimore years of study and theorising which he had often been tempted to think wasted began to bear golden fruit. He designed and drew with a rapidity and originality, a sense of perfect mastery of the various problems to be dealt with, and a delight in the working out of mass and detail, so intoxicating that he almost dreaded lest he should be the victim of some self-delusion.

His evenings were of course spent with the Futvoyes, in discovering Sylvia in some new and yet more adorable aspect. Altogether, he was very much in love, very happy, and very busy—three states not invariably found in combination.

And, as he had foreseen, he had effectually got rid of Fakrash, who was evidently too engrossed in the pursuit of Solomon to think of anything else. And there seemed no reason why he should abandon his search for a generation or two, for it would probably take all that time to convince him that that mighty monarch was no longer on the throne.

"It would have been too brutal to tell him myself," thought Horace, "when he was so keen on having his case reheard. And it gives him an object, poor old buffer, and keeps him from interfering in my affairs, so it's best for both of us."

Horace's little dinner-party had been twice postponed, till he had begun to have a superstitious fear that it would never come off; but at length the Professor had been induced to give an absolute promise for a certain evening.

On the day before, after breakfast, Horace had summoned his landlady to a consultation on the menu. "Nothing elaborate, you know, Mrs. Rapkin," said Horace, who, though he would have liked to provide a feast of all procurable delicacies for Sylvia's refection, was obliged to respect her father's prejudices. "Just a simple dinner, thoroughly well cooked, and nicely served—as you know so well how to do it."

"I suppose, sir, you would require Rapkin to wait?"

As the ex-butler was liable to trances on these occasions during which he could do nothing but smile and bow with speechless politeness as he dropped sauce-boats and plates, Horace replied that he thought of having someone in to avoid troubling Mr. Rapkin; but his wife expressed such confidence in her husband's proving equal to all emergencies, that Ventimore waived the point, and left it to her to hire extra help if she thought fit.

"Now, what soup can you give us?" he inquired, as Mrs. Rapkin stood at attention and quite unmollified.

After protracted mental conflict, she grudgingly suggested gravy soup—which Horace thought too unenterprising, and rejected in favour of mock turtle. "Well then, fish?" he continued; "how about fish?"

Mrs. Rapkin dragged the depths of her culinary resources for several seconds, and finally brought to the surface what she called "a nice fried sole." Horace would not hear of it, and urged her to aspire to salmon; she substituted smelts, which he opposed by a happy inspiration of turbot and lobster sauce. The sauce, however, presented insuperable difficulties to her mind, and she offered a compromise in the form of cod—which he finally accepted as a fish which the Professor could hardly censure for ostentation.

Next came the no less difficult questions of entrée or no entrée, of joint and bird. "What's in season just now?" said Horace; "let me see"—and glanced out of the window as he spoke, as though in search of some outside suggestion.... "Camels, by Jove!" he suddenly exclaimed.

"Camels, Mr. Ventimore, sir?" repeated Mrs. Rapkin, in some bewilderment; and then, remembering that he was given to untimely flippancy, she gave a tolerant little cough.

"I'll be shot if they aren't camels!" said Horace. "What do you make of 'em, Mrs. Rapkin?"

Out of the faint mist which hung over the farther end of the square advanced a procession of tall, dust-coloured animals, with long, delicately poised necks and a mincing gait. Even Mrs. Rapkin could not succeed in making anything of them except camels.

"What the deuce does a caravan of camels want in Vincent Square?" said Horace, with a sudden qualm for which he could not account.

"Most likely they belong to the Barnum Show, sir," suggested his landlady. "I did hear they were coming to Olympia again this year."

"Why, of course," cried Horace, intensely relieved. "It's on their way from the Docks—at least, it isn't out of their way. Or probably the main road's up for repairs. That's it—they'll turn off to the left at the corner. See, they've got Arab drivers with them. Wonderful how the fellows manage them."

"It seems to me, sir," said Mrs. Rapkin, "that they're coming our way—they seem to be stopping outside."

"Don't talk such infernal— I beg your pardon, Mrs. Rapkin; but why on earth should Barnum and Bailey's camels come out of their way to call on me? It's ridiculous, you know!" said Horace, irritably.

"Ridicklous it may be, sir," she retorted, "but they're all layin' down on the road opposite our door, as you can see—and them niggers is making signs to you to come out and speak to 'em."

It was true enough. One by one the camels, which were apparently of the purest breed, folded themselves up in a row like campstools at a sign from their attendants, who were now making profound salaams towards the window where Ventimore was standing.

"I suppose I'd better go down and see what they want," he said, with rather a sickly smile. "They may have lost the way to Olympia.... I only hope Fakrash isn't at the bottom of this," he thought, as he went downstairs. "But he'd come himself—at all events, he wouldn't send me a message on such a lot of camels!" As he appeared on the doorstep, all the drivers flopped down and rubbed their flat, black noses on the curbstone.

"For Heaven's sake get up!" said Horace angrily. "This isn't Hammersmith. Turn to the left, into the Vauxhall Bridge Road, and ask a policeman the nearest way to Olympia."

"Be not angry with thy slaves!" said the head driver, in excellent English. "We are here by command of Fakrash-el-Aamash, our lord, whom we are bound to obey. And we have brought thee these as gifts."

"My compliments to your master," said Horace, between his teeth, "and tell him that a London architect has no sort of occasion for camels. Say that I am extremely obliged—but am compelled to decline them."

"O highly born one," explained the driver, "the camels are not a gift—but the loads which are upon the camels. Suffer us, therefore, since we dare not disobey our lord's commands, to carry these trifling tokens of his good will into thy dwelling and depart in peace."

Horace had not noticed till then that every camel bore a heavy burden, which the attendants were now unloading. "Oh, if you must!" he said, not too graciously; "only do look sharp about it—there's a crowd collecting already, and I don't want to have a constable here."

He returned to his rooms, where he found Mrs. Rapkin paralysed with amazement. "It's—it's all right," he said; "I'd forgotten—it's only a few Oriental things from the place where that brass bottle came from, you know. They've left them here—on approval."

"Seems funny their sending their goods 'ome on camels, sir, doesn't it?" said Mrs. Rapkin.

"Not at all funny!" said Horace; "they—they're an enterprising firm—their way of advertising."

One after another, a train of dusky attendants entered, each of whom deposited his load on the floor with a guttural grunt and returned backward, until the sitting-room was blocked with piles of sacks, and bales, and chests, whereupon the head driver appeared and intimated that the tale of gifts was complete.

"I wonder what sort of tip this fellow expects," thought Horace; "a sovereign seems shabby—but it's all I can run to. I'll try him with that."

But the overseer repudiated all idea of a gratuity with stately dignity, and as Horace saw him to the gate, he found a stolid constable by the railings.

"This won't do, you know," said the constable; "these 'ere camels must move on—or I shall 'ave to interfere."

"It's all right, constable," said Horace, pressing into his hand the sovereign the head driver had rejected; "they're going to move on now. They've brought me a few presents from—from a friend of mine in the East."

By this time the attendants had mounted the kneeling camels, which rose with them, and swung off round the square in a long, swaying trot that soon left the crowd far behind, staring blankly after the caravan as camel after camel disappeared into the haze.

"I shouldn't mind knowin' that friend o' yours, sir," said the constable; "open-hearted sort o' gentleman, I should think?"

"Very!" said Horace, savagely, and returned to his room, which Mrs. Rapkin had now left.

His hands shook, though not with joy, as he untied some of the sacks and bales and forced open the outlandish-looking chests, the contents of which almost took away his breath.

For in the bales were carpets and tissues which he saw at a glance must be of fabulous antiquity and beyond all price; the sacks held golden ewers and vessels of strange workmanship and pantomimic proportions; the chests were full of jewels—ropes of creamy-pink pearls as large as average onions, strings of uncut rubies and emeralds, the smallest of which would have been a tight fit in an ordinary collar-box, and diamonds, roughly facetted and polished, each the size of a coconut, in whose hearts quivered a liquid and prismatic radiance.

On the most moderate computation, the total value of these gifts could hardly be less than several hundred millions; never probably in the world's history had any treasury contained so rich a store.

It would have been difficult for anybody, on suddenly finding himself the possessor of this immense incalculable wealth, to make any comment quite worthy of the situation, but, surely, none could have been more inadequate and indeed inappropriate than Horace's—which, heartfelt as it was, was couched in the simple monosyllable—"Damn!"

CHAPTER VII

"GRATITUDE—A LIVELY SENSE OF FAVOURS TO COME"

Most men on suddenly finding themselves in possession of such enormous wealth would have felt some elation. Ventimore, as we have seen, was merely exasperated. And, although this attitude of his may strike the reader as incomprehensible or absolutely wrong-headed, he had more reason on his side than might appear at a first view.

It was undoubtedly the fact that, with the money these treasures represented, he would be in a position to convulse the money markets of Europe and America, bring society to his feet, make and unmake kingdoms—dominate, in short, the entire world.

"But, then," as Horace told himself with a groan, "it wouldn't amuse me in the least to convulse money markets. Do I want to see the smartest people in London grovelling for anything they think they're likely to get out of me? As I should be perfectly well aware that their homage was not paid to any personal merit of mine, I could hardly consider it flattering. And why should I make kingdoms? The only thing I understand and care about is making houses. Then, am I likely to be a better hand at dominating the world than all the others who have tried the experiment? I doubt it."

He called to mind all the millionaires he had ever read or heard of; they didn't seem to get much fun out of their riches. The majority of them were martyrs to dyspepsia. They were often weighed down by the cares and responsibilities of their position; the only people who were unable to obtain an audience of them at any time were their friends; they lived in a glare of publicity, and every post brought them hundreds of begging letters, and a few threats; their children were in constant danger from kidnappers, and they themselves, after knowing no rest in life, could not be certain that even their tombs would be undisturbed. Whether they were extravagant or thrifty, they were equally maligned, and, whatever the fortune they left behind them, they could be absolutely certain that, in a couple of generations, it would be entirely dissipated.

"And the biggest millionaire living," concluded Horace, "is a pauper compared with me!"

But there was another consideration—how was he to realise all this wealth? He knew enough about precious stones to be aware that a ruby, for instance, of the true "pigeon's blood" colour and the size of a melon, as most of these rubies were, would be worth, even when cut, considerably over a million; but who would buy it?

"I think I see myself," he reflected grimly, "calling on some diamond merchant in Hatton Garden with half a dozen assorted jewels in a Gladstone bag. If he believed they were genuine, he'd probably have a fit; but most likely he'd think I'd invented some dodge for manufacturing them, and had been fool enough to overdo the size. Anyhow, he'd want to know how they came into my possession, and what could I say? That they were part of a little present made to me by a Jinnee in grateful acknowledgment of my having relieved him from a brass bottle in which he'd been shut up for nearly three thousand years? Look at it how you will, it's not convincing. I fancy I can guess what he'd say. And what an ass I should look! Then suppose the thing got into the papers?"

Got into the papers? Why, of course it would get into the papers. As if it were possible in these days for a young and hitherto unemployed architect suddenly to surround himself with wondrous carpets, and gold vessels, and gigantic jewels without attracting the notice of some enterprising journalist. He would be interviewed; the story of his curiously acquired riches would go the round of the papers; he would find himself the object of incredulity, suspicion, ridicule. In imagination he could already see the headlines on the news-sheets:

BOTTLED BILLIONS

AMAZING ARABESQUES BY AN ARCHITECT

HE SAYS THE JAR CONTAINED A JINNEE

SENSATIONAL STORY

DIVERTING DETAILS

And so on, through every phrase of alliterative ingenuity. He ground his teeth at the mere thought of it. Then Sylvia would come to hear of it, and what would she think? She would naturally be repelled, as any nice-minded girl would be, by the idea that her lover was in secret alliance with a supernatural being. And her father and mother—would they allow her to marry a man, however rich, whose wealth came from such a questionable source? No one would believe that he had not made some unholy bargain before consenting to set this incarcerated spirit free—he, who had acted in absolute ignorance, who had persistently declined all reward after realising what he had done!

No, it was too much. Try as he might to do justice to the Jinnee's gratitude and generosity, he could not restrain a bitter resentment at the utter want of consideration shown in overloading him with gifts so useless and so compromising. No Jinnee—however old, however unfamiliar with the world as it is now—had any right to be such a fool!

And at this, above the ramparts of sacks and bales, which occupied all the available space in the room, appeared Mrs. Rapkin's face.

"I was going to ask you, sir, before them parcels came," she began, with a dry cough of disapproval, "what you would like in the way of ongtray to-morrow night. I thought if I could find a sweetbread at all reasonable—"

To Horace—surrounded as he was by incalculable riches—sweetbreads seemed incongruous just then; the transition of thought was too violent.

"I can't bother about that now, Mrs. Rapkin," he said; "we'll settle it to-morrow. I'm too busy."

"I suppose most of these things will have to go back, sir, if they're only sent on approval like?"

If he only knew where and how he could send them back! "I—I'm not sure," he said; "I may have to keep them."

"Well, sir, bargain or none, I wouldn't have 'em as a gift myself, being so dirty and fusty; they can't be no use to anybody, not to mention there being no room to move with them blocking up all the place. I'd better tell Rapkin to carry 'em all upstairs out of people's way."

"Certainly not," said Horace, sharply, by no means anxious for the Rapkins to discover the real nature of his treasures. "Don't touch them, either of you. Leave them exactly as they are, do you understand?"

"As you please, Mr. Ventimore, sir; only, if they're not to be interfered with, I don't see myself how you're going to set your friends down to dinner to-morrow, that's all."

And, indeed, considering that the table and every available chair, and even the floor, were heaped so high with valuables that Horace himself could only just squeeze his way between the piles, it seemed as if his guests might find themselves inconveniently cramped.

"It will be all right," he said, with an optimism he was very far from feeling; "we'll manage somehow—leave it to me."

Before he left for his office he took the precaution to baffle any inquisitiveness on the part of his landlady by locking his sitting-room door and carrying away the key, but it was in a very different mood from his former light-hearted confidence that he sat down to his drawing-board in Great Cloister Street that morning. He could not concentrate his mind; his enthusiasm and his ideas had alike deserted him.

He flung down the dividers he had been using and pushed away the nest of saucers of Indian ink and colours in a fit of petulance. "It's no good," he exclaimed aloud; "I feel a perfect duffer this morning. I couldn't even design a decent dog-kennel!"

Even as he spoke he became conscious of a presence in the room, and, looking round, saw Fakrash the Jinnee standing at his elbow, smiling down on him more benevolently than ever, and with a serene expectation of being warmly welcomed and thanked, which made Horace rather ashamed of his own inability to meet it.

"He's a thoroughly good-natured old chap," he thought, self-reproachfully. "He means well, and I'm a beast not to feel more glad to see him. And yet, hang it all! I can't have him popping in and out of the office like a rabbit whenever the fancy takes him!"

"Peace be upon thee," said Fakrash. "Moderate the trouble of thy heart, and impart thy difficulties to me."

"Oh, they're nothing, thanks," said Horace, feeling decidedly embarrassed. "I got stuck over my work for the moment, and it worried me a little—that's all."

"Then thou hast not yet received the gifts which I commanded should be delivered at thy dwelling-place?"

"Oh, indeed I have!" replied Horace; "and—and I really don't know how to thank you for them."

"A few trifling presents," answered the Jinnee, "and by no means suited to thy dignity—yet the best in my power to bestow upon thee for the time being."

"My dear sir, they simply overwhelm me with their magnificence! They're beyond all price, and—and I've no idea what to do with such a superabundance."

"A superfluity of good things is good," was the Jinnee's sententious reply.

"Not in my particular case. I—I quite feel your goodness and generosity; but, indeed, as I told you before, it's really impossible for me to accept any such reward."

Fakrash's brows contracted slightly. "How sayest thou that it is impossible—seeing that these things are already in thy possession?"

"I know," said Horace; "but—you won't be offended if I speak quite plainly?"

"Art thou not even as a son to me, and can I be angered at any words of thine?"

"Well," said Horace, with sudden hope, "honestly, then, I would very much rather—if you're sure you don't mind—that you would take them all back again."

"What? Dost thou demand that I, Fakrash-el-Aamash, should consent to receive back the gifts I have bestowed? Are they, then, of so little value in thy sight?"

"They're of too much value. If I took such a reward for—for a very ordinary service, I should never be able to respect myself again."

"This is not the reasoning of an intelligent person," said the Jinnee, coldly.

"If you think me a fool, I can't help it. I'm not an ungrateful fool, at all events. But I feel very strongly that I can't keep these gifts of yours."

"So thou wouldst have me break the oath which I swore to reward thee fitly for thy kind action?"

"But you have rewarded me already," said Horace, "by contriving that a wealthy merchant should engage me to build him a residence. And—forgive my plain speaking—if you truly desire my happiness (as I am sure you do) you will relieve me of all these precious gems and merchandise, because, to be frank, they will not make me happy. On the contrary, they are making me extremely uncomfortable."

"In the days of old," said Fakrash, "all men pursued wealth; nor could any amass enough to satisfy his desires. Have riches, then, become so contemptible in mortal eyes that thou findest them but an encumbrance? Explain the matter."

Horace felt a natural delicacy in giving his real reasons. "I can't answer for other men," he said. "All I know is that I've never been accustomed to being rich, and I'd rather get used to it gradually, and be able to feel that I owed it, as far as possible, to my own exertions. For, as I needn't tell you, Mr. Fakrash, riches alone don't make any fellow happy. You must have observed that they're apt to—well, to land him in all kinds of messes and worries.... I'm talking like a confounded copybook," he thought, "but I don't care how priggish I am if I can only get my way!"

Fakrash was deeply impressed. "O young man of marvellous moderation!" he cried. "Thy sentiments are not inferior to those of the Great Suleyman himself (on whom be peace!). Yet even he doth not utterly despise them, for he hath gold and ivory and precious stones in abundance. Nor hitherto have I ever met a human being capable of rejecting them when offered. But, since thou seemest sincere in holding that my poor and paltry gifts will not advance thy welfare, and since I would do thee good and not evil— be it even as thou wouldst. For excellently was it said: 'The worth of a present depends not on itself, nor on the giver, but on the receiver alone.'"

Horace could hardly believe that he had really prevailed. "It's extremely good of you, sir," he said, "to take it so well. And if you could let that caravan call for them as soon as possible, it would be a great convenience to me. I mean—er—the fact is, I'm expecting a few friends to dine with me to-morrow, and, as my rooms are rather small at the best of times, I don't quite know how I can manage to entertain them at all unless something is done."

"It will be the easiest of actions," replied Fakrash; "therefore, have no fear that, when the time cometh, thou wilt not be able to entertain thy friends in a fitting manner. And for the caravan, it shall set out without delay."

"By Jove, though, I'd forgotten one thing," said Horace: "I've locked up the room where your presents are—they won't be able to get in without the key."

"Against the servants of the Jinn neither bolts nor bars can prevail. They shall enter therein and remove all that they brought thee, since it is thy desire."

"Very many thanks," said Horace. "And you do really understand that I'm every bit as grateful as if I could keep the things? You see, I want all my time and all my energies to complete the designs for this building, which," he added gracefully, "I should never be in a position to do at all, but for your assistance."

"On my arrival," said Fakrash, "I heard thee lamenting the difficulties of the task; wherein do they consist?"

"Oh," said Horace, "it's a little difficult to please all the different people concerned, and myself too. I want to make something of it that I shall be proud of, and that will give me a reputation. It's a large house, and there will be a good deal of work in it; but I shall manage it all right."

"This is a great undertaking indeed," remarked the Jinnee, after he had asked various by no means unintelligent questions and received the answers. "But be persuaded that it shall all turn out most fortunately and thou shalt obtain great renown. And now," he concluded, "I am compelled to take leave of thee, for I am still without any certain tidings of Suleyman."

"You mustn't let me keep you," said Horace, who had been on thorns for some minutes lest Beevor should return and find him with his mysterious visitor. "You see," he added instructively, "so long as you will neglect your own much more important affairs to look after mine, you can hardly expect to make much progress, can you?"

"How excellent is the saying," replied the Jinnee: "'The time which is spent in doing kindnesses, call it not wasted.'"

"Yes, that's very good," said Horace, feeling driven to silence this maxim, if possible, with one of his own invention. "But we have a saying too—how does it go? Ah, I remember. 'It is possible for a kindness to be more inconvenient than an injury.'"

"Marvellously gifted was he who discovered such a saying!" cried Fakrash.

"I imagine," said Horace, "he learnt it from his own experience. By the way, what place were you thinking of drawing—I mean trying—next for Suleyman?"

"I purpose to repair to Nineveh, and inquire there."

"Capital," said Ventimore, with hearty approval, for he hoped that this would take the Jinnee some little time. "Wonderful city, Nineveh, from all I've heard—though not quite what it used to be, perhaps. Then there's Babylon—you might go on there. And if you shouldn't hear of him there, why not strike down into Central Africa, and do that thoroughly? Or South America; it's a pity to lose any chance—you've never been to South America yet?"

"I have not so much as heard of such a country, and how should Suleyman be there?"

"Pardon me, I didn't say he was there. All I meant to convey was, that he's quite as likely to be there as anywhere else. But if you're going to Nineveh first, you'd better lose no more time, for I've always understood that it's rather an awkward place to get at—though probably you won't find it very difficult."

"I care not," said Fakrash, "though the search be long, for in travel there are five advantages—"

"I know," interrupted Horace, "so don't stop to describe them now. I should like to see you fairly started, and you really mustn't think it necessary to break off your search again on my account, because, thanks to you, I shall get on splendidly alone for the future—if you'll kindly see that that merchandise is removed."

"Thine abode shall not be encumbered with it for another hour," said the Jinnee. "O thou judicious one, in whose estimation wealth is of no value, know that I have never encountered a mortal who pleased me as thou hast; and moreover, be assured that such magnanimity as thine shall not go without a recompense!"

"How often must I tell you," said Horace, in a glow of impatience, "that I am already much more than recompensed? Now, my kind, generous old friend," he added, with an emotion that was not wholly insincere, "the time has come to bid you farewell—for ever. Let me picture you as revisiting your former haunts, penetrating to quarters of the globe (for, whether you are aware of it or not, this earth of ours is a globe) hitherto unknown to you, refreshing your mind by foreign travel and the study of mankind—but never, never for a moment losing sight of your main object, the eventual discovery of and reconciliation with Suleyman (on whom be peace!). That is the greatest, the only happiness you can give me now. Good-bye, and bon voyage!"

"May Allah never deprive thy friends of thy presence!" returned the Jinnee, who was apparently touched by this exordium, "for truly thou art a most excellent young man!"

And stepping back into the fireplace, he was gone in an instant.

Ventimore sank back in his chair with a sigh of relief. He had begun to fear that the Jinnee never would take himself off, but he had gone at last—and for good.

He was half ashamed of himself for feeling so glad, for Fakrash was a good-natured old thing enough in his way. Only he would overdo things: he had no sense of proportion. "Why," thought Horace, "if a fellow expressed a modest wish for a canary in a cage he's just the sort of old Jinnee to bring him a whole covey of rocs in an aviary about ten times the size of the Crystal Palace. However, he does understand now that I can't take anything more from him, and he isn't offended either, so that's all settled. Now I can set to work and knock off these plans in peace and quietness."

But he had not done much before he heard sounds in the next room which told him that Beevor had returned at last. He had been expected back from the country for the last day or two, and it was fortunate that he had delayed so long, thought Ventimore, as he went in to see him and to tell him the unexpected piece of good fortune that he himself had met with since they last met. It is needless to say that, in giving his account, he abstained from any mention of the brass bottle or the Jinnee, as unessential elements in his story.

Beevor's congratulations were quite as cordial as could be expected, as soon as he fully understood that no hoax was intended. "Well, old man," he said, "I am glad. I really am, you know. To think of a prize like that coming to you the very first time! And you don't even know how this Mr. Wackerbath came to hear of you—just happened to see your name up outside and came in, I expect. Why, I dare say, if I hadn't chanced to go away as I did—and about a couple of paltry two thousand pound houses, too! Ah, well, I don't grudge you your luck, though it does seem rather— It was worth waiting for; you'll be cutting me out before long—if you don't make a mess of this job. I mean, you know, old chap, if you don't go and give your City man a Gothic castle when what he wants is something with plenty of plate-glass windows and a Corinthian portico. That's the rock I see ahead of you. You mustn't mind my giving you a word of warning!"

"Oh no," said Ventimore; "but I shan't give him either a Gothic castle or plenty of plate-glass. I venture to think he'll be pleased with the general idea as I'm working it out."

"Let's hope so," said Beevor. "If you get into any difficulty, you know," he added, with a touch of patronage, "just you come to me."

"Thanks," said Horace, "I will. But I'm getting on very fairly at present."

"I should rather like to see what you've made of it. I might be able to give you a wrinkle here and there."

"It's awfully good of you, but I think I'd rather you didn't see the plans till they're quite finished," said Horace. The truth was that he was perfectly aware that the other would not be in sympathy with his ideas; and Horace, who had just been suffering from a cold fit of depression about his work, rather shrank from any kind of criticism.

"Oh, just as you please!" said Beevor, a little stiffly; "you always were an obstinate beggar. I've had a certain amount of experience, you know, in my poor little pottering way, and I thought I might possibly have saved you a cropper or two. But if you think you can manage better alone—only don't get bolted with by one of those architectural hobbies of yours, that's all."

"All right, old fellow. I'll ride my hobby on the curb," said Horace, laughing, as he went back to his own office, where he found that all his former certainty and enjoyment of his work had returned to him, and by the end of the day he had made so much progress that his designs needed only a few finishing touches to be complete enough for his client's inspection.

Better still, on returning to his rooms that evening to change before going to Kensington, he found that the admirable Fakrash had kept his promise—every chest, sack, and bale had been cleared away.

"Them camels come back for the things this afternoon, sir," said Mrs. Rapkin, "and it put me in a fluster at first, for I made sure you'd locked your door and took the key. But I must have been mistook—leastways, them Arabs got in somehow. I hope you meant everything to go back?"

"Quite," said Horace; "I saw the—the person who sent them this morning, and told him there was nothing I cared for enough to keep."

"And like his impidence sending you a lot o' rubbish like that on approval—and on camels, too!" declared Mrs. Rapkin. "I'm sure I don't know what them advertising firms will try next—pushing, I call it."

Now that everything was gone, Horace felt a little natural regret and doubt whether he need have been quite so uncompromising in his refusal of the treasures. "I might have kept some of those tissues and things for Sylvia," he thought; "and she loves pearls. And a prayer-carpet would have pleased the Professor tremendously. But no, after all, it wouldn't have done. Sylvia couldn't go about in pearls the size of new potatoes, and the Professor would only have ragged me for more reckless extravagance. Besides, if I'd taken any of the Jinnee's gifts, he might keep on pouring more in, till I should be just where I was before—or worse off, really, because I couldn't decently refuse them, then. So it's best as it is."

And really, considering his temperament and the peculiar nature of his position, it is not easy to see how he could have arrived at any other conclusion.

CHAPTER VIII

BACHELOR'S QUARTERS

Horace was feeling particularly happy as he walked back the next evening to Vincent Square. He had the consciousness of having done a good day's work, for the sketch-plans for Mr. Wackerbath's mansion were actually completed and despatched to his business address, while Ventimore now felt a comfortable assurance that his designs would more than satisfy his client.

But it was not that which made him so light of heart. That night his rooms were to be honoured for the first time by Sylvia's presence. She would tread upon his carpet, sit in his chairs, comment upon, and perhaps even handle, his books and ornaments—and all of them would retain something of her charm for ever after. If she only came! For even now he could not quite believe that she really would; that some untoward event would not make a point of happening to prevent her, as he sometimes doubted whether his engagement was not too sweet and wonderful to be true—or, at all events, to last.

As to the dinner, his mind was tolerably easy, for he had settled the remaining details of the menu with his landlady that morning, and he could hope that without being so sumptuous as to excite the Professor's wrath, it would still be not altogether unworthy—and what goods could be rare and dainty enough?—to be set before Sylvia.

He would have liked to provide champagne, but he knew that wine would savour of ostentation in the Professor's judgment, so he had contented himself instead with claret, a sound vintage which he knew he could depend upon. Flowers, he thought, were clearly permissible, and he had called at a florist's on his way and got some chrysanthemums of palest yellow and deepest terra-cotta, the finest he could see. Some of them would look well on the centre of the table in an old Nankin blue-and-white bowl he had; the rest he could arrange about the room: there would just be time to see to all that before dressing.

Occupied with these thoughts, he turned into Vincent Square, which looked vaster than ever with the murky haze, enclosed by its high railings, and under a wide expanse of steel-blue sky, across which the clouds were driving fast like ships in full sail scudding for harbour before a storm. Against the mist below, the young and nearly leafless trees showed flat, black profiles as of pressed seaweed, and the sky immediately above the house-tops was tinged with a sullen red from miles of lighted streets; from the river came the long-drawn tooting of tugs, mingled with the more distant wail and hysterical shrieks of railway engines on the Lambeth lines.

And now he reached the old semi-detached house in which he lodged, and noticed for the first time how the trellis-work of the veranda made, with the bared creepers and hanging baskets, a kind of decorative pattern against the windows, which were suffused with a roseate glow that looked warm and comfortable and hospitable. He wondered whether Sylvia would notice it when she arrived.

He passed under the old wrought-iron arch that once held an oil-lamp, and up a short but rather steep flight of steps, which led to a brick porch built out at the side. Then he let himself in, and stood spellbound with perplexed amazement,—for he was in a strange house.

In place of the modest passage with the yellow marble wall-paper, the mahogany hat-stand, and the elderly barometer in a state of chronic depression which he knew so well, he found an arched octagonal entrance-hall with arabesques of blue, crimson, and gold, and richly-embroidered hangings; the floor was marble, and from a shallow basin of alabaster in the centre a perfumed fountain rose and fell with a lulling patter.

"I must have mistaken the number," he thought, quite forgetting that his latch-key had fitted, and he was just about to retreat before his intrusion was discovered, when the hangings parted, and Mrs. Rapkin presented herself, making so deplorably incongruous a figure in such surroundings, and looking so bewildered and woebegone, that Horace, in spite of his own increasing uneasiness, had some difficulty in keeping his gravity.

"Oh, Mr. Ventimore, sir," she lamented; "whatever will you go and do next, I wonder? To think of your going and having the whole place done up and altered out of knowledge like this, without a word of warning! If any halterations were required, I do think as me and Rapkin had the right to be consulted."

Horace let all his chrysanthemums drop unheeded into the fountain. He understood now: indeed, he seemed in some way to have understood almost from the first, only he would not admit it even to himself.

The irrepressible Jinnee was at the bottom of this, of course. He remembered now having made that unfortunate remark the day before about the limited accommodation his rooms afforded.

Clearly Fakrash must have taken a mental note of it, and, with that insatiable munificence which was one of his worst failings, had determined, by way of a pleasant surprise, to entirely refurnish and redecorate the apartments according to his own ideas.

It was extremely kind of him; it showed a truly grateful disposition—"but, oh!" as Horace thought, in the bitterness of his soul, "if he would only learn to let well alone and mind his own business!"

However, the thing was done now, and he must accept the responsibility for it, since he could hardly disclose the truth. "Didn't I mention I was having some alterations made?" he said carelessly. "They've got the work done rather sooner than I expected. Were—were they long over it?"

"I'm sure I can't tell you, sir, having stepped out to get some things I wanted in for to-night; and Rapkin, he was round the corner at his reading-room; and when I come back it was all done and the workmen gone 'ome; and how they could have finished such a job in the time beats me altogether, for when we 'ad the men in to do the back kitchen they took ten days over it."

"Well," said Horace, evading this point, "however they've done this, they've done it remarkably well—you'll admit that, Mrs. Rapkin?"

"That's as may be sir," said Mrs. Rapkin, with a sniff, "but it ain't my taste, nor yet I don't think it will be Rapkin's taste when he comes to see it."

It was not Ventimore's taste either, though he was not going to confess it. "Sorry for that, Mrs. Rapkin," he said, "but I've no time to talk about it now. I must rush upstairs and dress."

"Begging your pardon, sir, but that's a total unpossibility—for they've been and took away the staircase.'

"Taken away the staircase? Nonsense!" cried Horace.

"So I think, Mr. Ventimore—but it's what them men have done, and if you don't believe me, come and see for yourself!"

She drew the hangings aside, and revealed to Ventimore's astonished gaze a vast pillared hall with a lofty domed roof, from which hung several lamps, diffusing a subdued radiance. High up in the wall, on his left, were the two windows which he judged to have formerly belonged to his sitting-room (for either from delicacy or inability, or simply because it had not occurred to him, the Jinnee had not interfered with the external structure), but the windows were now masked by a perforated and gilded lattice, which accounted for the pattern Horace had noticed from without. The walls were covered with blue-and-white Oriental tiles, and a raised platform of alabaster on which were divans ran round two sides of the hall, while the side opposite to him was pierced with horseshoe-shaped arches, apparently leading to other apartments. The centre of the marble floor was spread with costly rugs and piles of cushions, their rich hues glowing through the gold with which they were intricately embroidered.

"Well," said the unhappy Horace, scarcely knowing what he was saying, "it—it all looks very cosy, Mrs. Rapkin."

"It's not for me to say, sir; but I should like to know where you thought of dining?"

"Where?" said Horace. "Why, here, of course. There's plenty of room."

"There isn't a table left in the house," said Mrs. Rapkin; "so, unless you'd wish the cloth laid on the floor—"

"Oh, there must be a table somewhere," said Horace, impatiently, "or you can borrow one. Don't make difficulties, Mrs. Rapkin. Rig up anything you like.... Now I must be off and dress."

He got rid of her, and, on entering one of the archways, discovered a smaller room, in cedar-wood encrusted with ivory and mother-o'-pearl, which was evidently his bedroom. A gorgeous robe, stiff with gold and glittering with ancient gems, was laid out for him—for the Jinnee had thought of everything—but Ventimore, naturally, preferred his own evening clothes.

"Mr. Rapkin!" he shouted, going to another arch that seemed to communicate with the basement.

"Sir?" replied his landlord, who had just returned from his "reading-room," and now appeared, without a tie and in his shirt-sleeves, looking pale and wild, as was, perhaps, intelligible in the circumstances. As he entered his unfamiliar marble halls he staggered, and his red eyes rolled and his mouth gaped in a cod-like fashion. "They've been at it 'ere, too, seemin'ly," he remarked huskily.

"There have been a few changes," said Horace, quietly, "as you can see. You don't happen to know where they've put my dress-clothes, do you?"

"I don't 'appen to know where they've put nothink. Your dress clothes? Why, I dunno where they've bin and put our little parler where me and Maria 'ave set of a hevenin' all these years regular. I dunno where they've put the pantry, nor yet the bath-room, with 'ot and cold water laid on at my own expense. And you arsk me to find your hevenin' soot! I consider, sir, I consider that a unwall—that a most unwarrant-terrible liberty have bin took at my expense."

"My good man, don't talk rubbish!" said Horace.

"I'm talking to you about what I know, and I assert that an Englishman's 'ome is his cashle, and nobody's got the right when his backsh turned to go and make a 'Ummums of it. Not nobody 'asn't!"

"Make a what of it?" cried Ventimore.

"A 'Ummums—that's English, ain't it? A bloomin' Turkish baths! Who do you suppose is goin' to take apartments furnished in this 'ere ridic'loush style? What am I goin' to say to my landlord? It'll about ruing me, this will; and after you bein' a lodger 'ere for five year and more, and regarded by me and Maria in the light of one of the family. It's 'ard—it's damned 'ard!"

"Now, look here," said Ventimore, sharply—for it was obvious that Mr. Rapkin's studies had been lightened by copious refreshment—"pull yourself together, man, and listen to me."

"I respeckfully decline to pull myshelf togerrer f'r anybody livin'," said Mr. Rapkin, with a noble air. "I shtan' 'ere upon my dignity as a man, sir. I shay, I shtand 'ere upon—" Here he waved his hand, and sat down suddenly upon the marble floor.

"You can stand on anything you like—or can," said Horace; "but hear what I've got to say. The—the people who made all these alterations went beyond my instructions. I never wanted the house interfered with like this. Still, if your landlord doesn't see that its value is immensely improved, he's a fool, that's all. Anyway, I'll take care you shan't suffer. If I have to put everything back in its former state, I will, at my own expense. So don't bother any more about that."

"You're a gen'l'man, Mr. Ventimore," said Rapkin, cautiously regaining his feet. "There's no mishtaking a gen'l'man. I'm a gen'l'man."

"Of course you are," said Horace genially, "and I'll tell you how you're going to show it. You're going straight downstairs to get your good wife to pour some cold water over your head; and then you will finish dressing, see what you can do to get a table of some sort and lay it for dinner, and be ready to announce my friends when they arrive, and wait afterwards. Do you see?"

"That will be all ri', Mr. Ventimore," said Rapkin, who was not far gone enough to be beyond understanding or obeying. "You leave it entirely to me. I'll unnertake that your friends shall be made comforrable, perfferly comforrable. I've lived as butler in the besht, the mosht ecxlu—most arishto—you know the sort o' fam'lies I'm tryin' to r'member—and—and everything was always all ri', and I shall be all ri' in a few minutes."

With this assurance he stumbled downstairs, leaving Horace relieved to some extent. Rapkin would be sober enough after his head had been under the tap for a few minutes, and in any case there would be the hired waiter to rely upon.

If he could only find out where his evening clothes were! He returned to his room and made another frantic search—but they were nowhere to be found; and as he could not bring himself to receive his guests in his ordinary morning costume—which the Professor would probably construe as a deliberate slight, and which would certainly seem a solecism in Mrs. Futvoye's eyes, if not in her daughter's—he decided to put on the Eastern robes, with the exception of a turban, which he could not manage to wind round his head.

Thus arrayed he re-entered the domed hall, where he was annoyed to find that no attempt had been made as yet to prepare a dinner-table, and he was just looking forlornly round for a bell when Rapkin appeared. He had apparently followed Horace's advice, for his hair looked wet and sleek, and he was comparatively sober.

"This is too bad!" cried Horace; "my friends may be here at any moment now—and nothing done. You don't propose to wait at table like that, do you?" he added, as he noted the man's overcoat and the comforter round his throat.

"I do not propose to wait in any garments whatsoever," said Rapkin; "I'm a-goin' out, I am."

"Very well," said Horace; "then send the waiter up—I suppose he's come?"

"He come—but he went away again—I told him as he wouldn't be required."

"You told him that!" Horace said angrily, and then controlled himself. "Come, Rapkin, be reasonable. You can't really mean to leave your wife to cook the dinner, and serve it too!"

"She ain't intending to do neither; she've left the house already."

"You must fetch her back," cried Horace. "Good heavens, man, can't you see what a fix you're leaving me in? My friends have started long ago—it's too late to wire to them, or make any other arrangements."

There was a knock, as he spoke, at the front door; and odd enough was the familiar sound of the cast-iron knocker in that Arabian hall.

"There they are!" he said, and the idea of meeting them at the door and proposing an instant adjournment to a restaurant occurred to him—till he suddenly recollected that he would have to change and try to find some money, even for that. "For the last time, Rapkin," he cried in despair, "do you mean to tell me there's no dinner ready?"

"Oh," said Rapkin, "there's dinner right enough, and a lot o' barbarious furriners downstairs a cookin' of it—that's what broke Maria's 'art—to see it all took out of her 'ands, after the trouble she'd gone to."

"But I must have somebody to wait," exclaimed Horace.

"You've got waiters enough, as far as that goes. But if you expect a hordinary Christian man to wait along of a lot o' narsty niggers, and be at their beck and call, you're mistook, sir, for I'm going to sleep the night at my brother-in-law's and take his advice, he bein' a doorkeeper at a solicitor's orfice and knowing the law, about this 'ere business, and so I wish you a good hevening, and 'oping your dinner will be to your liking and satisfaction."

He went out by the farther archway, while from the entrance-hall Horace could hear voices he knew only too well. The Futvoyes had come; well, at all events, it seemed that there would be something for them to eat, since Fakrash, in his anxiety to do the thing thoroughly, had furnished both the feast and attendance himself—but who was there to announce the guests? Where were these waiters Rapkin had spoken of? Ought he to go and bring in his visitors himself?

These questions answered themselves the next instant, for, as he stood there under the dome, the curtains of the central arch were drawn with a rattle, and disclosed a double line of tall slaves in rich raiment, their onyx eyes rolling and their teeth flashing in their chocolate-hued countenances, as they salaamed.

Between this double line stood Professor and Mrs. Futvoye and Sylvia, who had just removed their wraps and were gazing in undisguised astonishment on the splendours which met their view.

Horace advanced to receive them; he felt he was in for it now, and the only course left him was to put as good a face as he could on the matter, and trust to luck to pull him through without discovery or disaster.

CHAPTER IX

"PERSICOS ODI, PUER, APPARATUS"

"So you've found your way here at last?" said Horace, as he shook hands heartily with the Professor and Mrs. Futvoye. "I can't tell you how delighted I am to see you."

As a matter of fact, he was very far from being at ease, which made him rather over-effusive, but he was determined that, if he could help it, he would not betray the slightest consciousness of anything bizarre or unusual in his domestic arrangements.

"And these," said Mrs. Futvoye, who was extremely stately in black, with old lace and steel embroidery—"these are the bachelor lodgings you were so modest about! Really," she added, with a humorous twinkle in her shrewd eyes, "you young men seem to understand how to make yourselves comfortable—don't they, Anthony?"

"They do, indeed," said the Professor, dryly, though it manifestly cost him some effort to conceal his appreciation. "To produce such results as these must, if I mistake not, have entailed infinite research— and considerable expense."

"No," said Horace, "no. You—you'd be surprised if you knew how little."

"I should have imagined," retorted the Professor, "that any outlay on apartments which I presume you do not contemplate occupying for an extended period must be money thrown away. But, doubtless, you know best."

"But your rooms are quite wonderful, Horace!" cried Sylvia, her charming eyes dilating with admiration. "And where, where did you get that magnificent dressing-gown? I never saw anything so lovely in my life!"

She herself was lovely enough in a billowy, shimmering frock of a delicate apple-green hue, her only ornament a deep-blue Egyptian scarab with spread wings, which was suspended from her neck by a slender gold chain.

"I—I ought to apologise for receiving you in this costume," said Horace, with embarrassment; "but the fact is, I couldn't find my evening clothes anywhere, so—so I put on the first things that came to hand."

"It is hardly necessary," said the Professor, conscious of being correctly clad, and unconscious that his shirt-front was bulging and his long-eared white tie beginning to work up towards his left jaw—"hardly necessary to offer any apology for the simplicity of your costume—which is entirely in keeping with the—ah—strictly Oriental character of your interior."

"I feel dreadfully out of keeping!" said Sylvia, "for there's nothing in the least Oriental about me—unless it's my scarab—and he's I don't know how many centuries behind the time, poor dear!"

"If you said 'thousands of years,' my dear," corrected the Professor, "you would be more accurate. That scarab was taken out of a tomb of the thirteenth dynasty."

"Well, I'm sure he'd rather be where he is," said Sylvia, and Ventimore entirely agreed with her. "Horace, I must look at everything. How clever and original of you to transform an ordinary London house into this!"

"Oh, well, you see," explained Horace, "it—it wasn't exactly done by me."

"Whoever did it," said the Professor, "must have devoted considerable study to Eastern art and architecture. May I ask the name of the firm who executed the alterations?"

"I really couldn't tell you, sir," answered Horace, who was beginning to understand how very bad a mauvais quart d'heure can be.

"You can't tell me!" exclaimed the Professor. "You order these extensive, and I should say expensive, decorations, and you don't know the firm you selected to carry them out!"

"Of course I know," said Horace, "only I don't happen to remember at this moment. Let me see, now. Was it Liberty? No, I'm almost certain it wasn't Liberty. It might have been Maple, but I'm not sure. Whoever did do it, they were marvellously cheap."

"I am glad to hear it," said the Professor, in his most unpleasant tone. "Where is your dining-room?"

"Why, I rather think," said Horace, helplessly, as he saw a train of attendants laying a round cloth on the floor, "I rather think this is the dining-room."

"You appear to be in some doubt?" said the Professor.

"I leave it to them—it depends where they choose to lay the cloth," said Horace. "Sometimes in one place; sometimes in another. There's a great charm in uncertainty," he faltered.

"Doubtless," said the Professor.

By this time two of the slaves, under the direction of a tall and turbaned black, had set a low ebony stool, inlaid with silver and tortoiseshell in strange devices, on the round carpet, when other attendants followed with a circular silver tray containing covered dishes, which they placed on the stool and salaamed.

"Your—ah—groom of the chambers," said the Professor, "seems to have decided that we should dine here. I observe they are making signs to you that the food is on the table."

"So it is," said Ventimore. "Shall we sit down?"

"But, my dear Horace," said Mrs. Futvoye, "your butler has forgotten the chairs."

"You don't appear to realise, my dear," said the Professor, "that in such an interior as this chairs would be hopelessly incongruous."

"I'm afraid there aren't any," said Horace, for there was nothing but four fat cushions. "Let's sit down on these," he proposed. "It—it's more fun!"

"At my time of life," said the Professor, irritably, as he let himself down on the plumpest cushion, "such fun as may be derived from eating one's meals on the floor fails to appeal to my sense of humour. However, I admit that it is thoroughly Oriental."

"I think it's delightful," said Sylvia; "ever so much nicer than a stiff, conventional dinner-party."

"One may be unconventional," remarked her father, "without escaping the penalty of stiffness. Go away, sir! go away!" he added snappishly, to one of the slaves, who was attempting to pour water over his hands. "Your servant, Ventimore, appears to imagine that I go out to dinner without taking the trouble to wash my hands previously. This, I may mention, is not the case."

"It's only an Eastern ceremony, Professor," said Horace.

"I am perfectly well aware of what is customary in the East," retorted the Professor; "it does not follow that such—ah—hygienic precautions are either necessary or desirable at a Western table."

Horace made no reply; he was too much occupied in gazing blankly at the silver dish-covers and wondering what in the world might be underneath; nor was his perplexity relieved when the covers were removed, for he was quite at a loss to guess how he was supposed to help the contents without so much as a fork.

The chief attendant, however, solved that difficulty by intimating in pantomime that the guests were expected to use their fingers.

Sylvia accomplished this daintily and with intense amusement, but her father and mother made no secret of their repugnance. "If I were dining in the desert with a Sheik, sir," observed the Professor, "I should, I hope, know how to conform to his habits and prejudices. Here, in the heart of London, I confess all this strikes me as a piece of needless pedantry."

"I'm very sorry," said Horace; "I'd have some knives and forks if I could—but I'm afraid these fellows don't even understand what they are, so it's useless to order any. We—we must rough it a little, that's all. I hope that—er—fish is all right, Professor?"

He did not know precisely what kind of fish it was, but it was fried in oil of sesame and flavoured with a mixture of cinnamon and ginger, and the Professor did not appear to be making much progress with it. Ventimore himself would have infinitely preferred the original cod and oyster sauce, but that could not be helped now.

"Thank you," said the Professor, "it is curious—but characteristic. Not any more, thank you."

Horace could only trust that the next course would be more of a success. It was a dish of mutton, stewed with peaches, jujubes and sugar, which Sylvia declared was delicious. Her parents made no comment.

"Might I ask for something to drink?" said the Professor, presently; whereupon a cupbearer poured him a goblet of iced sherbet perfumed with conserve of violets.

"I'm very sorry, my dear fellow," he said, after sipping it, "but if I drink this I shall be ill all next day. If I might have a glass of wine—"

Another slave instantly handed him a cup of wine, which he tasted and set down with a wry face and a shudder. Horace tried some afterwards, and was not surprised. It was a strong, harsh wine, in which goatskin and resin struggled for predominance.

"It's an old and, I make no doubt, a fine wine," observed the Professor, with studied politeness, "but I fancy it must have suffered in transportation. I really think that, with my gouty tendency, a little whisky and Apollinaris would be better for me—if you keep such occidental fluids in the house?"

Horace felt convinced that it would be useless to order the slaves to bring whisky or Apollinaris, which were of course, unknown in the Jinnee's time, so he could do nothing but apologise for their absence.

"No matter," said the Professor; "I am not so thirsty that I cannot wait till I get home."

It was some consolation that both Sylvia and her mother commended the sherbet, and even appreciated—or were so obliging as to say they appreciated—the entrée, which consisted of rice and mincemeat wrapped in vine-leaves, and certainly was not appetising in appearance, besides being difficult to dispose of gracefully.

It was followed by a whole lamb fried in oil, stuffed with pounded pistachio nuts, pepper, nutmeg, and coriander seeds, and liberally besprinkled with rose-water and musk.

Only Horace had sufficient courage to attack the lamb—and he found reason to regret it. Afterwards came fowls stuffed with raisins, parsley, and crumbled bread, and the banquet ended with pastry of weird forms and repellent aspect.

"I hope," said Horace, anxiously, "you don't find this Eastern cookery very—er—unpalatable?"—he himself was feeling distinctly unwell: "it's rather a change from the ordinary routine."

"I have made a truly wonderful dinner, thank you," replied the Professor, not, it is to be feared, without intention. "Even in the East I have eaten nothing approaching this."

"But where did your landlady pick up this extraordinary cooking, my dear Horace?" said Mrs. Futvoye. "I thought you said she was merely a plain cook. Has she ever lived in the East?"

"Not exactly in the East," exclaimed Horace; "not what you would call living there. The fact is," he continued, feeling that he was in danger of drivelling, and that he had better be as candid as he could, "this dinner wasn't cooked by her. She—she was obliged to go away quite suddenly. So the dinner was all sent in by—by a sort of contractor, you know. He supplies the whole thing, waiters and all."

"I was thinking," said the Professor, "that for a bachelor—an engaged bachelor—you seemed to maintain rather a large establishment."

"Oh, they're only here for the evening, sir," said Horace. "Capital fellows—more picturesque than the local greengrocer—and they don't breathe on the top of your head."

"They're perfect dears, Horace," remarked Sylvia; "only—well, just a little creepy-crawly to look at!"

"It would ill become me to criticise the style and method of our entertainment," put in the Professor, acidly, "otherwise I might be tempted to observe that it scarcely showed that regard for economy which I should have—"

"Now, Anthony," put in his wife, "don't let us have any fault-finding. I'm sure Horace has done it all delightfully—yes, delightfully; and even if he has been just a little extravagant, it's not as if he was obliged to be as economical now, you know!"

"My dear," said the Professor, "I have yet to learn that the prospect of an increased income in the remote future is any justification for reckless profusion in the present."

"If you only knew," said Horace, "you wouldn't call it profusion. It—it's not at all the dinner I meant it to be, and I'm afraid it wasn't particularly nice—but it's certainly not expensive."

"Expensive is, of course, a very relative term. But I think I have the right to ask whether this is the footing on which you propose to begin your married life?"

It was an extremely awkward question, as the reader will perceive. If Ventimore replied—as he might with truth—that he had no intention whatever of maintaining his wife in luxury such as that, he stood convicted of selfish indulgence as a bachelor; if, on the other hand, he declared that he did propose to maintain his wife in the same fantastic and exaggerated splendour as the present, it would certainly confirm her father's disbelief in his prudence and economy.

And it was that egregious old ass of a Jinnee, as Horace thought, with suppressed rage, who had let him in for all this, and who was now far beyond all remonstrance or reproach!

Before he could bring himself to answer the question, the attendants had noiselessly removed the tray and stool, and were handing round rosewater in a silver ewer and basin, the character of which, luckily or otherwise, turned the Professor's inquisitiveness into a different channel.

"These are not bad—really not bad at all," he said, inspecting the design. "Where did you manage to pick them up?"

"I didn't," said Horace; "they're provided by the—the person who supplies the dinner."

"Can you give me his address?" said the Professor, scenting a bargain; "because really, you know, these things are probably antiques—much too good to be used for business purposes."

"I'm wrong," said Horace, lamely; "these particular things are—are lent by an eccentric Oriental gentleman, as a great favour."

"Do I know him? Is he a collector of such things?"

"You wouldn't have met him; he—he's lived a very retired life of late."

"I should very much like to see his collection. If you could give me a letter of introduction—"

"No," said Horace, in a state of prickly heat; "it wouldn't be any use. His collection is never shown. He—he's a most peculiar man. And just now he's abroad."

"Ah! pardon me if I've been indiscreet; but I concluded from what you said that this—ah—banquet was furnished by a professional caterer."

"Oh, the banquet? Yes, that came from the Stores," said Horace, mendaciously. "The—the Oriental Cookery Department. They've just started it, you know; so—so I thought I'd give them a trial. But it's not what I call properly organised yet."

The slaves were now, with low obeisances, inviting them to seat themselves on the divan which lined part of the hall.

"Ha!" said the Professor, as he rose from his cushion, cracking audibly, "so we're to have our coffee and what not over there, hey?... Well, my boy, I shan't be sorry, I confess, to have something to lean my back against—and a cigar, a mild cigar, will—ah—aid digestion. You do smoke here?"

"Smoke?" said Horace, "Why, of course! All over the place. Here," he said, clapping his hands, which brought an obsequious slave instantly to his side; "just bring coffee and cigars, will you?"

The slave rolled his brandy-ball eyes in obvious perplexity.

"Coffee," said Horace; "you must know what coffee is. And cigarettes. Well, chibouks, then—'hubble-bubbles'—if that's what you call them."

But the slave clearly did not understand, and it suddenly struck Horace that, since 'tobacco and coffee were not introduced, even in the East, till long after the Jinnee's time, he, as the founder of the feast, would naturally be unaware how indispensable they had become at the present day.

"I'm really awfully sorry," he said; "but they don't seem to have provided any. I shall speak to the manager about it. And, unfortunately, I don't know where my own cigars are."

"It's of no consequence," said the Professor, with the sort of stoicism that minds very much. "I am a moderate smoker at best, and Turkish coffee, though delicious, is apt to keep me awake. But if you could let me have a look at that brass bottle you got at poor Collingham's sale, I should be obliged to you."

Horace had no idea where it was then, nor could he, until the Professor came to the rescue with a few words of Arabic, manage to make the slaves comprehend what he wished them to find.

At length, however, two of them appeared, bearing the brass bottle with every sign of awe, and depositing it at Ventimore's feet.

Professor Futvoye, after wiping and adjusting his glasses, proceeded to examine the vessel. "It certainly is a most unusual type of brassware," he said, "as unique in its way as the silver ewer and basin; and, as you thought, there does seem to be something resembling an inscription on the cap, though in this dim light it is almost impossible to be sure."

While he was poring over it, Horace seated himself on the divan by Sylvia's side, hoping for one of the whispered conversations permitted to affianced lovers; he had pulled through the banquet somehow, and on the whole he felt thankful things had not gone off worse. The noiseless and uncanny attendants, whom he did not know whether to regard as Efreets, or demons, or simply illusions, but whose services he had no wish to retain, had all withdrawn. Mrs. Futvoye was peacefully slumbering, and her husband was in a better humour than he had been all the evening.

Suddenly from behind the hangings of one of the archways came strange, discordant sounds, barbaric janglings and thumpings, varied by yowls as of impassioned cats.

Sylvia drew involuntarily closer to Horace; her mother woke with a start, and the Professor looked up from the brass bottle with returning irritation.

"What's this? What's this?" he demanded; "some fresh surprise in store for us?"

It was quite as much of a surprise for Horace, but he was spared the humiliation of owning it by the entrance of some half-dozen dusky musicians swathed in white and carrying various strangely fashioned instruments, with which they squatted down in a semi-circle by the opposite wall, and began to twang, and drub, and squall with the complacent cacophony of an Eastern orchestra. Clearly Fakrash was determined that nothing should be wanting to make the entertainment a complete success.

"What a very extraordinary noise!" said Mrs. Futvoye; "surely they can't mean it for music?"

"Yes, they do," said Horace; "it—it's really more harmonious than it sounds—you have to get accustomed to the—er—notation. When you do, it's rather soothing than otherwise."

"I dare say," said the poor lady. "And do they come from the Stores, too?"

"No," said Horace, with a fine assumption of candour, "they don't; they come from—the Arab Encampment at Earl's Court—parties and fêtes attended, you know. But they play here for nothing; they—they want to get their name known, you see; very deserving and respectable set of fellows."

"My dear Horace!" remarked Mrs. Futvoye, "if they expect to get engagements for parties and so on, they really ought to try and learn a tune of some sort."

"I understand, Horace," whispered Sylvia, "it's very naughty of you to have gone to all this trouble and expense (for, of course, it has cost you a lot) just to please us; but, whatever, dad may say, I love you all the better for doing it!"

And her hand stole softly into his, and he felt that he could forgive Fakrash everything, even—even the orchestra.

But there was something unpleasantly spectral about their shadowy forms, which showed in grotesquely baggy and bulgy shapes in the uncertain light. Some of them wore immense and curious white head-dresses, which gave them the appearance of poulticed thumbs; and they all went on scraping and twiddling and caterwauling with a doleful monotony that Horace felt must be getting on his guests' nerves, as it certainly was on his own.

He did not know how to get rid of them, but he sketched a kind of gesture in the air, intended to intimate that, while their efforts had afforded the keenest pleasure to the company generally, they were unwilling to monopolise them any longer, and the artists were at liberty to retire.

Perhaps there is no art more liable to misconstruction than pantomime; certainly, Ventimore's efforts in this direction were misunderstood, for the music became wilder, louder, more aggressively and abominably out of tune—and then a worse thing happened.

For the curtains separated, and, heralded by sharp yelps from the performers, a female figure floated into the hall and began to dance with a slow and sinuous grace.

Her beauty, though of a pronounced Oriental type, was unmistakable, even in the subdued light which fell on her; her diaphanous robe indicated a faultless form; her dark tresses were braided with sequins; she had the long, lustrous eyes, the dusky cheeks artificially whitened, and the fixed scarlet smile of the Eastern dancing-girl of all time.

And she paced the floor with her tinkling feet, writhing and undulating like some beautiful cobra, while the players worked themselves up to yet higher and higher stages of frenzy.

Ventimore, as he sat there looking helplessly on, felt a return of his resentment against the Jinnee. It was really too bad of him; he ought, at his age, to have known better!

Not that there was anything objectionable in the performance itself; but still, it was not the kind of entertainment for such an occasion. Horace wished now he had mentioned to Fakrash who the guests were whom he expected, and then perhaps even the Jinnee would have exercised more tact in his arrangements.

"And does this girl come from Earl's Court?" inquired Mrs. Futvoye, who was now thoroughly awake.

"Oh dear, no," said Horace; "I engaged her at—at Harrod's—the Entertainment Bureau. They told me there she was rather good—struck out a line of her own, don't you know. But perfectly correct; she—she only does this to support an invalid aunt."

These statements were, as he felt even in making them, not only gratuitous, but utterly unconvincing, but he had arrived at that condition in which a man discovers with terror the unsuspected amount of mendacity latent in his system.

"I should have thought there were other ways of supporting invalid aunts," remarked Mrs. Futvoye. "What is this young lady's name?"

"Tinkler," said Horace, on the spur of the moment. "Miss Clementine Tinkler."

"But surely she is a foreigner?"

"Mademoiselle, I ought to have said. And Tinkla—with an 'a,' you know. I believe her mother was of Arabian extraction—but I really don't know," explained Horace, conscious that Sylvia had withdrawn her hand from his, and was regarding him with covert anxiety.

"I really must put a stop to this," he thought.

"You're getting bored by all this, darling," he said aloud; "so am I. I'll tell them to go." And he rose and held out his hand as a sign that the dance should cease.

It ceased at once; but, to his unspeakable horror, the dancer crossed the floor with a swift jingling rush, and sank in a gauzy heap at his feet, seizing his hand in both hers and covering it with kisses, while she murmured speeches in some tongue unknown to him.

"Is this a usual feature in Miss Tinkla's entertainments, may I ask?" said Mrs. Futvoye, bristling with not unnatural indignation.

"I really don't know," said the unhappy Horace; "I can't make out what she's saying."

"If I understand her rightly," said the Professor, "she is addressing you as the 'light of her eyes and the vital spirit of her heart.'"

"Oh!" said Horace, "she's quite mistaken, you know. It—it's the emotional artist temperament—they don't mean anything by it. My—my dear young lady," he added, "you've danced most delightfully, and

I'm sure we're all most deeply indebted to you; but we won't detain you any longer. Professor," he added, as she made no offer to rise, "will you kindly explain to them in Arabic that I should be obliged by their going at once?"

The Professor said a few words, which had the desired effect. The girl gave a little scream and scudded through the archway, and the musicians seized their instruments and scuttled after her.

"I am so sorry," said Horace, whose evening seemed to him to have been chiefly spent in apologies; "it's not at all the kind of entertainment one would expect from a place like Whiteley's."

"By no means," agreed the Professor; "but I understood you to say Miss Tinkla was recommended to you by Harrod's?"

"Very likely, sir," said Horace; "but that doesn't affect the case. I shouldn't expect it from them."

"Probably they don't know how shamelessly that young person conducts herself," said Mrs. Futvoye. "And I think it only right that they should be told."

"I shall complain, of course," said Horace. "I shall put it very strongly."

"A protest would have more weight coming from a woman," said Mrs. Futvoye; "and, as a shareholder in the company, I shall feel bound—"

"No, I wouldn't," said Horace; "in fact, you mustn't. For, now I come to think of it, she didn't come from Harrod's, after all, or Whiteley's either."

"Then perhaps you will be good enough to inform us where she did come from?"

"I would if I knew," said Horace; "but I don't."

"What!" cried the Professor, sharply, "do you mean to say you can't account for the existence of a dancing-girl who—in my daughter's presence—kisses your hand and addresses you by endearing epithets?"

"Oriental metaphor!" said Horace. "She was a little overstrung. Of course, if I had had any idea she would make such a scene as that— Sylvia," he broke off, "you don't doubt me?"

"No, Horace," said Sylvia, simply, "I'm sure you must have some explanation—only I do think it would be better if you gave it."

"If I told you the truth," said Horace, slowly, "you would none of you believe me!"

"Then you admit," put in the Professor, "that hitherto you have not been telling the truth?"

"Not as invariably as I could have wished," Horace confessed.

"So I suspected. Then, unless you can bring yourself to be perfectly candid, you can hardly wonder at our asking you to consider your engagement as broken off?"

"Broken off!" echoed Horace. "Sylvia, you won't give me up! You know I wouldn't do anything unworthy of you!"

"I'm certain that you can't have done anything which would make me love you one bit the less if I knew it. So why not be quite open with us?"

"Because, darling," said Horace, "I'm in such a fix that it would only make matters worse."

"In that case," said the Professor, "and as it is already rather late, perhaps you will allow one of your numerous retinue to call a four-wheeler?"

Horace clapped his hands, but no one answered the summons, and he could not find any of the slaves in the antechamber.

"I'm afraid all the servants have left," he explained; and it is to be feared he would have added that they were all obliged to return to the contractor by eleven, only he caught the Professor's eye and decided that he had better refrain. "If you will wait here, I'll go out and fetch a cab," he added.

"There is no occasion to trouble you," said the Professor; "my wife and daughter have already got their things on, and we will walk until we find a cab. Now, Mr. Ventimore, we will bid you good-night and good-bye. For, after what has happened, you will, I trust, have the good taste to discontinue your visits and make no attempt to see Sylvia again."

"Upon my honour," protested Horace, "I have done nothing to warrant you in shutting your doors against me."

"I am unable to agree with you. I have never thoroughly approved of your engagement, because, as I told you at the time, I suspected you of recklessness in money matters. Even in accepting your invitation to-night I warned you, as you may remember, not to make the occasion an excuse for foolish extravagance. I come here, and find you in apartments furnished and decorated (as you informed us) by yourself, and on a scale which would be prodigal in a millionaire. You have a suite of retainers which (except for their nationality and imperfect discipline) a prince might envy. You provide a banquet of—hem!—delicacies which must have cost you infinite trouble and unlimited expense—this, after I had expressly stipulated for a quiet family dinner! Not content with that, you procure for our diversion Arab music and dancing of a—of a highly recondite character. I should be unworthy of the name of father, sir, if I were to entrust my only daughter's happiness to a young man with so little common sense, so little self-restraint. And she will understand my motives and obey my wishes."

"You're right, Professor, according to your lights," admitted Horace. "And yet—confound it all!—you're utterly wrong, too!"

"Oh, Horace," cried Sylvia; "if you had only listened to dad, and not gone to all this foolish, foolish expense, we might have been so happy!"

"But I have gone to no expense. All this hasn't cost me a penny!"

"Ah, there is some mystery! Horace, if you love me, you will explain—here, now, before it's too late!"

"My darling," groaned Horace, "I would, like a shot, if I thought it would be of the least use!"

"Hitherto," said the Professor, "you cannot be said to have been happy in your explanations—and I should advise you not to venture on any more. Good-night, once more. I only wish it were possible, without needless irony, to make the customary acknowledgments for a pleasant evening."

Mrs. Futvoye had already hurried her daughter away, and, though she had left her husband to express his sentiments unaided, she made it sufficiently clear that she entirely agreed with them.

Horace stood in the outer hall by the fountain, in which his drowned chrysanthemums were still floating, and gazed in stupefied despair after his guests as they went down the path to the gate. He knew only too well that they would never cross his threshold, nor he theirs, again.

Suddenly he came to himself with a start. "I'll try it!" he cried. "I can't and won't stand this!" And he rushed after them bareheaded.

"Professor!" he said breathlessly, as he caught him up, "one moment. On second thoughts, I will tell you my secret, if you will promise me a patient hearing."

"The pavement is hardly the place for confidences," replied the Professor, "and, if it were, your costume is calculated to attract more remark than is desirable. My wife and daughter have gone on—if you will permit me, I will overtake them—I shall be at home to-morrow morning, should you wish to see me."

"No—to-night, to-night!" urged Horace. "I can't sleep in that infernal place with this on my mind. Put Mrs. Futvoye and Sylvia into a cab, Professor, and come back. It's not late, and I won't keep you long— but for Heaven's sake, let me tell you my story at once."

Probably the Professor was not without some curiosity on the subject; at all events he yielded. "Very well," he said, "go into the house and I will rejoin you presently. Only remember," he added, "that I shall accept no statement without the fullest proof. Otherwise you will merely be wasting your time and mine."

"Proof!" thought Horace, gloomily, as he returned to his Arabian halls, "The only decent proof I could produce would be old Fakrash, and he's not likely to turn up again—especially now I want him."

A little later the Professor returned, having found a cab and despatched his women-folk home. "Now, young man," he said, as he unwound his wrapper and seated himself on the divan by Horace's side, "I can give you just ten minutes to tell your story in, so let me beg you to make it as brief and as comprehensible as you can."

It was not exactly an encouraging invitation in the circumstances, but Horace took his courage in both hands and told him everything, just as it had happened.

"And that's your story?" said the Professor, after listening to the narrative with the utmost attention, when Horace came to the end.

"That's my story, sir," said Horace. "And I hope it has altered your opinion of me."

"It has," replied the Professor, in an altered tone; "it has indeed. Yours is a sad case—a very sad case."

"It's rather awkward, isn't it? But I don't mind so long as you understand. And you'll tell Sylvia—as much as you think proper?"

"Yes—yes; I must tell Sylvia."

"And I may go on seeing her as usual?"

"Well—will you be guided by my advice—the advice of one who has lived more than double your years?"

"Certainly," said Horace.

"Then, if I were you, I should go away at once, for a complete change of air and scene."

"That's impossible, sir—you forget my work!"

"Never mind your work, my boy: leave it for a while, try a sea-voyage, go round the world, get quite away from these associations."

"But I might come across the Jinnee again," objected Horace; "he's travelling, as I told you."

"Yes, yes, to be sure. Still, I should go away. Consult any doctor, and he'll tell you the same thing."

"Consult any— Good God!" cried Horace; "I see what it is—you think I'm mad!"

"No, no, my dear boy," said the Professor, soothingly, "not mad—nothing of the sort; perhaps your mental equilibrium is just a trifle—it's quite intelligible. You see, the sudden turn in your professional prospects, coupled with your engagement to Sylvia—I've known stronger minds than yours thrown off their balance—temporarily, of course, quite temporarily—by less than that."

"You believe I am suffering from delusions?"

"I don't say that. I think you may see ordinary things in a distorted light."

"Anyhow, you don't believe there really was a Jinnee inside that bottle?"

"Remember, you yourself assured me at the time you opened it that you found nothing whatever inside it. Isn't it more credible that you were right then than that you should be right now?"

"Well," said Horace, "you saw all those black slaves; you ate, or tried to eat, that unutterably beastly banquet; you heard that music—and then there was the dancing-girl. And this hall we're in, this robe I've got on—are they delusions? Because if they are, I'm afraid you will have to admit that you're mad too."

"Ingeniously put," said the Professor. "I fear it is unwise to argue with you. Still, I will venture to assert that a strong imagination like yours, over-heated and saturated with Oriental ideas—to which I fear I may have contributed—is not incapable of unconsciously assisting in its own deception. In other words, I think that you may have provided all this yourself from various quarters without any clear recollection of the fact."

"That's very scientific and satisfactory as far as it goes, my dear Professor," said Horace; "but there's one piece of evidence which may upset your theory—and that's this brass bottle."

"If your reasoning powers were in their normal condition," said the Professor, compassionately, "you would see that the mere production of an empty bottle can be no proof of what it contained—or, for that matter, that it ever contained anything at all!"

"Oh, I see that," said Horace; "but this bottle has a stopper with what you yourself admit to be an inscription of some sort. Suppose that inscription confirms my story—what then? All I ask you to do is to make it out for yourself before you decide that I'm either a liar or a lunatic."

"I warn you," said the Professor, "that if you are trusting to my being unable to decipher the inscription, you are deceiving yourself. You represent that this bottle belongs to the period of Solomon—that is, about a thousand years B.C. Probably you are not aware that the earliest specimens of Oriental metal-work in existence are not older than the tenth century of our era. But, granting that it is as old as you allege, I shall certainly be able to read any inscription there may be on it. I have made out clay tablets in Cuneiform which were certainly written a thousand years before Solomon's time."

"So much the better," said Horace. "I'm as certain as I can be that, whatever is written on that lid—whether it's Phoenician, or Cuneiform, or anything else—must have some reference to a Jinnee confined in the bottle, or at least bear the seal of Solomon. But there the thing is—examine it for yourself."

"Not now," said the Professor; "it's too late, and the light here is not strong enough. But I'll tell you what I will do. I'll take this stopper thing home with me, and examine it carefully to-morrow—on one condition."

"You have only to name it," said Horace.

"My condition is, that if I, and one or two other Orientalists to whom I may submit it, come to the conclusion that there is no real inscription at all—or, if any, that a date and meaning must be assigned to it totally inconsistent with your story—you will accept our finding and acknowledge that you have been under a delusion, and dismiss the whole affair from your mind."

"Oh, I don't mind agreeing to that," said Horace, "particularly as it's my only chance."

"Very well, then," said the Professor, as he removed the metal cap and put it in his pocket; "you may depend upon hearing from me in a day or two. Meantime, my boy," he continued, almost affectionately, "why not try a short bicycle tour somewhere, hey? You're a cyclist, I know—anything but allow yourself to dwell on Oriental subjects."

"It's not so easy to avoid dwelling on them as you think!" said Horace, with rather a dreary laugh. "And I fancy, Professor, that—whether you like it or not—you'll have to believe in that Jinnee of mine sooner or later."

"I can scarcely conceive," replied the Professor, who was by this time at the outer door, "any degree of evidence which could succeed in convincing me that your brass bottle had ever contained an Arabian Jinnee. However, I shall endeavour to preserve an open mind on the subject. Good evening to you."

As soon as he was alone, Horace paced up and down his deserted halls in a state of simmering rage as he thought how eagerly he had looked forward to his little dinner-party; how intimate and delightful it might have been, and what a monstrous and prolonged nightmare it had actually proved. And at the end of it there he was—in a fantastic, impossible dwelling, deserted by every one, his chances of setting himself right with Sylvia hanging on the slenderest thread; unknown difficulties and complications threatening him from every side!

He owed all this to Fakrash. Yes, that incorrigibly grateful Jinnee, with his antiquated notions and his high-flown professions, had contrived to ruin him more disastrously than if he had been his bitterest foe! Ah! if he could be face to face with him once more—if only for five minutes—he would be restrained by no false delicacy: he would tell him fairly and plainly what a meddling, blundering old fool he was. But Fakrash had taken his flight for ever: there were no means of calling him back—nothing to be done now but go to bed and sleep—if he could!

Exasperated by the sense of his utter helplessness, Ventimore went to the arch which led to his bed-chamber and drew the curtain back with a furious pull. And just within the archway, standing erect with folded arms and the smile of fatuous benignity which Ventimore was beginning to know and dread, was the form of Fakrash-el-Aamash, the Jinnee!

CHAPTER X

NO PLACE LIKE HOME!

"May thy head long survive!" said Fakrash, by way of salutation, as he stepped through the archway.

"You're very good," said Horace, whose anger had almost evaporated in the relief of the Jinnee's unexpected return, "but I don't think any head can survive this sort of thing long."

"Art thou content with this dwelling I have provided for thee?" inquired the Jinnee, glancing around the stately hall with perceptible complacency.

It would have been positively brutal to say how very far from contented he felt, so Horace could only mumble that he had never been lodged like that before in all his life.

"It is far below thy deserts," Fakrash observed graciously. "And were thy friends amazed at the manner of their entertainment?"

"They were," said Horace.

"A sure method of preserving friends is to feast them with liberality," remarked the Jinnee.

This was rather more than Horace's temper could stand. "You were kind enough to provide my friends with such a feast," he said, "that they'll never come here again."

"How so? Were not the meats choice and abounding in fatness? Was not the wine sweet, and the sherbet like unto perfumed snow?"

"Oh, everything was—er—as nice as possible," said Horace. "Couldn't have been better."

"Yet thou sayest that thy friends will return no more—for what reason?"

"Well, you see," explained Horace, reluctantly, "there's such a thing as doing people too well. I mean, it isn't everybody that appreciates Arabian cooking. But they might have stood that. It was the dancing-girl that did for me."

"I commanded that a houri, lovelier than the full moon, and graceful as a young gazelle, should appear for the delight of thy guests."

"She came," said Horace, gloomily.

"Acquaint me with that which hath occurred—for I perceive plainly that something hath fallen out contrary to thy desires."

"Well," said Horace, "if it had been a bachelor party, there would have been no harm in the houri; but, as it happened, two of my guests were ladies, and they—well, they not unnaturally put a wrong construction on it all."

"Verily," exclaimed the Jinnee, "thy words are totally incomprehensible to me."

"I don't know what the custom may be in Arabia," said Horace, "but with us it is not usual for a man to engage a houri to dance after dinner to amuse the lady he is proposing to marry. It's the kind of attention she'd be most unlikely to appreciate.

"Then was one of thy guests the damsel whom thou art seeking to marry?"

"She was," said Horace, "and the other two were her father and mother. From which you may imagine that it was not altogether agreeable for me when your gazelle threw herself at my feet and hugged my knees and declared that I was the light of her eyes. Of course, it all meant nothing—it's probably the conventional behaviour for a gazelle, and I'm not reflecting upon her in the least. But, in the circumstances, it was compromising."

"I thought," said Fakrash, "that thou assuredst me that thou wast not contracted to any damsel?"

"I think I only said that there was no one whom I would trouble you to procure as a wife for me," replied Horace; "I certainly was engaged—though, after this evening, my engagement is at an end—unless ...

that reminds me, do you happen to know whether there really was an inscription on the seal of your bottle, and what it said?"

"I know naught of any inscription," said the Jinnee; "bring me the seal that I may see it."

"I haven't got it by me at this moment," said Horace; "I lent it to my friend—the father of this young lady I told you of. You see, Mr. Fakrash, you got me into—I mean, I was in such a hole over this affair that I was obliged to make a clean breast of it to him. And he wouldn't believe it, so it struck me that there might be an inscription of some sort on the seal, saying who you were, and why Solomon had you confined in the bottle. Then the Professor would be obliged to admit that there's something in my story."

"Truly, I wonder at thee and at the smallness of thy penetration," the Jinnee commented; "for if there were indeed any writing upon this seal, it is not possible that one of thy race should be able to decipher it."

"Oh, I beg your pardon," said Horace; "Professor Futvoye is an Oriental scholar; he can make out any inscription, no matter how many thousands of years old it may be. If anything's there, he'll decipher it. The question is whether anything is there."

The effect of this speech on Fakrash was as unexpected as it was inexplicable: the Jinnee's features, usually so mild, began to work convulsively until they became terrible to look at, and suddenly, with a fierce howl, he shot up to nearly double his ordinary stature.

"O thou of little sense and breeding!" he cried, in a loud voice; "how camest thou to deliver the bottle in which I was confined into the hands of this learned man?"

Ventimore, startled as he was, did not lose his self-possession. "My dear sir," he said, "I did not suppose you could have any further use for it. And, as a matter of fact, I didn't give Professor Futvoye the bottle—which is over there in the corner—but merely the stopper. I wish you wouldn't tower over me like that—it gives me a crick in the neck to talk to you. Why on earth should you make such a fuss about my lending the seal; what possible difference can it make to you even if it does confirm my story? And it's of immense importance to me that the Professor should believe I told the truth."

"I spoke in haste," said the Jinnee, slowly resuming his normal size, and looking slightly ashamed of his recent outburst as well as uncommonly foolish. "The bottle truly is of no value; and as for the stopper, since it is but lent, it is no great matter. If there be any legend upon the seal, perchance this learned man of whom thou speakest will by this time have deciphered it?"

"No," said Horace, "he won't tackle it till to-morrow. And it's as likely as not that when he does he won't find any reference to you—and I shall be up a taller tree than ever!"

"Art thou so desirous that he should receive proof that thy story is true?"

"Why, of course I am! Haven't I been saying so all this time?"

"Who can satisfy him so surely as I?"

"You!" cried Horace. "Do you mean to say you really would? Mr. Fakrash, you are an old brick! That would be the very thing!"

"There is naught," said the Jinnee, smiling indulgently, "that I would not do to promote thy welfare, for thou hast rendered me inestimable service. Acquaint me therefore with the abode of this sage, and I will present myself before him, and if haply he should find no inscription upon the seal, or its purport should be hidden from him, then will I convince him that thou hast spoken the truth and no lie."

Horace very willingly gave him the Professor's address. "Only don't drop in on him to-night, you know," he thought it prudent to add, "or you might startle him. Call any time after breakfast to-morrow, and you'll find him in."

"To-night," said Fakrash, "I return to pursue my search after Suleyman (on whom be peace!). For not yet have I found him."

"If you will try to do so many things at once," said Horace, "I don't see how you can expect much result."

"At Nineveh they knew him not—for where I left a city I found but a heap of ruins, tenanted by owls and bats."

"They say the lion and the lizard keep the Courts—" murmured Horace, half to himself. "I was afraid you might be disappointed with Nineveh myself. Why not run over to Sheba? You might hear of him there."

"Seba of El-Yemen—the country of Bilkees, the Queen beloved of Suleyman," said the Jinnee. "It is an excellent suggestion, and I will follow it without delay."

"But you won't forget to look in on Professor Futvoye to-morrow, will you?"

"Assuredly I will not. And now, ere I depart, tell me if there be any other service I may render thee."

Horace hesitated. "There is just one," he said, "only I'm afraid you'll be offended if I mention it."

"On the head and the eye be thy commands!" said the Jinnee; "for whatsoever thou desirest shall be accomplished, provided that it lie within my power to perform it."

"Well," said Horace, "if you're sure you don't mind, I'll tell you. You've transformed this house into a wonderful place, more like the Alhambra—I don't mean the one in Leicester Square—than a London lodging-house. But then I am only a lodger here, and the people the house belongs to—excellent people in their way—would very much rather have the house as it was. They have a sort of idea that they won't be able to let these rooms as easily as the others."

"Base and sordid dogs!" said the Jinnee, with contempt.

"Possibly," said Horace, "it's narrow-minded of them—but that's the way they look at it. They've actually left rather than stay here. And it's their house—not mine."

"If they abandon this dwelling, thou wilt remain in the more secure possession."

"Oh, shall I, though? They'll go to law and have me turned out, and I shall have to pay ruinous damages into the bargain. So, you see, what you intended as a kindness will only bring me bad luck."

"Come—without more words—to the statement of thy request," said Fakrash, "for I am in haste."

"All I want you to do," replied Horace, in some anxiety as to what the effect of his request would be, "is to put everything here back to what it was before. It won't take you a minute."

"Of a truth," exclaimed Fakrash, "to bestow a favour upon thee is but a thankless undertaking, for not once, but twice, hast thou rejected my benefits—and now, behold, I am at a loss to devise means to gratify thee!"

"I know I've abused your good nature," said Horace; "but if you'll only do this, and then convince the Professor that my story is true, I shall be more than satisfied. I'll never ask another favour of you!"

"My benevolence towards thee hath no bounds—as thou shalt see; and I can deny thee nothing, for truly thou art a worthy and temperate young man. Farewell, then, and be it according to thy desire."

He raised his arms above his head, and shot up like a rocket towards the lofty dome, which split asunder to let him pass. Horace, as he gazed after him, had a momentary glimpse of deep blue sky, with a star or two that seemed to be hurrying through the transparent opal scud, before the roof closed in once more.

Then came a low, rumbling sound, with a shock like a mild earthquake: the slender pillars swayed under their horseshoe arches; the big hanging-lanterns went out; the walls narrowed, and the floor heaved and rose—till Ventimore found himself up in his own familiar sitting-room once more, in the dark. Outside he could see the great square still shrouded in grey haze—the street lamps flickering in the wind; a belated reveller was beguiling his homeward way by rattling his stick against the railings as he passed.

Inside the room everything was exactly as before, and Horace found it difficult to believe that a few minutes earlier he had been standing on that same site, but twenty feet or so below his present level, in a spacious blue-tiled hall, with a domed ceiling and gaudy pillared arches.

But he was very far from regretting his short-lived splendour; he burnt with shame and resentment whenever he thought of that nightmare banquet, which was so unlike the quiet, unpretentious little dinner he had looked forward to.

However, it was over now, and it was useless to worry himself about what could not be helped. Besides, fortunately, there was no great harm done; the Jinnee had been brought to see his mistake, and, to do him justice, had shown himself willing enough to put it right. He had promised to go and see the Professor next day, and the result of the interview could not fail to be satisfactory. And after this, Ventimore thought, Fakrash would have the sense and good feeling not to interfere in his affairs again.

Meanwhile he could sleep now with a mind free from his worst anxieties, and he went to his room in a spirit of intense thankfulness that he had a Christian bed to sleep in. He took off his gorgeous robes—the only things that remained to prove to him that the events of that evening had been no delusion—and locked them in his wardrobe with a sense of relief that he would never be required to wear them again, and his last conscious thought before he fell asleep was the comforting reflection that, if there were any barrier between Sylvia and himself, it would be removed in the course of a very few more hours.

CHAPTER XI

A FOOL'S PARADISE

Ventimore found next morning that his bath and shaving-water had been brought up, from which he inferred, quite correctly, that his landlady must have returned.

Secretly he was by no means looking forward to his next interview with her, but she appeared with his bacon and coffee in a spirit so evidently chastened that he saw that he would have no difficulty so far as she was concerned.

"I'm sure, Mr. Ventimore, sir," she began, apologetically, "I don't know what you must have thought of me and Rapkin last night, leaving the house like we did!"

"It was extremely inconvenient," said Horace, "and not at all what I should have expected from you. But possibly you had some reason for it?"

"Why, sir," said Mrs. Rapkin, running her hand nervously along the back of a chair, "the fact is, something come over me, and come over Rapkin, as we couldn't stop here another minute not if it was ever so."

"Ah!" said Horace, raising his eyebrows, "restlessness—eh, Mrs. Rapkin? Awkward that it should come on just then, though, wasn't it?"

"It was the look of the place, somehow," said Mrs. Rapkin. "If you'll believe me, sir, it was all changed like—nothing in it the same from top to bottom!"

"Really?" said Horace. "I don't notice any difference myself."

"No more don't I, sir, not by daylight; but last night it was all domes and harches and marble fountings let into the floor, with parties moving about downstairs all silent and as black as your hat—which Rapkin saw them as well as what I did."

"From the state your husband was in last night," said Horace, "I should say he was capable of seeing anything—and double of most things."

"I won't deny, sir, that Rapkin mayn't have been quite hisself, as a very little upsets him after he's spent an afternoon studying the papers and what-not at the libery. But I see the niggers too, Mr. Ventimore, and no one can say I ever take more than is good for me."

"I don't suggest that for a moment, Mrs. Rapkin," said Horace; "only, if the house was as you describe last night, how do you account for its being all right this morning?"

Mrs. Rapkin in her embarrassment was reduced to folding her apron into small pleats. "It's not for me to say, sir," she replied, "but, if I was to give my opinion, it would be as them parties as called 'ere on camels the other day was at the bottom of it."

"I shouldn't wonder if you were right, Mrs. Rapkin," said Horace blandly; "you see, you had been exerting yourself over the cooking, and no doubt were in an over-excited state, and, as you say, those camels had taken hold of your imagination until you were ready to see anything that Rapkin saw, and he was ready to see anything you did. It's not at all uncommon. Scientific people, I believe, call it 'Collective Hallucination.'"

"Law, sir!" said the good woman, considerably impressed by this diagnosis, "you don't mean to say I had that? I was always fanciful from a girl, and could see things in coffee-grounds as nobody else could—but I never was took like that before. And to think of me leaving my dinner half cooked, and you expecting your young lady and her pa and ma! Well, there, now, I am sorry. Whatever did you do, sir?"

"We managed to get food of sorts from somewhere," said Horace, "but it was most uncomfortable for me, and I trust, Mrs. Rapkin—I sincerely trust that it will not occur again."

"That I'll answer for it shan't, sir. And you won't take no notice to Rapkin, sir, will you? Though it was his seein' the niggers and that as put it into my 'ed; but I 'ave spoke to him pretty severe already, and he's truly sorry and ashamed for forgetting hisself as he did."

"Very well, Mrs. Rapkin," said Horace; "we will understand that last night's—hem—rather painful experience is not to be alluded to again—on either side."

He felt sincerely thankful to have got out of it so easily, for it was impossible to say what gossip might not have been set on foot if the Rapkins had not been brought to see the advisability of reticence on the subject.

"There's one more thing, sir, I wished for to speak to you about," said Mrs. Rapkin; "that great brass vawse as you bought at an action some time back. I dunno if you remember it?"

"I remember it," said Horace. "Well, what about it?"

"Why, sir, I found it in the coal-cellar this morning, and I thought I'd ask if that was where you wished it kep' in future. For, though no amount o' polish could make it what I call a tasty thing, it's neither horniment nor yet useful where it is at present."

"Oh," said Horace, rather relieved, for he had an ill-defined dread from her opening words that the bottle might have been misbehaving itself in some way. "Put it wherever you please, Mrs. Rapkin; do whatever you like with it—so long as I don't see the thing again!"

"Very good, sir; I on'y thought I'd ask the question," said Mrs. Rapkin, as she closed the door upon herself.

Altogether, Horace walked to Great Cloister Street that morning in a fairly cheerful mood and amiably disposed, even towards the Jinnee. With all his many faults, he was a thoroughly good-natured old devil—very superior in every way to the one the Arabian Nights fisherman found in his bottle.

"Ninety-nine Jinn out of a hundred," thought Horace, "would have turned nasty on finding benefit after benefit 'declined with thanks.' But one good point in Fakrash is that he does take a hint in good part, and, as soon as he can be made to see where he's wrong, he's always ready to set things right. And he thoroughly understands now that these Oriental dodges of his won't do nowadays, and that when people see a penniless man suddenly wallowing in riches they naturally want to know how he came by them. I don't suppose he will trouble me much in future. If he should look in now and then, I must put up with it. Perhaps, if I suggested it, he wouldn't mind coming in some form that would look less outlandish. If he would get himself up as a banker, or a bishop—the Bishop of Bagdad, say—I shouldn't care how often he called. Only, I can't have him coming down the chimney in either capacity. But he'll see that himself. And he's done me one real service—I mustn't let myself forget that. He sent me old Wackerbath. By the way, I wonder if he's seen my designs yet, and what he thinks of them."

He was at his table, engaged in jotting down some rough ideas for the decoration of the reception-rooms in the projected house, when Beevor came in.

"I've got nothing doing just now," he said; "so I thought I'd come in and have a squint at those plans of yours, if they're forward enough to be seen yet."

Ventimore had to explain that even the imperfect method of examination proposed was not possible, as he had despatched the drawings to his client the night before.

"Phew!" said Beevor; "that's sharp work, isn't it?"

"I don't know. I've been sticking hard at it for over a fortnight."

"Well, you might have given me a chance of seeing what you've made of it. I let you see all my work!"

"To tell you the honest truth, old fellow, I wasn't at all sure you'd like it, and I was afraid you'd put me out of conceit with what I'd done, and Wackerbath was in a frantic hurry to have the plans—so there it was."

"And do you think he'll be satisfied with them?"

"He ought to be. I don't like to be cock-sure, but I believe—I really do believe—that I've given him rather more than he expected. It's going to be a devilish good house, though I say it myself."

"Something new-fangled and fantastic, eh? Well, he mayn't care about it, you know. When you've had my experience, you'll realise that a client is a rum bird to satisfy."

"I shall satisfy my old bird," said Horace, gaily. "He'll have a cage he can hop about in to his heart's content."

"You're a clever chap enough," said Beevor; "but to carry a big job like this through you want one thing—and that's ballast."

"Not while you heave yours at my head! Come, old fellow, you aren't really riled because I sent off those plans without showing them to you? I shall soon have them back, and then you can pitch into 'em as much as you please. Seriously, though, I shall want all the help you can spare when I come to the completed designs."

"'Um," said Beevor, "you've got along very well alone so far—at least, by your own account; so I dare say you'll be able to manage without me to the end. Only, you know," he added, as he left the room, "you haven't won your spurs yet. A fellow isn't necessarily a Gilbert Scott, or a Norman Shaw, or a Waterhouse just because he happens to get a sixty-thousand pound job the first go off!"

"Poor old Beevor!" thought Horace, repentantly, "I've put his back up. I might just as well have shown him the plans, after all; it wouldn't have hurt me and it would have pleased him. Never mind, I'll make my peace with him after lunch. I'll ask him to give me his idea for a—no, hang it all, even friendship has its limits!"

He returned from lunch to hear what sounded like an altercation of some sort in his office, in which, as he neared his door, Beevor's voice was distinctly audible.

"My dear sir," he was saying, "I have already told you that it is no affair of mine."

"But I ask you, sir, as a brother architect," said another voice, "whether you consider it professional or reasonable—?"

"As a brother architect," replied Beevor, as Ventimore opened the door, "I would rather be excused from giving an opinion.... Ah, here is Mr. Ventimore himself."

Horace entered, to find himself confronted by Mr. Wackerbath, whose face was purple and whose white whiskers were bristling with rage. "So, sir!" he began. "So, sir!—" and choked ignominiously.

"There appears to have been some misunderstanding, my dear Ventimore," explained Beevor, with a studious correctness which was only a shade less offensive than open triumph. "I think I'd better leave you and this gentleman to talk it over quietly."

"Quietly?" exclaimed Mr. Wackerbath, with an apoplectic snort; "quietly!!"

"I've no idea what you are so excited about, sir," said Horace. "Perhaps you will explain?"

"Explain!" Mr. Wackerbath gasped; "why—no, if I speak just now, I shall be ill: you tell him," he added, waving a plump hand in Beevor's direction.

"I'm not in possession of all the facts," said Beevor, smoothly; "but, so far as I can gather, this gentleman thinks that, considering the importance of the work he intrusted to your hands, you have given less time to it than he might have expected. As I have told him, that is a matter which does not concern me, and which he must discuss with you."

So saying, Beevor retired to his own room, and shut the door with the same irreproachable discretion, which conveyed that he was not in the least surprised, but was too much of a gentleman to show it.

"Well, Mr. Wackerbath," began Horace, when they were alone, "so you're disappointed with the house?"

"Disappointed!" said Mr. Wackerbath, furiously. "I am disgusted, sir, disgusted!"

Horace's heart sank lower still; had he deceived himself after all, then? Had he been nothing but a conceited fool, and—most galling thought of all—had Beevor judged him only too accurately? And yet, no, he could not believe it—he knew his work was good!

"This is plain speaking with a vengeance," he said; "I'm sorry you're dissatisfied. I did my best to carry out your instructions."

"Oh, you did?" sputtered Mr. Wackerbath. "That's what you call—but go on, sir, go on!"

"I got it done as quickly as possible," continued Horace, "because I understood you wished no time to be lost."

"No one can accuse you of dawdling over it. What I should like to know is how the devil you managed to get it done in the time?"

"I worked incessantly all day and every day," said Horace. "That's how I managed it—and this is all the thanks I get for it!"

"Thanks?" Mr. Wackerbath well-nigh howled. "You—you insolent young charlatan; you expect thanks!"

"Now look here, Mr. Wackerbath," said Horace, whose own temper was getting a little frayed. "I'm not accustomed to being treated like this, and I don't intend to submit to it. Just tell me—in as moderate language as you can command—what you object to?"

"I object to the whole damned thing, sir! I mean, I repudiate the entire concern. It's the work of a raving lunatic—a place that no English gentleman, sir, with any self-respect or—ah!—consideration for his reputation and position in the county, could consent to occupy for a single hour!"

"Oh," said Horace, feeling deathly sick, "in that case it is useless, of course, to suggest any modifications."

"Absolutely!" said Mr. Wackerbath.

"Very well, then; there's no more to be said," replied Horace. "You will have no difficulty in finding an architect who will be more successful in realising your intentions. Mr. Beevor, the gentleman you met just now," he added, with a touch of bitterness, "would probably be just your man. Of course I retire altogether. And really, if any one is the sufferer over this, I fancy it's myself. I can't see how you are any the worse."

"Not any the worse?" cried Mr. Wackerbath, "when the infernal place is built!"

"Built!" echoed Horace feebly.

"I tell you, sir, I saw it with my own eyes driving to the station this morning; my coachman and footman saw it; my wife saw it—damn it, sir, we all saw it!"

Then Horace understood. His indefatigable Jinnee had been at work again! Of course, for Fakrash it must have been what he would term "the easiest of affairs"—especially after a glance at the plans (and Ventimore remembered that the Jinnee had surprised him at work upon them, and even requested to have them explained to him)—to dispense with contractors and bricklayers and carpenters, and construct the entire building in the course of a single night.

It was a generous and spirited action—but, particularly now that the original designs had been found faulty and rejected, it placed the unfortunate architect in a most invidious position.

"Well, sir," said Mr. Wackerbath, with elaborate irony, "I presume it is you whom I have to thank for improving my land by erecting this precious palace on it?"

"I—I—" began Horace, utterly broken down; and then he saw, with emotions that may be imagined, the Jinnee himself, in his green robes, standing immediately behind Mr. Wackerbath.

"Greeting to you," said Fakrash, coming forward with his smile of amiable cunning. "If I mistake not," he added, addressing the startled estate agent, who had jumped visibly, "thou art the merchant for whom my son here," and he laid a hand on Horace's shrinking shoulder, "undertook to construct a mansion?"

"I am," said Mr. Wackerbath, in some mystification. "Have I the pleasure of addressing Mr. Ventimore, senior?"

"No, no," put in Horace; "no relation. He's a sort of informal partner."

"Hast thou not found him an architect of divine gifts?" inquired the Jinnee, beaming with pride. "Is not the palace that he hath raised for thee by his transcendent accomplishments a marvel of beauty and stateliness, and one that Sultans might envy?"

"No, sir!" shouted the infuriated Mr. Wackerbath; "since you ask my opinion, it's nothing of the sort! It's a ridiculous tom-fool cross between the palm-house at Kew and the Brighton Pavilion! There's no billiard-room, and not a decent bedroom in the house. I've been all over it, so I ought to know; and as for drainage, there isn't a sign of it. And he has the brass—ah, I should say, the unblushing effrontery—to call that a country house!"

Horace's dismay was curiously shot with relief. The Jinnee, who was certainly very far from being a genius except by courtesy, had taken it upon himself to erect the palace according to his own notions of Arabian domestic luxury—and Horace, taught by bitter experience, could sympathise to some extent with his unfortunate client. On the other hand, it was balm to his smarting self-respect to find that it was not his own plans, after all, which had been found so preposterous; and, by some obscure mental process, which I do not propose to explain, he became reconciled, and almost grateful, to the officious Fakrash. And then, too, he was his Jinnee, and Horace had no intention of letting him be bullied by an outsider.

"Let me explain, Mr. Wackerbath," he said. "Personally I've had nothing to do with this. This gentleman, wishing to spare me the trouble, has taken upon himself to build your house for you, without consulting either of us, and, from what I know of his powers in the direction, I've no doubt that—that it's a devilish fine place, in its way. Anyhow, we make no charge for it—he presents it to you as a free gift. Why not accept it as such and make the best of it?"

"Make the best of it?" stormed Mr. Wackerbath. "Stand by and see the best site in three counties defaced by a jimcrack Moorish nightmare like that! Why, they'll call it 'Wackerbath's Folly,' sir. I shall be the laughing-stock of the neighbourhood. I can't live in the beastly building. I couldn't afford to keep it up, and I won't have it cumbering my land. Do you hear? I won't! I'll go to law, cost me what it may, and compel you and your Arabian friends there to pull the thing down. I'll take the case up to the House of Lords, if necessary, and fight you as long as I can stand!"

"As long as thou canst stand!" repeated Fakrash, gently. "That is a long time truly, O thou litigious one!... On all fours, ungrateful dog that thou art!" he cried, with an abrupt and entire change of manner, "and crawl henceforth for the remainder of thy days. I, Fakrash-el-Aamash, command thee!"

It was both painful and grotesque to see the portly and intensely respectable Mr. Wackerbath suddenly drop forward on his hands while desperately striving to preserve his dignity. "How dare you, sir?" he almost barked, "how dare you, I say? Are you aware that I could summon you for this? Let me up. I insist upon getting up!"

"O contemptible in aspect!" replied the Jinnee, throwing open the door. "Begone to thy kennel."

"I won't! I can't!" whimpered the unhappy man. "How do you expect me—me!—to cross Westminster Bridge on all fours? What will the officials think at Waterloo, where I have been known and respected for years? How am I to face my family in—in this position? Do, for mercy's sake, let me get up!"

Horace had been too shocked and startled to speak before, but now humanity, coupled with disgust for the Jinnee's high-handed methods, compelled him to interfere. "Mr. Fakrash," he said, "this has gone far enough. Unless you stop tormenting this unfortunate gentleman, I've done with you."

"Never," said Fakrash. "He hath dared to abuse my palace, which is far too sumptuous a dwelling for such a son of a burnt dog as he. Therefore, I will make his abode to be in the dust for ever."

"But I don't find fault," yelped poor Mr. Wackerbath. "You—you entirely misunderstood the—the few comments I ventured to make. It's a capital mansion, handsome, and yet 'homey,' too. I'll never say another word against it. I'll—yes, I'll live in it—if only you'll let me up?"

"Do as he asks you," said Horace to the Jinnee, "or I swear I'll never speak to you again."

"Thou art the arbiter of this matter," was the reply. "And if I yield, it is at thy intercession, and not his. Rise then," he said to the humiliated client; "depart, and show us the breadth of thy shoulders."

It was this precise moment which Beevor, who was probably unable to restrain his curiosity any longer, chose to re-enter the room. "Oh, Ventimore," he began, "did I leave my—?... I beg your pardon. I thought you were alone again."

"Don't go, sir," said Mr. Wackerbath, as he scrambled awkwardly to his feet, his usually florid face mottled in grey and lilac. "I—I should like you to know that, after talking things quietly over with your friend Mr. Ventimore and his partner here, I am thoroughly convinced that my objections were quite untenable. I retract all I said. The house is—ah—admirably planned: most convenient, roomy, and—ah—unconventional. The—the entire freedom from all sanitary appliances is a particular recommendation. In short, I am more than satisfied. Pray forget anything I may have said which might be taken to imply the contrary.... Gentlemen, good afternoon!"

He bowed himself past the Jinnee in a state of deference and apprehension, and was heard stumbling down the staircase. Horace hardly dared to meet Beevor's eyes, which were fixed upon the green-turbaned Jinnee, as he stood apart in dreamy abstraction, smiling placidly to himself.

"I say," Beevor said to Horace, at last, in an undertone, "you never told me you had gone into partnership."

"He's not a regular partner," whispered Ventimore; "he does odd things for me occasionally, that's all."

"He soon managed to smooth your client down," remarked Beevor.

"Yes," said Horace; "he's an Oriental, you see, and, he has a—a very persuasive manner. Would you like to be introduced?"

"If it's all the same to you," replied Beevor, still below his voice, "I'd rather be excused. To tell you the truth, old fellow, I don't altogether fancy the looks of him, and it's my opinion," he added, "that the less you have to do with him the better. He strikes me as a wrong'un, old man."

"No, no," said Horace; "eccentric, that's all—you don't understand him."

"Receive news!" began the Jinnee, after Beevor, with suspicion and disapproval evident even on his back and shoulders, had retreated to his own room, "Suleyman, the son of Daood, sleeps with his fathers."

"I know," retorted Horace, whose nerves were unequal to much reference to Solomon just then. "So does Queen Anne."

"I have not heard of her. But art thou not astounded, then, by my tidings?"

"I have matters nearer home to think about," said Horace, dryly. "I must say, Mr. Fakrash, you have landed me in a pretty mess!"

"Explain thyself more fully, for I comprehend thee not."

"Why on earth," Horace groaned, "couldn't you let me build that house my own way?"

"Did I not hear thee with my own ears lament thy inability to perform the task? Thereupon, I determined that no disgrace should fall upon thee by reason of such incompetence, since I myself would erect a palace so splendid that it should cause thy name to live for ever. And, behold, it is done."

"It is," said Horace. "And so am I. I don't want to reproach you. I quite feel that you have acted with the best intentions; but, oh, hang it all! can't you see that you've absolutely wrecked my career as an architect?"

"That is a thing that cannot be," returned the Jinnee, "seeing that thou hast all the credit."

"The credit! This is England, not Arabia. What credit can I gain from being supposed to be the architect of an Oriental pavilion, which might be all very well for Haroun-al-Raschid, but I can assure you is preposterous as a home for an average Briton?"

"Yet that overfed hound," remarked the Jinnee, "expressed much gratification therewith."

"Naturally, after he had found that he could not give a candid opinion except on all-fours. A valuable testimonial, that! And how do you suppose I can take his money? No, Mr. Fakrash, if I have to go on all-fours myself for it, I must say, and I will say, that you've made a most frightful muddle of it!"

"Acquaint me with thy wishes," said Fakrash, a little abashed, "for thou knowest that I can refuse thee naught."

"Then," said Horace, boldly, "couldn't you remove that palace—dissipate it into space or something?"

"Verily," said the Jinnee, in an aggravated tone, "to do good acts unto such as thee is but wasted time, for thou givest me no peace till they are undone!"

"This is the last time," urged Horace; "I promise never to ask you for anything again."

"Not for the first time hast thou made such a promise," said Fakrash. "And save for the magnitude of thy service unto me, I would not hearken to this caprice of thine, nor wilt thou find me so indulgent on another occasion. But for this once"—and he muttered some words and made a sweeping gesture with his right hand—"thy desire is granted unto thee. Of the palace and all that is therein there remaineth no trace!"

"Another surprise for poor old Wackerbath," thought Horace, "but a pleasant one this time. My dear Mr. Fakrash," he said aloud, "I really can't say how grateful I am to you. And now—I hate bothering you like this, but if you could manage to look in on Professor Futvoye—"

"What!" cried the Jinnee, "yet another request? Already!"

"Well, you promised you'd do that before, you know!" said Horace.

"For that matter," remarked Fakrash, "I have already fulfilled my promise."

"You have?" Horace exclaimed. "And does he believe now that it's all true about that bottle?"

"When I left him," answered the Jinnee, "all his doubts were removed."

"By Jove, you are a trump!" cried Horace, only too glad to be able to commend with sincerity. "And do you think, if I went to him now, I should find him the same as usual?"

"Nay," said Fakrash, with his weak and yet inscrutable smile, "that is more than I can promise thee."

"But why?" asked Horace, "if he knows all?"

There was the oddest expression in the Jinnee's furtive eyes: a kind of elfin mischief combined with a sense of wrong-doing, like a naughty child whose palate is still reminiscent of illicit jam. "Because," he replied, with a sound between a giggle and a chuckle, "because, in order to overcome his unbelief, it was necessary to transform him into a one-eyed mule of hideous appearance."

"What!" cried Horace. But, whether to avoid thanks or explanations, the Jinnee had disappeared with his customary abruptness.

"Fakrash!" shouted Horace, "Mr. Fakrash! Come back! Do you hear? I must speak to you!" There was no answer; the Jinnee might be well on his way to Lake Chad, or Jericho, by that time—he was certainly far enough from Great Cloister Street.

Horace sat down at his drawing-table, and, his head buried in his hands, tried to think out this latest complication. Fakrash had transformed Professor Futvoye into a one-eyed mule. It would have seemed incredible, almost unthinkable, once, but so many impossibilities had happened to Horace of late that one more made little or no strain upon his credulity.

What he felt chiefly was the new barrier that this event must raise between himself and Sylvia; to do him justice, the mere fact that the father of his fiancée was a mule did not lessen his ardour in the slightest. Even if he had felt no personal responsibility for the calamity, he loved Sylvia far too well to be deterred by it, and few family cupboards are without a skeleton of some sort.

With courage and the determination to look only on the bright side of things, almost any domestic drawback can be lived down.

But the real point, as he instantly recognised, was whether in the changed condition of circumstances Sylvia would consent to marry him. Might she not, after the experiences of that abominable dinner of his the night before, connect him in some way with her poor father's transformation? She might even suspect him of employing this means of compelling the Professor to renew their engagement; and, indeed, Horace was by no means certain himself that the Jinnee might not have acted from some muddle-headed motive of this kind. It was likely enough that the Professor, after learning the truth, should have refused to allow his daughter to marry the protégé of so dubious a patron, and that Fakrash had then resorted to pressure.

In any case, Ventimore knew Sylvia well enough to feel sure that pride would steel her heart against him so long as this obstacle remained.

It would be unseemly to set down here all that Horace said and thought of the person who had brought all this upon them, but after some wild and futile raving he became calm enough to recognise that his proper place was by Sylvia's side. Perhaps he ought to have told her at first, and then she would have been less unprepared for this—and yet how could he trouble her mind so long as he could cling to the hope that the Jinnee would cease to interfere?

But now he could be silent no longer; naturally the prospect of calling at Cottesmore Gardens just then was anything but agreeable, but he felt it would be cowardly to keep away.

Besides, he could cheer them up; he could bring with him a message of hope. No doubt they believed that the Professor's transformation would be permanent—a harrowing prospect for so united a family; but, fortunately, Horace would be able to reassure them on this point.

Fakrash had always revoked his previous performances as soon as he could be brought to understand their fatuity—and Ventimore would take good care that he revoked this.

Nevertheless, it was with a sinking heart and an unsteady hand that he pulled the visitors' bell at the Futvoyes' house that afternoon, for he neither knew in what state he should find that afflicted family, nor how they would regard his intrusion at such a time.

CHAPTER XII

THE MESSENGER OF HOPE

Jessie, the neat and pretty parlour-maid, opened the door with a smile of welcome which Horace found reassuring. No girl, he thought, whose master had suddenly been transformed into a mule could possibly smile like that. The Professor, she told him, was not at home, which again was comforting. For a savant, however careless about his personal appearance, would scarcely venture to brave public opinion in the semblance of a quadruped.

"Is the Professor out?" he inquired, to make sure.

"Not exactly out, sir," said the maid, "but particularly engaged, working hard in his study, and not to be disturbed on no account."

This was encouraging, too, since a mule could hardly engage in literary labour of any kind. Evidently the Jinnee must either have overrated his supernatural powers, or else have been deliberately amusing himself at Horace's expense.

"Then I will see Miss Futvoye," he said.

"Miss Sylvia is with the master, sir," said the girl; "but if you'll come into the drawing-room I'll let Mrs. Futvoye know you are here."

He had not been in the drawing-room long before Mrs. Futvoye appeared, and one glance at her face confirmed Ventimore's worst fears. Outwardly she was calm enough, but it was only too obvious that her calmness was the result of severe self-repression; her eyes, usually so shrewdly and placidly observant, had a haggard and hunted look; her ears seemed on the strain to catch some distant sound.

"I hardly thought we should see you to-day," she began, in a tone of studied reserve; "but perhaps you came to offer some explanation of the extraordinary manner in which you thought fit to entertain us last night? If so—"

"The fact is," said Horace, looking into his hat, "I came because I was rather anxious about the Professor.

"About my husband?" said the poor lady, with a really heroic effort to appear surprised. "He is—as well as could be expected. Why should you suppose otherwise?" she asked, with a flash of suspicion.

"I fancied perhaps that—that he mightn't be quite himself to-day," said Horace, with his eyes on the carpet.

"I see," said Mrs. Futvoye, regaining her composure; "you were afraid that all those foreign dishes might not have agreed with him. But—except that he is a little irritable this afternoon—he is much as usual."

"I'm delighted to hear it," said Horace, with reviving hope. "Do you think he would see me for a moment?"

"Great heavens, no!" cried Mrs. Futvoye, with an irrepressible start; "I mean," she explained, "that, after what took place last night, Anthony—my husband—very properly feels that an interview would be too painful."

"But when we parted he was perfectly friendly."

"I can only say," replied the courageous woman, "that you would find him considerably altered now."

Horace had no difficulty in believing it.

"At least, I may see Sylvia?" he pleaded.

"No," said Mrs. Futvoye; "I really can't have Sylvia disturbed just now. She is very busy, helping her father. Anthony has to read a paper at one of his societies to-morrow night, and she is writing it out from his dictation."

If any departure from strict truth can ever be excusable, this surely was one; unfortunately, just then Sylvia herself burst into the room.

"Mother," she cried, without seeing Horace in her agitation, "do come to papa, quick! He has just begun kicking again, and I can't manage him alone.... Oh, you here?" she broke off, as she saw who was in the room. "Why do you come here now, Horace? Please, please go away! Papa is rather unwell—nothing serious, only—oh, do go away!"

"Darling!" said Horace, going to her and taking both her hands, "I know all—do you understand?—all!"

"Mamma!" cried Sylvia, reproachfully, "have you told him—already? When we settled that even Horace wasn't to know till—till papa recovers!"

"I have told him nothing, my dear," replied her mother. "He can't possibly know, unless—but no, that isn't possible. And, after all," she added, with a warning glance at her daughter, "I don't know why we should make any mystery about a mere attack of gout. But I had better go and see if your father wants anything." And she hurried out of the room.

Sylvia sat down and gazed silently into the fire. "I dare say you don't know how dreadfully people kick when they've got gout," she remarked presently.

"Oh yes, I do," said Horace, sympathetically; "at least, I can guess."

"Especially when it's in both legs," continued Sylvia.

"Or," said Horace gently, "in all four."

"Ah, you do know!" cried Sylvia. "Then it's all the more horrid of you to come!"

"Dearest," said Horace, "is not this just the time when my place should be near you—and him?"

"Not near papa, Horace!" she put in anxiously; "it wouldn't be at all safe."

"Do you really think I have any fear for myself?"

"Are you sure you quite know—what he is like now?"

"I understand," said Horace, trying to put it as considerately as possible, "that a casual observer, who didn't know your father, might mistake him, at first sight, for—for some sort of quadruped."

"He's a mule," sobbed Sylvia, breaking down entirely. "I could bear it better if he had been a nice mule.... B—but he isn't!"

"Whatever he may be," declared Horace, as he knelt by her chair endeavouring to comfort her, "nothing can alter my profound respect for him. And you must let me see him, Sylvia; because I fully believe I shall be able to cheer him up."

"If you imagine you can persuade him to—to laugh it off!" said Sylvia, tearfully.

"I wasn't proposing to try to make him see the humorous side of his situation," Horace mildly explained. "I trust I have more tact than that. But he may be glad to know that, at the worst, it is only a temporary inconvenience. I'll take care that he's all right again before very long."

She started up and looked at him, her eyes widened with dawning dread and mistrust.

"If you can speak like that," she said, "it must have been you who—no, I can't believe it—that would be too horrible!"

"I who did what, Sylvia? Weren't you there when—when it happened?"

"No," she replied. "I was only told of it afterwards. Mother heard papa talking loudly in his study this morning, as if he was angry with somebody, and at last she grew so uneasy she couldn't bear it any longer, and went in to see what was the matter with him. Dad was quite alone and looked as usual, only a little excited; and then, without the slightest warning, just as she entered the room, he—he changed slowly into a mule before her eyes! Anybody but mamma would have lost her head and roused the whole house."

"Thank Heaven she didn't!" said Horace, fervently. "That was what I was most afraid of."

"Then—oh, Horace, it was you! It's no use denying it. I feel more certain of it every moment!"

"Now, Sylvia!" he protested, still anxious, if possible, to keep the worst from her, "what could have put such an idea as that into your head?"

"I don't know," she said slowly. "Several things last night. No one who was really nice, and like everybody else, would live in such queer rooms like those, and dine on cushions, with dreadful black slaves, and—and dancing-girls and things. You pretended you were quite poor."

"So I am, darling. And as for my rooms, and—and the rest, they're all gone, Sylvia. If you went to Vincent Square to-day, you wouldn't find a trace of them!"

"That only shows!" said Sylvia. "But why should you play such a cruel, and—and ungentlemanly trick on poor dad? If you had ever really loved me—!"

"But I do, Sylvia, you can't really believe me capable of such an outrage! Look at me and tell me so."

"No, Horace," said Sylvia frankly. "I don't believe you did it. But I believe you know who did. And you had better tell me at once!"

"If you're quite sure you can stand it," he replied, "I'll tell you everything." And, as briefly as possible, he told her how he had unsealed the brass bottle, and all that had come of it.

She bore it, on the whole, better than he had expected; perhaps, being a woman, it was some consolation to her to remind him that she had foretold something of this kind from the very first.

"But, of course, I never really thought it would be so awful as this!" she said. "Horace, how could you be so careless as to let a great wicked thing like that escape out of its bottle?"

"I had a notion it was a manuscript," said Horace—"till he came out. But he isn't a great wicked thing, Sylvia. He's an amiable old Jinnee enough. And he'd do anything for me. Nobody could be more grateful and generous than he has been."

"Do you call it generous to change the poor, dear dad into a mule?" inquired Sylvia, with a little curl of her upper lip.

"That was an oversight," said Horace; "he meant no harm by it. In Arabia they do these things—or used to in his day. Not that that's much excuse for him. Still, he's not so young as he was, and besides, being bottled up for all those centuries must have narrowed him rather. You must try and make allowances for him, darling."

"I shan't," said Sylvia, "unless he apologises to poor father, and puts him right at once."

"Why, of course, he'll do that," Horace answered confidently. "I'll see that he does. I don't mean to stand any more of his nonsense. I'm afraid I've been just a little too slack for fear of hurting his feelings; but this time he's gone too far, and I shall talk to him like a Dutch uncle. He's always ready to do the right thing when he's once shown where he has gone wrong—only he takes such a lot of showing, poor old chap!"

"But when do you think he'll—do the right thing?"

"Oh, as soon as I see him again."

"Yes; but when will you see him again?"

"That's more than I can say. He's away just now—in China, or Peru, or somewhere."

"Horace! Then he won't be back for months and months!"

"Oh yes, he will. He can do the whole trip, aller et retour, you know, in a few hours. He's an active old beggar for his age. In the meantime, dearest, the chief thing is to keep up your father's spirits. So I think I'd better— I was just telling Sylvia, Mrs. Futvoye," he said, as that lady re-entered the room, "that I should like to see the Professor at once."

"It's quite, quite impossible!" was the nervous reply. "He's in such a state that he's unable to see any one. You don't know how fractious gout makes him!"

"Dear Mrs. Futvoye," said Horace, "believe me, I know more than you suppose."

"Yes, mother, dear," put in Sylvia, "he knows everything—really everything. And perhaps it might do dad good to see him."

Mrs. Futvoye sank helplessly down on a settee. "Oh, dear me!" she said. "I don't know what to say. I really don't. If you had seen him plunge at the mere suggestion of a doctor!"

Privately, though naturally he could not say so, Horace thought a vet. might be more appropriate, but eventually he persuaded Mrs. Futvoye to conduct him to her husband's study.

"Anthony, love," she said, as she knocked gently at the door, "I've brought Horace Ventimore to see you for a few moments, if he may."

It seemed from the sounds of furious snorting and stamping within, that the Professor resented this intrusion on his privacy. "My dear Anthony," said his devoted wife, as she unlocked the door and turned the key on the inside after admitting Horace, "try to be calm. Think of the servants downstairs. Horace is so anxious to help."

As for Ventimore, he was speechless—so inexpressibly shocked was he by the alteration in the Professor's appearance. He had never seen a mule in sorrier condition or in so vicious a temper. Most of the lighter furniture had been already reduced to matchwood; the glass doors of the bookcase were starred or shivered; precious Egyptian pottery and glass were strewn in fragments on the carpets, and even the mummy, though it still smiled with the same enigmatic cheerfulness, seemed to have suffered severely from the Professorial hoofs.

Horace instinctively felt that any words of conventional sympathy would jar here; indeed, the Professor's attitude and expression reminded him irresistibly of a certain "Blondin Donkey" he had seen enacted by music-hall artists, at the point where it becomes sullen and defiant. Only, he had laughed helplessly at the Blondin Donkey, and somehow he felt no inclination to laugh now.

"Believe me, sir," he began, "I would not disturb you like this unless—steady there, for Heaven's sake Professor, don't kick till you've heard me out!" For, the mule, in a clumsy, shambling way which betrayed the novice, was slowly revolving on his own axis so as to bring his hind-quarters into action, while still keeping his only serviceable eye upon his unwelcome visitor.

"Listen to me, sir," said Horace, manoeuvring in his turn. "I'm not to blame for this, and if you brain me, as you seem to be endeavouring to do, you'll simply destroy the only living man who can get you out of this."

The mule appeared impressed by this, and backed cumbrously into a corner, from which he regarded Horace with a mistrustful, but attentive, eye. "If, as I imagine, sir," continued Horace, "you are, though temporarily deprived of speech, perfectly capable of following an argument, will you kindly signify it by raising your right ear?" The mule's right ear rose with a sharp twitch.

"Now we can get on," said Horace. "First let me tell you that I repudiate all responsibility for the proceedings of that infernal Jinnee.... I wouldn't stamp like that—you might go through the floor, you know.... Now, if you will only exercise a little patience—"

At this the exasperated animal made a sudden run at him with his mouth open, which obliged Horace to shelter himself behind a large leather arm-chair. "You really must keep cool, sir," he remonstrated; "your nerves are naturally upset. If I might suggest a little champagne—you could manage it in—in a bucket, and it would help you to pull yourself together. A whisk of your—er—tail would imply consent." The Professor's tail instantly swept some rare Arabian glass lamps and vases from a shelf at his rear, whereupon Mrs. Futvoye went out, and returned presently with a bottle of champagne and a large china jardinière, as the best substitute she could find for a bucket.

When the mule had drained the flower-pot greedily and appeared refreshed, Horace proceeded: "I have every hope, sir," he said, "that before many hours you will be smiling—pray don't prance like that, I mean what I say—smiling over what now seems to you, very justly, a most annoying and serious catastrophe. I shall speak seriously to Fakrash (the Jinnee, you know), and I am sure that, as soon as he realises what a frightful blunder he has made, he will be the first to offer you every reparation in his power. For, old foozle as he is, he's thoroughly good-hearted."

The Professor drooped his ears at this, and shook his head with a doleful incredulity that made him look more like the Pantomime Donkey than ever.

"I think I understand him fairly well by this time, sir," said Horace, "and I'll answer for it that there's no real harm in him. I give you my word of honour that, if you'll only remain quiet and leave everything to me, you shall very soon be released from this absurd position. That's all I came to tell you, and now I won't trouble you any longer. If you could bring yourself, as a sign that you bear me no ill-feeling, to give me your—your off-foreleg at parting, I—"

But the Professor turned his back in so pointed and ominous a manner that Horace judged it better to withdraw without insisting further. "I'm afraid," he said to Mrs. Futvoye, after they had rejoined Sylvia in the drawing-room—"I'm afraid your husband is still a little sore with me about this miserable business."

"I don't know what else you can expect," replied the lady, rather tartly; "he can't help feeling—as we all must and do, after what you said just now—that, but for you, this would never have happened!"

"If you mean it was all through my attending that sale," said Horace, "you might remember that I only went there at the Professor's request. You know that, Sylvia."

"Yes, Horace," said Sylvia; "but papa never asked you to buy a hideous brass bottle with a nasty Genius in it. And any one with ordinary common sense would have kept it properly corked!"

"What, you against me too, Sylvia!" cried Horace, cut to the quick.

"No, Horace, never against you. I didn't mean to say what I did. Only it is such a relief to put the blame on somebody. I know, I know you feel it almost as much as we do. But so long as poor, dear papa remains as he is, we can never be anything to one another. You must see that, Horace!"

"Yes, I see that," he said; "but trust me, Sylvia, he shall not remain as he is. I swear he shall not. In another day or two, at the outside, you will see him his own self once more. And then—oh, darling, darling, you won't let anything or anybody separate us? Promise me that!"

He would have held her in his arms, but she kept him at a distance. "When papa is himself again," she said, "I shall know better what to say. I can't promise anything now, Horace."

Horace recognised that no appeal would draw a more definite answer from her just then; so he took his leave, with the feeling that, after all, matters must improve before very long, and in the meantime he must bear the suspense with patience.

He got through dinner as well as he could in his own rooms, for he did not like to go to his club lest the Jinnee should suddenly return during his absence.

"If he wants me he'd be quite equal to coming on to the club after me," he reflected, "for he has about as much sense of the fitness of things as Mary's lamb. I shouldn't care about seeing him suddenly bursting through the floor of the smoking-room. Nor would the committee."

He sat up late, in the hope that Fakrash would appear; but the Jinnee made no sign, and Horace began to get uneasy. "I wish there was some way of ringing him up," he thought. "If he were only the slave of a ring or a lamp, I'd rub it; but it wouldn't be any use to rub that bottle—and, besides, he isn't a slave. Probably he has a suspicion that he has not exactly distinguished himself over his latest feat, and thinks it prudent to keep out of my way for the present. But if he fancies he'll make things any better for himself by that he'll find himself mistaken."

It was maddening to think of the unhappy Professor still fretting away hour after hour in the uncongenial form of a mule, waiting impatiently for the relief that never came. If it lingered much longer, he might actually starve, unless his family thought of getting in some oats for him, and he could be prevailed upon to touch them. And how much longer could they succeed in concealing the nature of his affliction? How long before all Kensington, and the whole civilised world, would know that one of the leading Orientalists in Europe was restlessly prancing on four legs around his study in Cottesmore Gardens?

Racked by speculations such as these, Ventimore lay awake till well into the small hours, when he dropped off into troubled dreams that, wild as they were, could not be more grotesquely fantastic than the realities to which they were the alternative.

CHAPTER XIII

A CHOICE OF EVILS

Not even his morning tub could brace Ventimore's spirits to their usual cheerfulness. After sending away his breakfast almost untasted he stood at his window, looking drearily out over the crude green turf of Vincent Square at the indigo masses of the Abbey and the Victoria Tower and the huge gasometers to the right which loomed faintly through a dun-coloured haze.

He felt a positive loathing for his office, to which he had gone with such high hopes and enthusiasm of late. There was no work for him to do there any longer, and the sight of his drawing-table and materials would, he knew, be intolerable in their mute mockery.

Nor could he with any decency present himself again at Cottesmore Gardens while the situation still remained unchanged, as it must do until he had seen Fakrash.

When would the Jinnee return, or—horrible suspicion!—did he never intend to return at all?

"Fakrash!" he groaned aloud, "you can't really mean to leave me in such a regular deuce of a hole as this?"

"At thy service!" said a well-known voice behind him, and he turned to see the Jinnee standing smiling on the hearthrug—and at this accomplishment of his dearest desire all his indignation surged back.

"Oh, there you are!" he said irritably. "Where on earth have you been all this time?"

"Nowhere on earth," was the bland reply; "but in the regions of the air, seeking to promote thy welfare."

"If you have been as brilliantly successful up there as you have down here," retorted Horace, "I have much to thank you for."

"I am more than repaid," answered the Jinnee, who, like many highly estimable persons, was almost impervious to irony, "by such assurances of thy gratitude."

"I'm not grateful," said Horace, fuming. "I'm devilish annoyed!"

"Well hath it been written," replied the Jinnee:—

"'Be disregardful of thine affairs, and commit them to the course of Fate, For often a thing that enrages thee may eventually be to thee pleasing.'"

"I don't see the remotest chance of that, in my case," said Horace.

"Why is thy countenance thus troubled, and what new complaint hast thou against me?"

"What the devil do you mean by turning a distinguished and perfectly inoffensive scholar into a wall-eyed mule?" Horace broke out. "If that is your idea of a practical joke—!"

"It is one of the easiest affairs possible," said the Jinnee, complacently running his fingers through the thin strands of his beard. "I have accomplished such transformations on several occasions."

"Then you ought to be ashamed of yourself, that's all. The question is now—how do you propose to restore him again?"

"Far from undoing be that which is accomplished!" was the sententious answer.

"What?" cried Horace, hardly believing his ears; "you surely don't mean to allow that unhappy Professor to remain like that for ever, do you?"

"None can alter what is predestined."

"Very likely not. But it wasn't decreed that a learned man should be suddenly degraded to a beastly mule for the rest of his life. Destiny wouldn't be such a fool!"

"Despise not mules, for they are useful and valuable animals in the household."

"But, confound it all, have you no imagination? Can't you enter at all into the feelings of a man—a man of wide learning and reputation—suddenly plunged into such a humiliating condition?"

"Upon his own head be it," said Fakrash, coldly. "For he hath brought this fate upon himself."

"Well, how do you suppose that you have helped me by this performance? Will it make him any the more disposed to consent to my marrying his daughter? Is that all you know of the world?"

"It is not my intention that thou shouldst take his daughter to wife."

"Whether you approve or not, it's my intention to marry her."

"Assuredly she will not marry thee so long as her father remaineth a mule."

"There I agree with you. But is that your notion of doing me a good turn?"

"I did not consider thy interest in this matter."

"Then will you be good enough to consider it now? I have pledged my word that he shall be restored to his original form. Not only my happiness is at stake, but my honour."

"By failure to perform the impossible none can lose honour. And this is a thing that cannot be undone."

"Cannot be undone?" repeated Horace, feeling a cold clutch at his heart. "Why?"

"Because," said the Jinnee, sullenly, "I have forgotten the way."

"Nonsense!" retorted Horace; "I don't believe it. Why," he urged, descending to flattery, "you're such a clever old Johnny—I beg your pardon, I meant such a clever old Jinnee—you can do anything, if you only give your mind to it. Just look at the way you changed this house back again to what it was. Marvellous!"

"That was the veriest trifle," said Fakrash, though he was obviously pleased by this tribute to his talent; "this would be a different affair altogether."

"But child's play to you!" insinuated Horace. "Come, you know very well you can do it if you only choose."

"It may be as thou sayest. But I do not choose."

"Then I think," said Horace, "that, considering the obligation you admit yourself you are under to me, I have a right to know the reason—the real reason—why you refuse."

"Thy claim is not without justice," answered the Jinnee, after a pause, "nor can I decline to gratify thee."

"That's right," cried Horace; "I knew you'd see it in the proper light when it was once put to you. Now, don't lose any more time, but restore that unfortunate man at once, as you've promised."

"Not so," said the Jinnee; "I promised thee a reason for my refusal—and that thou shalt have. Know then, O my son, that this indiscreet one had, by some vile and unhallowed arts, divined the hidden meaning of what was written upon the seal of the bottle wherein I was confined, and was preparing to reveal the same unto all men."

"What would it matter to you if he did?"

"Much—for the writing contained a false and lying record of my actions."

"If it is all lies, it can't do you any harm. Why not treat them with the contempt they deserve?"

"They are not all lies," the Jinnee admitted reluctantly.

"Well, never mind. Whatever you've done, you've expiated it by this time."

"Now that Suleyman is no more, it is my desire to seek out my kinsmen of the Green Jinn, and live out my days in amity and honour. How can that be if they hear my name execrated by all mortals?"

"Nobody would think of execrating you about an affair three thousand years old. It's too stale a scandal."

"Thou speakest without understanding. I tell thee that if men knew but the half of my misdoings," said Fakrash, in a tone not altogether free from a kind of sombre complacency, "the noise of them would rise even unto the uppermost regions, and scorn and loathing would be my portion."

"Oh, it's not so bad as all that," said Horace, who had a private impression that the Jinnee's "past" would probably turn out to be chiefly made up of peccadilloes. "But, anyway, I'm sure the Professor will readily agree to keep silence about it; and, as you have of course, got the seal in your own possession again—"

"Nay; the seal is still in his possession, and it is naught to me where it is deposited," said Fakrash, "since the only mortal who hath deciphered it is now a dumb animal."

"Not at all," said Horace. "There are several friends of his who could decipher that inscription quite as easily as he did."

"Is this the truth?" said the Jinnee, in visible alarm.

"Certainly," said Horace. "Within the last quarter of a century archæology has made great strides. Our learned men can now read Babylonian bricks and Chaldean tablets as easily as if they were advertisements on galvanised iron. You may think you've been extremely clever in turning the Professor into an animal, but you'll probably find you've only made another mistake."

"How so?" inquired Fakrash.

"Well," said Horace, seeing his advantage, and pushing it unscrupulously, "now, that, in your infinite wisdom, you have ordained that he should be a mule, he naturally can't possess property. Therefore all his effects will have to be sold, and amongst them will be that seal of yours, which, like many other things in his collection, will probably be bought up by the British Museum, where it will be examined and commented upon by every Orientalist in Europe. I suppose you've thought of all that?"

"O young man of marvellous sagacity!" said the Jinnee; "truly I had omitted to consider these things, and thou hast opened my eyes in time. For I will present myself unto this man-mule and adjure him to reveal where he hath bestowed this seal, so that I may regain it."

"He can't do that, you know, so long as he remains a mule."

"I will endow him with speech for the purpose."

"Let me tell you this," said Horace: "he's in a very nasty temper just now, naturally enough, and you won't get anything out of him until you have restored him to human form. If you do that, he'll agree to anything."

"Whether I restore him or not will depend not on me, but on the damsel who is his daughter, and to whom thou art contracted in marriage. For first of all I must speak with her."

"So long as I am present and you promise not to play any tricks," said Horace, "I've no objection, for I believe, if you once saw her and heard her plead for her poor father, you wouldn't have the heart to hold out any longer. But you must give me your word that you'll behave yourself."

"Thou hast it," said the Jinnee; "I do but desire to see her on thine account."

"Very well," agreed Horace; "but I really can't introduce you in that turban—she'd be terrified. Couldn't you contrive to get yourself up in commonplace English clothes, just for once—something that wouldn't attract so much attention?"

"Will this satisfy thee?" inquired the Jinnee, as his green turban and flowing robes suddenly resolved themselves into the conventional chimney-pot hat, frock-coat, and trousers of modern civilisation.

He bore a painful resemblance in them to the kind of elderly gentleman who comes on in the harlequinade to be bonneted by the clown; but Horace was in no mood to be critical just then.

"That's better," he said encouragingly; "much better. Now," he added, as he led the way to the hall and put on his own hat and overcoat, "we'll go out and find a hansom and be at Kensington in less than twenty minutes."

"We shall be there in less than twenty seconds," said the Jinnee, seizing him by the arm above the elbow; and Horace found himself suddenly carried up into the air and set down, gasping with surprise and want of breath, on the pavement opposite the Futvoyes' door.

"I should just like to observe," he said, as soon as he could speak, "that if we've been seen, we shall probably cause a sensation. Londoners are not accustomed to seeing people skimming over the chimney-pots like amateur rooks."

"Trouble not for that," said Fakrash, "for no mortal eyes are capable of following our flight."

"I hope not," said Horace, "or I shall lose any reputation I have left. I think," he added, "I'd better go in alone first and prepare them, if you don't mind waiting outside. I'll come to the window and wave my pocket-handkerchief when they're ready. And do come in by the door like an ordinary person, and ask the maidservant if you may see me."

"I will bear it in mind," answered the Jinnee, and suddenly sank, or seemed to sink, through a chink in the pavement.

Horace, after ringing at the Futvoyes' door, was admitted and shown into the drawing-room, where Sylvia presently came to him, looking as lovely as ever, in spite of the pallor due to sleeplessness and anxiety. "It is kind of you to call and inquire," she said, with the unnatural calm of suppressed hysteria. "Dad is much the same this morning. He had a fairly good night, and was able to take part of a carrot for breakfast—but I'm afraid he has just remembered that he has to read a paper on 'Oriental Occultism' before the Asiatic Society this evening, and it's worrying him a little.... Oh, Horace," she broke out, unexpectedly, "how perfectly awful all this is! How are we to bear it?"

"Don't give way, darling!" said Horace; "you will not have to bear it much longer."

"It's all very well, Horace, but unless something is done soon it will be too late. We can't go on keeping a mule in the study without the servants suspecting something, and where are we to put poor, dear papa? It's too ghastly to think of his having to be sent away to—to a Home of Rest for Horses—and yet what is to be done with him?... Why do you come if you can't do anything?"

"I shouldn't be here unless I could bring you good news. You remember what I told you about the Jinnee?"

"Remember!" cried Sylvia. "As if I could forget! Has he really come back, Horace?"

"Yes. I think I have brought him to see that he has made a foolish mistake in enchanting your unfortunate father, and he seems willing to undo it on certain conditions. He is somewhere within call at this moment, and will come in whenever I give the signal. But he wishes to speak to you first."

"To me? Oh, no, Horace!" exclaimed Sylvia, recoiling. "I'd so much rather not. I don't like things that have come out of brass bottles. I shouldn't know what to say, and it would frighten me horribly."

"You must be brave, darling!" said Horace. "Remember that it depends on you whether the Professor is to be restored or not. And there's nothing alarming about old Fakrash, either, I've got him to put on ordinary things, and he really doesn't look so bad in them. He's quite a mild, amiable old noodle, and he'll do anything for you, if you'll only stroke him down the right way. You will see him, won't you, for your father's sake?"

"If I must," said Sylvia, with a shudder, "I—I'll be as nice to him as I can."

Horace went to the window and gave the signal, though there was no one in sight. However, it was evidently seen, for the next moment there was a resounding blow at the front door, and a little later Jessie, the parlour-maid, announced "Mr. Fatrasher Larmash—to see Mr. Ventimore," and the Jinnee stalked gravely in, with his tall hat on his head.

"You are probably not aware of it, sir," said Horace, "but it is the custom here to uncover in the presence of a lady." The Jinnee removed his hat with both hands, and stood silent and impassive.

"Let me present you to Miss Sylvia Futvoye," Ventimore continued, "the lady whose name you have already heard."

There was a momentary gleam in Fakrash's odd, slanting eyes as they lighted on Sylvia's shrinking figure, but he made no acknowledgment of the introduction.

"The damsel is not without comeliness," he remarked to Horace; "but there are lovelier far than she."

"I didn't ask you for either criticisms or comparisons," said Ventimore, sharply; "there is nobody in the world equal to Miss Futvoye, in my opinion, and you will be good enough to remember that fact. She is exceedingly distressed (as any dutiful daughter would be) by the cruel and senseless trick you have played her father, and she begs that you will rectify it at once. Don't you, Sylvia?"

"Yes, indeed!" said Sylvia, almost in a whisper, "if—if it isn't troubling you too much!"

"I have been turning over thy words in my mind," said Fakrash to Horace, still ignoring Sylvia, "and I am convinced that thou art right. Even if the contents of the seal were known of all men, they would raise no clamour about affairs that concern them not. Therefore it is nothing to me in whose hands the seal may be. Dost thou not agree with me in this?"

"Of course I do," said Horace. "And it naturally follows that—"

"It naturally follows, as thou sayest," said the Jinnee, with a cunning assumption of indifference, "that I have naught to gain by demanding back the seal as the price of restoring this damsel's father to his original form. Wherefore, so far as I am concerned, let him remain a mule for ever; unless, indeed, thou art ready to comply with my conditions."

"Conditions!" cried Horace, utterly unprepared for this conclusion. "What can you possibly want from me? But state them. I'll agree to anything, in reason!"

"I demand that thou shouldst renounce the hand of this damsel."

"That's out of all reason," said Horace, "and you know it. I will never give her up, so long as she is willing to keep me."

"Maiden," said the Jinnee, addressing Sylvia for the first time, "the matter rests with thee. Wilt thou release this my son from his contract, since thou art no fit wife for such as he?"

"How can I," cried Sylvia, "when I love him and he loves me? What a wicked tyrannical old thing you must be to expect it! I can't give him up."

"It is but giving up what can never be thine," said Fakrash. "And be not anxious for him, for I will reward and console him a thousandfold for the loss of thy society. A little while, and he shall remember thee no more."

"Don't believe him, darling," said Horace; "you know me better than that."

"Remember," said the Jinnee, "that by thy refusal thou wilt condemn thy parent to remain a mule throughout all his days. Art thou so unnatural and hard-hearted a daughter as to do this thing?"

"Oh, I couldn't!" cried Sylvia. "I can't let poor father remain a mule all his life when one word—and yet what am I to do? Horace, what shall I say? Advise me.... Advise me!"

"Heaven help us both!" groaned Ventimore. "If I could only see the right thing to do. Look here, Mr. Fakrash," he added, "this is a matter that requires consideration. Will you relieve us of your presence for a short time, while we talk it over?"

"With all my heart," said the Jinnee, in the most obliging manner in the world, and vanished instantly.

"Now, darling," began Horace, after he had gone, "if that unspeakable old scoundrel is really in earnest, there's no denying that he's got us in an extremely tight place. But I can't bring myself to believe that he does mean it. I fancy he's only trying us. And what I want you to do is not to consider me in the matter at all."

"How can I help it?" said poor Sylvia. "Horace, you—you don't want to be released, do you?"

"I?" said Horace, "when you are all I have in the world! That's so likely, Sylvia! But we are bound to look facts in the face. To begin with, even if this hadn't happened, your people wouldn't let our engagement continue. For my prospects have changed again, dearest. I'm even worse off than when we first met, for that confounded Jinnee has contrived to lose my first and only client for me—the one thing worth having he ever gave me." And he told her the story of the mushroom palace and Mr. Wackerbath's withdrawal. "So you see, darling," he concluded, "I haven't even a home to offer you; and if I had, it would be miserably uncomfortable for you with that old Marplot continually dropping in on us—especially if, as I'm afraid he has, he's taken some unreasonable dislike to you."

"But surely you can talk him over?" said Sylvia; "you said you could do anything you liked with him."

"I'm beginning to find," he replied, ruefully enough, "that he's not so easily managed as I thought. And for the present, I'm afraid, if we are to get the Professor out of this, that there's nothing for it but to humour old Fakrash."

"Then you actually advise me to—to break it off?" she cried; "I never thought you would do that!"

"For your own sake," said Horace; "for your father's sake. If you won't, Sylvia, I must. And you will spare me that? Let us both agree to part and—and trust that we shall be united some day."

"Don't try to deceive me or yourself, Horace," she said; "if we part now, it will be for ever."

He had a dismal conviction that she was right. "We must hope for the best," he said drearily; "Fakrash may have some motive in all this we don't understand. Or he may relent. But part we must, for the present."

"Very well," she said. "If he restores dad, I will give you up. But not unless."

"Hath the damsel decided?" asked the Jinnee, suddenly re-appearing; "for the period of deliberation is past."

"Miss Futvoye and I," Horace answered for her, "are willing to consider our engagement at an end, until you approve of its renewal, on condition that you restore her father at once."

"Agreed!" said Fakrash. "Conduct me to him, and we will arrange the matter without delay."

Outside they met Mrs. Futvoye on her way from the study. "You here, Horace?" she exclaimed. "And who is this—gentleman?"

"This," said Horace, "is the—er—author of the Professor's misfortunes, and he had come here at my request to undo his work."

"It would be so kind of him!" exclaimed the distressed lady, who was by this time far beyond either surprise or resentment. "I'm sure, if he knew all we have gone through—!" and she led the way to her husband's room.

As soon as the door was opened the Professor seemed to recognise his tormentor in spite of his changed raiment, and was so powerfully agitated that he actually reeled on his four legs, and "stood over" in a lamentable fashion.

"O man of distinguished attainments!" began the Jinnee, "whom I have caused, for reasons that are known unto thee, to assume the shape of a mule, speak, I adjure thee, and tell me where thou hast deposited the inscribed seal which is in thy possession."

The Professor spoke; and the effect of articulate speech proceeding from the mouth of what was to all outward seeming an ordinary mule was strange beyond description. "I'll see you damned first," he said sullenly. "You can't do worse to me than you've done already!"

"As thou wilt," said Fakrash; "but unless I regain it, I will not restore thee to what thou wast."

"Well, then," said the mule, savagely, "you'll find it in the top right-hand drawer of my writing-table: the key is in that diorite bowl on the mantelpiece."

The Jinnee unlocked the drawer, and took out the metal cap, which he placed in the breast pocket of his incongruous frock-coat. "So far, well," he said; "next thou must deliver up to me the transcription thou hast made, and swear to preserve an inviolable secrecy regarding the meaning thereof."

"Do you know what you're asking, sir?" said the mule, laying back his ears viciously. "Do you think that to oblige you I'm going to suppress one of the most remarkable discoveries of my whole scientific career? Never, sir—never!"

"Since if thou refusest I shall assuredly deprive thee of speech once more and leave thee a mule, as thou art now, of hideous appearance," said the Jinnee, "thou art like to gain little by a discovery which thou wilt be unable to impart. However, the choice rests with thee."

The mule rolled his one eye, and showed all his teeth in a vicious snarl. "You've got the whip-hand of me," he said, "and I may as well give in. There's a transcript inside my blotting-case—it's the only copy I've made."

Fakrash found the paper, which he rubbed into invisibility between his palms, as any ordinary conjurer might do.

"Now raise thy right forefoot," he said, "and swear by all thou holdest sacred never to divulge what thou hast learnt"—which oath the Professor, in the vilest of tempers, took, clumsily enough.

"Good," said the Jinnee, with a grim smile. "Now let one of thy women bring me a cup of fair water."

Sylvia went out, and came back with a cup of water. "It's filtered," she said anxiously; "I don't know if that will do?"

"It will suffice," said Fakrash. "Let both the women withdraw."

"Surely," remonstrated Mrs. Futvoye, "you don't mean to turn his wife and daughter out of the room at such a moment as this? We shall be perfectly quiet, and we may even be of some help."

"Do as you're told, my dear!" snapped the ungrateful mule; "do as you're told. You'll only be in the way here. Do you suppose he doesn't know his own beastly business?"

They left accordingly; whereupon Fakrash took the cup—an ordinary breakfast cup with a Greek key-border pattern in pale blue round the top—and, drenching the mule with the contents, exclaimed, "Quit this form and return to the form in which thou wast!"

For a dreadful moment or two it seemed as if no effect was to be produced; the animal simply stood and shivered, and Ventimore began to feel an agonising suspicion that the Jinnee really had, as he had first asserted, forgotten how to perform this particular incantation.

All at once the mule reared, and began to beat the air frantically with his fore-hoofs; after which he fell heavily backward into the nearest armchair (which was, fortunately, a solid and capacious piece of furniture) with his fore-legs hanging limply at his side, in a semi-human fashion. There was a brief convulsion, and then, by some gradual process unspeakably impressive to witness, the man seemed to break through the mule, the mule became merged in the man—and Professor Futvoye, restored to his own natural form and habit, sat gasping and trembling in the chair before them.

CHAPTER XIV

"SINCE THERE'S NO HELP, COME, LET US KISS AND PART!"

As soon as the Professor seemed to have regained his faculties, Horace opened the door and called in Sylvia and her mother, who were, as was only to be expected, overcome with joy on seeing the head of the family released from his ignoble condition of a singularly ill-favoured quadruped.

"There, there," said the Professor, as he submitted to their embraces and incoherent congratulations, "it's nothing to make a fuss about. I'm quite myself again, as you can see. And," he added, with an unreasonable outburst of ill-temper, "if one of you had only had the common sense to think of such a simple remedy as sprinkling a little cold water over me when I was first taken like that, I should have been spared a great deal of unnecessary inconvenience. But that's always the way with women—lose their heads the moment anything goes wrong! If I had not kept perfectly cool myself—"

"It was very, very stupid of us not to think of it, papa," said Sylvia, tactfully ignoring the fact that there was scarcely an undamaged article in the room; "still, you know, if we had thrown the water it mightn't have had the same effect."

"I'm not in a condition to argue now," said her father; "you didn't trouble to try it, and there's no more to be said."

"No more to be said!" exclaimed Fakrash. "O thou monster of ingratitude, hast thou no thanks for him who hath delivered thee from thy predicament?"

"As I am already indebted to you, sir," said the Professor, "for about twenty-four hours of the most poignant and humiliating mental and bodily anguish a human being can endure, inflicted for no valid reason that I can discover, except the wanton indulgence of your unholy powers, I can only say that any gratitude of which I am conscious is of a very qualified description. As for you, Ventimore," he added, turning to Horace, "I don't know—I can only guess at—the part you have played in this wretched business; but in any case you will understand, once for all, that all relations between us must cease."

"Papa," said Sylvia, tremulously, "Horace and I have already agreed that—that we must separate."

"At my bidding," explained Fakrash, suavely; "for such an alliance would be totally unworthy of his merits and condition."

This frankness was rather too much for the Professor, whose temper had not been improved by his recent trials.

"Nobody asked for your opinion, sir!" he snapped. "A person who has only recently been released from a term of long and, from all I have been able to ascertain, well-deserved imprisonment, is scarcely entitled to pose as an authority on social rank. Have the decency not to interfere again with my domestic affairs."

"Excellent is the saying," remarked the imperturbable Jinnee, "'Let the rat that is between the paws of the leopard observe rigidly all the rules of politeness and refrain from words of provocation.' For to return thee to the form of a mule once more would be no difficult undertaking."

"I think I failed to make myself clear," the Professor hastened to observe—"failed to make myself clear. I—I merely meant to congratulate you on your fortunate escape from the consequences of what I—I don't doubt was an error of justice. I—I am sure that, in the future, you will employ your—your very remarkable abilities to better purpose, and I would suggest that the greatest service you can do this unfortunate young man here is to abstain from any further attempts to promote his interests."

"Hear, hear!" Horace could not help throwing in, though in so discreet an undertone that it was inaudible.

"Far be this from me," replied Fakrash. "For he has become unto me even as a favourite son, whom I design to place upon the golden pinnacle of felicity. Therefore, I have chosen for him a wife, who is unto this damsel of thine as the full moon to the glow-worm, and as the bird of Paradise to an unfledged sparrow. And the nuptials shall be celebrated before many hours."

"Horace!" cried Sylvia, justly incensed, "why—why didn't you tell me this before?"

"Because," said the unhappy Horace, "this is the very first I've heard of it. He's always springing some fresh surprise on me," he added, in a whisper—"but they never come to anything much. And he can't marry me against my will, you know."

"No," said Sylvia, biting her lip. "I never supposed he could do that, Horace."

"I'll settle this at once," he replied. "Now, look here, Mr. Jinnee," he added, "I don't know what new scheme you have got in your head—but if you are proposing to marry me to anybody in particular—"

"Have I not informed thee that I have it in contemplation to obtain for thee the hand of a King's daughter of marvellous beauty and accomplishments?"

"You know perfectly well you never mentioned it before," said Horace, while Sylvia gave a little low cry.

"Repine not, O damsel," counselled the Jinnee, "since it is for his welfare. For, though as yet he believeth it not, when he beholds the resplendent beauty of her countenance he will swoon away with delight and forget thy very existence."

"I shall do nothing of the sort," said Horace, savagely. "Just understand that I don't intend to marry any Princess. You may prevent me—in fact, you have—from marrying this lady, but you can't force me to marry anybody else. I defy you!"

"When thou hast seen thy bride's perfections thou wilt need no compulsion," said Fakrash. "And if thou shouldst refuse, know this: that thou wilt be exposing those who are dear to thee in this household to calamities of the most unfortunate description."

The awful vagueness of this threat completely crushed Horace; he could not think, he did not even dare to imagine, what consequences he might bring upon his beloved Sylvia and her helpless parents by persisting in his refusal.

"Give me time," he said heavily; "I want to talk this over with you."

"Pardon me, Ventimore," said the Professor, with acidulous politeness; "but, interesting as the discussion of your matrimonial arrangements is to you and your—a—protector, I should greatly prefer that you choose some more fitting place for arriving at a decision which is in the circumstances a foregone conclusion. I am rather tired and upset, and I should be obliged if you and this gentleman could bring this most trying interview to a close as soon as you conveniently can."

"You hear, Mr. Fakrash?" said Horace, between his teeth, "it is quite time we left. If you go at once, I will follow you very shortly."

"Thou wilt find me awaiting thee," answered the Jinnee, and, to Mrs. Futvoye's and Sylvia's alarm, disappeared through one of the bookcases.

"Well," said Horace, gloomily, "you see how I'm situated? That obstinate old devil has cornered me. I'm done for!"

"Don't say that," said the Professor; "you appear to be on the eve of a most brilliant alliance, in which I am sure you have our best wishes—the best wishes of us all," he added pointedly.

"Sylvia," said Horace, still lingering, "before I go, tell me that, whatever I may have to do, you will understand that—that it will be for your sake!"

"Please don't talk like that," she said. "We may never see one another again. Don't let my last recollection of you be of—of a hypocrite, Horace!"

"A hypocrite!" he cried. "Sylvia, this is too much! What have I said or done to make you think me that?"

"Oh, I am not so simple as you suppose, Horace," she replied. "I see now why all this has happened: why poor dad was tormented; why you insisted on my setting you free. But I would have released you without that! Indeed, all this elaborate artifice wasn't in the least necessary!"

"You believe I was an accomplice in that old fool's plot?" he said. "You believe me such a cur as that?"

"I don't blame you," she said. "I don't believe you could help yourself. He can make you do whatever he chooses. And then, you are so rich now, it is natural that you should want to marry some one—some one more suited to you—like this lovely Princess of yours."

"Of mine!" groaned the exasperated Horace. "When I tell you I've never even seen her! As if any Princess in the world would marry me to please a Jinnee out of a brass bottle! And if she did, Sylvia, you can't believe that any Princess would make me forget you!"

"It depends so very much on the Princess," was all Sylvia could be induced to say.

"Well," said Horace, "if that's all the faith you have in me, I suppose it's useless to say any more. Good-bye, Mrs. Futvoye; good-bye, Professor. I wish I could tell you how deeply I regret all the trouble I have brought on you by my own folly. All I can say is, that I will bear anything in future rather than expose you or any of you to the smallest risk."

"I trust, indeed," said the Professor, stiffly, "that you will use all the influence at your command to secure me from any repetition of an experience that might well have unmanned a less equable temperament than my own."

"Good-bye, Horace," said Mrs. Futvoye, more kindly. "I believe you are more to be pitied than blamed, whatever others may think. And I don't forget—if Anthony does—that, but for you, he might, instead of sitting there comfortably in his armchair, be lashing out with his hind legs and kicking everything to pieces at this very moment!"

"I deny that I lashed out!" said the Professor. "My—a—hind quarters may have been under imperfect control—but I never lost my reasoning powers or my good humour for a single instant. I can say that truthfully."

If the Professor could say that truthfully amidst the general wreck in which he sat, like another Marius, he had little to learn in the gentle art of self-deception; but there was nothing to gain by contradicting him then.

"Good-bye, Sylvia," said Horace, and held out his hand.

"Good-bye," she said, without offering to take it or look at him—and, after a miserable pause, he left the study. But before he had reached the front door he heard a swish and swirl of drapery behind him, and felt her light hand on his arm. "Ah, no!" she said, clinging to him, "I can't let you go like this. I didn't mean all the things I said just now. I do believe in you, Horace—at least, I'll try hard to.... And I shall always, always love you, Horace.... I shan't care—very much—even if you do forget me, so long as you are happy.... Only don't be too happy. Think of me sometimes!"

"I shall not be too happy," he said, as he held her close to his heart and kissed her pathetically drawn mouth and flushed cheeks. "And I shall think of you always."

"And you won't fall in love with your Princess?" entreated Sylvia, at the end of her altruism. "Promise!"

"If I am ever provided with one," he replied, "I shall loathe her—for not being you. But don't let us lose heart, darling. There must be some way of talking that old idiot out of this nonsense and bringing him round to common sense. I'm not going to give in just yet!"

These were brave words—but, as they both felt, the situation had little enough to warrant them, and, after one last long embrace, they parted, and he was no sooner on the steps than he felt himself caught up as before and borne through the air with breathless speed, till he was set down, he could not have well said how, in a chair in his own sitting-room at Vincent Square.

"Well," he said, looking at the Jinnee, who was standing opposite with a smile of intolerable complacency, "I suppose you feel satisfied with yourself over this business?"

"It hath indeed been brought to a favourable conclusion," said Fakrash. "Well hath the poet written—"

"I don't think I can stand any more 'Elegant Extracts' this afternoon," interrupted Horace. "Let us come to business. You seem," he went on, with a strong effort to keep himself in hand, "to have formed some plan for marrying me to a King's daughter. May I ask you for full particulars?"

"No honour and advancement can be in excess of thy deserts," answered the Jinnee.

"Very kind of you to say so—but you are probably unaware that, as society is constituted at the present time, the objections to such an alliance would be quite insuperable."

"For me," said the Jinnee, "few obstacles are insuperable. But speak thy mind freely."

"I will," said Horace. "To begin with, no European Princess of the Blood Royal would entertain the idea for a moment. And if she did, she would forfeit her rank and cease to be a Princess, and I should probably be imprisoned in a fortress for lèse majesté or something."

"Dismiss thy fears, for I do not propose to unite thee to any Princess that is born of mortals. The bride I intend for thee is a Jinneeyeh; the peerless Bedeea-el-Jemal, daughter of my kinsman Shahyal, the Ruler of the Blue Jann."

"Oh, is she, though?" said Horace, blankly. "I'm exceedingly obliged, but, whatever may be the lady's attractions—"

"Her nose," recited the Jinnee, with enthusiasm, "is like unto the keen edge of a polished sword; her hair resembleth jewels, and her cheeks are ruddy as wine. She hath heavy lips, and when she looketh aside she putteth to shame the wild cows...."

"My good, excellent friend," said Horace, by no means impressed by this catalogue of charms, "one doesn't marry to mortify wild cows."

"When she walketh with a vacillating gait," continued Fakrash, as though he had not been interrupted, "the willow branch itself turneth green with envy."

"Personally," said Horace, "a waddle doesn't strike me as particularly fascinating—it's quite a matter of taste. Do you happen to have seen this enchantress lately?"

"My eyes have not been refreshed by her manifold beauties since I was enclosed by Suleyman—whose name be accursed—in the brass bottle of which thou knowest. Why dost thou ask?"

"Merely because it occurred to me that, after very nearly three thousand years, your charming kinswoman may—well, to put it as mildly as possible, not have altogether escaped the usual effects of Time. I mean, she must be getting on, you know!"

"O, silly-bearded one!" said the Jinnee, in half-scornful rebuke; "art thou, then, ignorant that we of the Jinn are not as mortals, that we should feel the ravages of age?"

"Forgive me if I'm personal," said Horace; "but surely your own hair and beard might be described as rather inclining to grey."

"Not from age," said Fakrash, "This cometh from long confinement."

"I see," said Horace. "Like the Prisoner of Chillon. Well, assuming that the lady in question is still in the bloom of early youth, I see one fatal difficulty to becoming her suitor."

"Doubtless," said the Jinnee, "thou art referring to Jarjarees, the son of Rejmoos, the son of Iblees?"

"No, I wasn't," said Horace; "because, you see, I don't remember having ever heard of him. However, he's another fatal difficulty. That makes two of them."

"Surely I have spoken of him to thee as my deadliest foe? It is true that he is a powerful and vindictive Efreet, who hath long persecuted the beauteous Bedeea with hateful attentions. Yet it may be possible, by good fortune, to overthrow him."

"Then I gather that any suitor for Bedeea's hand would be looked upon as a rival by the amiable Jarjarees?"

"Far is he from being of an amiable disposition," answered the Jinnee, simply, "and he would be so transported by rage and jealousy that he would certainly challenge thee to mortal combat."

"Then that settles it," said Horace. "I don't think any one can fairly call me a coward, but I do draw the line at fighting an Efreet for the hand of a lady I've never seen. How do I know he'll fight fair?"

"He would probably appear unto thee first in the form of a lion, and if he could not thus prevail against thee, transform himself into a serpent, and then into a buffalo or some other wild beast."

"And I should have to tackle the entire menagerie?" said Horace. "Why, my dear sir, I should never get beyond the lion!"

"I would assist thee to assume similar transformations," said the Jinnee, "and thus thou mayst be enabled to defeat him. For I burn with desire to behold mine enemy reduced to cinders."

"It's much more likely that you would have to sweep me up!" said Horace, who had a strong conviction that anything in which the Jinnee was concerned would be bungled somehow. "And if you're so anxious to destroy this Jarjarees, why don't you challenge him to meet you in some quiet place in the desert and settle him yourself? It's much more in your line than it is in mine!"

He was not without hopes that Fakrash might act on this suggestion, and that so he would be relieved of him in the simplest and most satisfactory way; but any such hopes were as usual doomed to disappointment.

"It would be of no avail," said the Jinnee, "for it hath been written of old that Jarjarees shall not perish save by the hand of a mortal. And I am persuaded that thou wilt turn out to be that mortal, since thou art both strong and fearless, and, moreover, it is also predestined that Bedeea shall wed one of the sons of men."

"Then," said Horace, feeling that this line of defence must be abandoned, "I fall back on objection number one. Even if Jarjarees were obliging enough to retire in my favour, I should still decline to become the—a—consort of a Jinneeyeh whom I've never seen, and don't love."

"Thou hast heard of her incomparable charms, and verily the ear may love before the eye."

"It may," admitted Horace, "but neither of my ears is the least in love at present."

"These reasons are of no value," said Fakrash, "and if thou hast none better—"

"Well," said Ventimore, "I think I have. You profess to be anxious to—to requite the trifling service I rendered you, though hitherto, you'll admit yourself, you haven't made a very brilliant success of it. But, putting the past aside," he continued, with a sudden dryness in his throat; "putting the past aside, I ask you to consider what possible benefit or happiness such a match as this—I'm afraid I'm not so fortunate as to secure your attention?" he broke off, as he observed the Jinnee's eyes beginning to film over in the disagreeable manner characteristic of certain birds.

"Proceed," said Fakrash, unskinning his eyes for a second; "I am hearkening unto thee."

"It seems to me," stammered Horace, inconsequently enough, "that all that time inside a bottle—well, you can't call it experience exactly; and possibly in the interval you've forgotten all you knew about feminine nature. I think you must have."

"It is not possible that such knowledge should be forgotten," said the Jinnee, resenting this imputation in quite a human way. "Thy words appear to me to lack sense. Interpret them, I pray thee."

"Why," explained Horace, "you don't mean to tell me that this young and lovely relation of yours, a kind of immortal, and—and with the devil's own pride, would be gratified by your proposal to bestow her hand upon an insignificant and unsuccessful London architect? She'd turn up that sharp and polished nose of hers at the mere idea of so unequal a match!"

"An excellent rank is that conferred by wealth," remarked the Jinnee.

"But I'm not rich, and I've already declined any riches from you," said Horace. "And, what's more to the point, I'm perfectly and hopelessly obscure. If you had the slightest sense of humour—which I fear you have not—you would at once perceive the absurdity of proposing to unite a radiant, ethereal, superhuman being to a commonplace professional nonentity in a morning coat and a tall hat. It's really too ridiculous!"

"What thou hast just said is not altogether without wisdom," said Fakrash, to whom this was evidently a new point of view. "Art thou, indeed, so utterly unknown?"

"Unknown?" repeated Horace; "I should rather think I was! I'm simply an inconsiderable unit in the population of the vastest city in the world; or, rather, not a unit—a cipher. And, don't you see, a man to be worthy of your exalted kinswoman ought to be a celebrity. There are plenty of them about."

"What meanest thou by a celebrity?" inquired Fakrash, falling into the trap more readily than Horace had ventured to hope.

"Oh, well, a distinguished person, whose name is on everybody's lips, who is honoured and praised by all his fellow-citizens. Now, that kind of man no Jinneeyeh could look down upon."

"I perceive," said Fakrash, thoughtfully. "Yes, I was in danger of committing a rash action. How do men honour such distinguished individuals in these days?"

"They generally overfeed them," said Horace. "In London the highest honour a hero can be paid is to receive the freedom of the City, which is only conferred in very exceptional cases, and for some notable service. But, of course, there are other sorts of celebrities, as you could see if you glanced through the society papers."

"I cannot believe that thou, who seemest a gracious and talented young man, can be indeed so obscure as thou hast represented."

"My good sir, any of the flowers that blush unseen in the desert air, or the gems concealed in ocean caves, so excellently described by one of our poets, could give me points and a beating in the matter of notoriety. I'll make you a sporting offer. There are over five million inhabitants in this London of ours. If you go out into the streets and ask the first five hundred you meet whether they know me, I don't mind betting you—what shall I say? a new hat—that you won't find half a dozen who've ever even heard of my existence. Why not go out and see for yourself?"

To his surprise and gratification the Jinnee took this seriously. "I will go forth and make inquiry," he said, "for I desire further enlightenment concerning thy statements. But, remember," he added: "should I still require thee to wed the matchless Bedeea-el-Jemal, and thou shouldst disobey me, thou wilt bring disaster, not on thine own head, but on those thou art most desirous of protecting."

"Yes, so you told me before," said Horace, brusquely. "Good evening." But Fakrash was already gone. In spite of all he had gone through and the unknown difficulties before him, Ventimore was seized with what Uncle Remus calls "a spell of the dry grins" at the thought of the probable replies that the Jinnee would meet with in the course of his inquiries. "I'm afraid he won't be particularly impressed by the politeness of a London crowd," he thought; "but at least they'll convince him that I am not exactly a prominent citizen. Then he'll give up this idiotic match of his—I don't know, though. He's such a pig-headed old fool that he may stick to it all the same. I may find myself encumbered with a Jinneeyeh bride several centuries my senior before I know where I am. No, I forget; there's the jealous Jarjarees to be polished off first. I seem to remember something about a quick-change combat with an Efreet in the "Arabian Nights." I may as well look it up, and see what may be in store for me."

And after dinner he went to his shelves and took down Lane's three-volume edition of "The Arabian Nights," which he set himself to study with a new interest. It was long since he had looked into these wondrous tales, old beyond all human calculation, and fresher, even now, than the most modern of successful romances. After all, he was tempted to think, they might possess quite as much historical value as many works with graver pretentions to accuracy.

He found a full account of the combat with the Efreet in "The Story of the Second Royal Mendicant" in the first volume, and was unpleasantly surprised to discover that the Efreet's name was actually given as "Jarjarees, the son of Rejmoos, the son of Iblees"—evidently the same person to whom Fakrash had referred as his bitterest foe. He was described as "of hideous aspect," and had, it seemed, not only carried off the daughter of the Lord of the Ebony Island on her wedding night, but, on discovering her in the society of the Royal Mendicant, had revenged himself by striking off her hands, her feet, and her head, and transforming his human rival into an ape. "Between this fellow and old Fakrash," he reflected ruefully, at this point, "I seem likely to have a fairly lively time of it!"

He read on till he reached the memorable encounter between the King's daughter and Jarjarees, who presented himself "in a most hideous shape, with hands like winnowing forks, and legs like masts, and eyes like burning torches"—which was calculated to unnerve the stoutest novice. The Efreet began by transforming himself from a lion to a scorpion, upon which the Princess became a serpent; then he changed to an eagle, and she to a vulture; he to a black cat, and she to a cock; he to a fish, and she to a larger fish still.

"If Fakrash can shove me through all that without a fatal hitch somewhere," Ventimore told himself, "I shall be agreeably disappointed in him," But, after reading a few more lines, he cheered up. For the Efreet finished as a flame, and the Princess as a "body of fire." "And when we looked towards him," continued the narrator, "we perceived that he had become a heap of ashes."

"Come," said Horace to himself, "that puts Jarjarees out of action, any way! The odd thing is that Fakrash should never have heard of it."

But, as he saw on reflection, it was not so very odd, after all, as the incident had probably happened after the Jinnee had been consigned to his brass bottle, where intelligence of any kind would be most unlikely to reach him.

He worked steadily through the whole of the second volume and part of the third; but, although he picked up a certain amount of information upon Oriental habits and modes of thought and speech which might come in useful later, it was not until he arrived at the 24th Chapter of the third volume that his interest really revived.

For the 24th Chapter contained "The Story of Seyf-el-Mulook and Bedeea-el-Jemal," and it was only natural that he should be anxious to know all that there was to know concerning the antecedents of one who might be his fiancée before long. He read eagerly.

Bedeea, it appeared, was the lovely daughter of Shahyal, one of the Kings of the Believing Jann; her father—not Fakrash himself, as the Jinnee had incorrectly represented—had offered her in marriage to no less a personage than King Solomon himself, who, however, had preferred the Queen of Sheba. Seyf, the son of the King of Egypt, afterwards fell desperately in love with Bedeea, but she and her grandmother both declared that between mankind and the Jann there could be no agreement.

"And Seyf was a King's son!" commented Horace. "I needn't alarm myself. She wouldn't be likely to have anything to say to me. It's just as I told Fakrash."

His heart grew lighter still as he came to the end, for he learnt that, after many adventures which need not be mentioned here, the devoted Seyf did actually succeed in gaining the proud Bedeea as his wife. "Even Fakrash could not propose to marry me to some one who has a husband already," he thought. "Still, she may be a widow!"

To his relief, however, the conclusion ran thus; "Seyf-el-Mulook lived with Bedeea-el-Jemal a most pleasant and agreeable life ... until they were visited by the terminator of delights and the separator of companions."

"If that means anything at all," he reasoned, "it means that Seyf and Bedeea are both deceased. Even Jinneeyeh seem to be mortal. Or perhaps she became so by marrying a mortal; I dare say that Fakrash himself wouldn't have lasted all this time if he hadn't been bottled, like a tinned tomato. But I'm glad I found this out, because Fakrash is evidently unaware of it, and, if he should persist in any more of this nonsense, I think I see my way now to getting the better of him."

So, with renewed hope and in vastly improved spirits, he went to bed and was soon sound asleep.

CHAPTER XV

BLUSHING HONOURS

It was rather late the next morning when Ventimore opened his eyes, to discover the Jinnee standing by the foot of his bed. "Oh, it's you, is it?" he said sleepily. "How did you—a—get on last night?"

"I gained such information as I desired," said Fakrash, guardedly; "and now, for the last time, I am come to ask thee whether thou wilt still persist in refusing to wed the illustrious Bedeea-el-Jemal? And have a care how thou answerest."

"So you haven't given up the idea?" said Horace. "Well, since you make such a point of it, I'll meet you as far as this. If you produce the lady, and she consents to marry me, I won't decline the honour. But there's one condition I really must insist on."

"It is not for thee to make stipulations. Still, yet this once I will hear thee."

"I'm sure you'll see that it's only fair. Supposing, for any reason, you can't persuade the Princess to meet me within a reasonable time—shall we say a week?—"

"Thou shalt be admitted to her presence within twenty-four hours," said the Jinnee.

"That's better still. Then, if I don't see her within twenty-four hours, I am to be at liberty to infer that the negotiations are off, and I may marry anybody else I please, without any opposition from you? Is that understood?"

"It is agreed," said Fakrash, "for I am confident that Bedeea will accept thee joyfully."

"We shall see," said Horace. "But it might be as well if you went and prepared her a little. I suppose you know where to find her—and you've only twenty-four hours, you know."

"More than is needed," answered the Jinnee, with such childlike confidence, that Horace felt almost ashamed of so easy a victory. "But the sun is already high. Arise, my son, put on these robes"—and with this he flung on the bed the magnificent raiment which Ventimore had last worn on the night of his disastrous entertainment—"and when thou hast broken thy fast, prepare to accompany me."

"Before I agree to that," said Horace, sitting up in bed, "I should like to know where you're taking me to."

"Obey me without demur," said Fakrash, "or thou knowest the consequences."

It seemed to Horace that it was as well to humour him, and he got up accordingly, washed and shaved, and, putting on his dazzling robe of cloth-of-gold thickly sewn with gems, he joined Fakrash—who, by the way, was similarly, if less gorgeously, arrayed—in the sitting-room, in a state of some mystification.

"Eat quickly," commanded the Jinnee, "for the time is short." And Horace, after hastily disposing of a cold poached egg and a cup of coffee, happened to go to the windows.

"Good Heavens!" he cried. "What does all this mean?"

He might well ask. On the opposite side of the road, by the railings of the square, a large crowd had collected, all staring at the house in eager expectation. As they caught sight of him they raised a cheer, which caused him to retreat in confusion, but not before he had seen a great golden chariot with six magnificent coal-black horses, and a suite of swarthy attendants in barbaric liveries, standing by the pavement below. "Whose carriage is that?" he asked.

"It belongs to thee," said the Jinnee; "descend then, and make thy progress in it through the City."

"I will not," said Horace. "Even to oblige you I simply can't drive along the streets in a thing like the band-chariot of a travelling circus."

"It is necessary," declared Fakrash. "Must I again recall to thee the penalty of disobedience?"

"Oh, very well," said Horace, irritably. "If you insist on my making a fool of myself, I suppose I must. But where am I to drive, and why?"

"That," replied Fakrash, "thou shalt discover at the fitting moment." And so, amidst the shouts of the spectators, Ventimore climbed up into the strange-looking vehicle, while the Jinnee took his seat by his side. Horace had a parting glimpse of Mr. and Mrs. Rapkin's respective noses flattened against the basement window, and then two dusky slaves mounted to a seat at the back of the chariot, and the horses started off at a stately trot in the direction of Rochester Row.

"I think you might tell me what all this means," he said. "You've no conception what an ass I feel, stuck up here like this!"

"Dismiss bashfulness from thee, since all this is designed to render thee more acceptable in the eyes of the Princess Bedeea," said the Jinnee.

Horace said no more, though he could not but think that this parade would be thrown away.

But as they turned into Victoria Street and seemed to be heading straight for the Abbey, a horrible thought occurred to him. After all, his only authority for the marriage and decease of Bedeea was the "Arabian Nights," which was not unimpeachable evidence. What if she were alive and waiting for the arrival of the bridegroom? No one but Fakrash would have conceived such an idea as marrying him to a Jinneeyeh in Westminster Abbey; but he was capable of any extravagance, and there were apparently no limits to his power.

"Mr. Fakrash," he said hoarsely, "surely this isn't my—my wedding day? You're not going to have the ceremony there?"

"Nay," said the Jinnee, "be not impatient. For this edifice would be totally unfitted for the celebration of such nuptials as thine."

As he spoke, the chariot left the Abbey on the right and turned down the Embankment. The relief was so intense that Horace's spirits rose irrepressibly. It was absurd to suppose that even Fakrash could have arranged the ceremony in so short a time. He was merely being taken for a drive, and fortunately his best friends could not recognise him in his Oriental disguise. And it was a glorious morning, with a touch of frost in the air and a sky of streaky turquoise and pale golden clouds; the broad river glittered in the sunshine; the pavements were lined with admiring crowds, and the carriage rolled on amidst frantic enthusiasm, like some triumphal car.

"How they're cheering us!" said Horace. "Why, they couldn't make more row for the Lord Mayor himself."

"What is this Lord Mayor of whom thou speakest?" inquired Fakrash.

"The Lord Mayor?" said Horace. "Oh, he's unique. There's nobody in the world quite like him. He administers the law, and if there's any distress in any part of the earth he relieves it. He entertains monarchs and Princes and all kinds of potentates at his banquets, and altogether he's a tremendous swell."

"Hath he dominion over the earth and the air and all that is therein?"

"Within his own precincts, I believe he has," said Horace, rather lazily, "but I really don't know precisely how wide his powers are." He was vainly trying to recollect whether such matters as sky-signs, telephones, and telegraphs in the City were within the Lord Mayor's jurisdiction or the County Council's.

Fakrash remained silent just as they were driving underneath Charing Cross Railway Bridge, when he started perceptibly at the thunder of the trains overhead and the piercing whistles of the engines. "Tell me," he said, clutching Horace by the arm, "what meaneth this?"

"You don't mean to say," said Horace, "that you have been about London all these days, and never noticed things like these before?"

"Till now," said the Jinnee, "I have had no leisure to observe them and discover their nature."

"Well," said Horace, anxious to let the Jinnee see that he had not the monopoly of miracles, "since your days we have discovered how to tame or chain the great forces of Nature and compel them to do our will. We control the Spirits of Earth, Air, Fire, and Water, and make them give us light and heat, carry our messages, fight our quarrels for us, transport us wherever we wish to go, with a certainty and precision that throw even your performances, my dear sir, entirely into the shade."

Considering what a very large majority of civilised persons would be as powerless to construct the most elementary machine as to create the humblest kind of horse, it is not a little odd how complacently we credit ourselves with all the latest achievements of our generation. Most of us accept the amazement of the simple-minded barbarian on his first introduction to modern inventions as a gratifying personal tribute: we feel a certain superiority, even if we magnanimously refrain from boastfulness. And yet our own particular share in these discoveries is limited to making use of them under expert guidance, which any barbarian, after overcoming his first terror, is quite as competent to do as we are.

It is a harmless vanity enough, and especially pardonable in Ventimore's case, when it was so desirable to correct any tendency to "uppishness" on the part of the Jinnee.

"And doth the Lord Mayor dispose of these forces at his will?" inquired Fakrash, on whom Ventimore's explanation had evidently produced some impression.

"Certainly," said Horace; "whenever he has occasion."

The Jinnee seemed engrossed in his own thoughts, for he said no more just then.

They were now nearing St. Paul's Cathedral, and Horace's first suspicion returned with double force.

"Mr. Fakrash, answer me," he said. "Is this my wedding day or not? If it is, it's time I was told!"

"Not yet," said the Jinnee, enigmatically, and indeed it proved to be another false alarm, for they turned down Cannon Street and towards the Mansion House.

"Perhaps you can tell me why we're going through Victoria Street, and what all this crowd has come out for?" asked Ventimore. For the throng was denser than ever; the people surged and swayed in serried ranks behind the City police, and gazed with a wonder and awe that for once seemed to have entirely silenced the Cockney instinct of persiflage.

"For what else but to do thee honour?" answered Fakrash.

"What bosh!" said Horace. "They mistake me for the Shah or somebody—and no wonder, in this get-up."

"Not so," said the Jinnee. "Thy names are familiar to them."

Horace glanced up at the hastily improvised decorations; on one large strip of bunting which spanned the street he read: "Welcome to the City's most distinguished guest!" "They can't mean me," he thought; and then another legend caught his eye: "Well done, Ventimore!" And an enthusiastic householder next door had burst into poetry and displayed the couplet—

"Would we had twenty more   Like Horace Ventimore!"

"They do mean me!" he exclaimed. "Now, Mr. Fakrash, will you kindly explain what tomfoolery you've been up to now? I know you're at the bottom of this business."

It struck him that the Jinnee was slightly embarrassed. "Didst thou not say," he replied, "that he who should receive the freedom of the City from his fellow-men would be worthy of Bedeea-el-Jemal?"

"I may have said something of the sort. But, good heavens! you don't mean that you have contrived that I should receive the freedom of the City?"

"It was the easiest affair possible," said the Jinnee, but he did not attempt to meet Horace's eye.

"Was it, though?" said Horace, in a white rage. "I don't want to be inquisitive, but I should like to know what I've done to deserve it?"

"Why trouble thyself with the reason? Let it suffice thee that such honour is bestowed upon thee."

By this time the chariot had crossed Cheapside and was entering King Street.

"This really won't do!" urged Horace. "It's not fair to me. Either I've done something, or you must have made the Corporation believe I've done something, to be received like this. And, as we shall be in the Guildhall in a very few seconds, you may as well tell me what it is!"

"Regarding that matter," replied the Jinnee, in some confusion, "I am truly as ignorant as thyself."

As he spoke they drove through some temporary wooden gates into the courtyard, where the Honourable Artillery Company presented arms to them, and the carriage drew up before a large marquee decorated with shields and clustered banners.

"Well, Mr. Fakrash," said Horace, with suppressed fury, as he alighted, "you have surpassed yourself this time. You've got me into a nice scrape, and you'll have to pull me through it as well as you can."

"Have no uneasiness," said the Jinnee, as he accompanied his protégé into the marquee, which was brilliant with pretty women in smart frocks, officers in scarlet tunics and plumed hats, and servants in State liveries.

Their entrance was greeted by a politely-subdued buzz of applause and admiration, and an official, who introduced himself as the Prime Warden of the Candlestick-makers' Company, advanced to meet them. "The Lord Mayor will receive you in the library," he said. "If you will have the kindness to follow me—"

Horace followed him mechanically. "I'm in for it now," he thought, "whatever it is. If I can only trust Fakrash to back me up—but I'm hanged if I don't believe he's more nervous than I am!"

As they came into the noble Library of the Guildhall a fine string band struck up, and Horace, with the Jinnee in his rear, made his way through a lane of distinguished spectators towards a dais, on the steps of which, in his gold-trimmed robes and black-feather hat, stood the Lord Mayor, with his sword and mace-bearers on either hand, and behind him a row of beaming sheriffs.

A truly stately and imposing figure did the Chief Magistrate for that particular year present: tall, dignified, with a lofty forehead whose polished temples reflected the light, an aquiline nose, and piercing black eyes under heavy white eyebrows, a frosty pink in his wrinkled cheeks, and a flowing silver beard with a touch of gold still lingering under the lower lip: he seemed, as he stood there, a worthy representative of the greatest and richest city in the world.

Horace approached the steps with an unpleasant sensation of weakness at the knees, and no sort of idea what he was expected to do or say when he arrived.

And, in his perplexity, he turned for support and guidance to his self-constituted mentor—only to discover that the Jinnee, whose short-sightedness and ignorance had planted him in this present false position, had mysteriously and perfidiously disappeared, and left him to grapple with the situation single-handed.

CHAPTER XVI

A KILLING FROST

Fortunately for Ventimore, the momentary dismay he had felt on finding himself deserted by his unfathomable Jinnee at the very outset of the ceremony passed unnoticed, as the Prime Warden of the Candlestick-makers' Company immediately came to his rescue by briefly introducing him to the Lord Mayor, who, with dignified courtesy, had descended to the lowest step of the dais to receive him.

"Mr. Ventimore," said the Chief Magistrate, cordially, as he pressed Horace's hand, "you must allow me to say that I consider this one of the greatest privileges—if not the greatest privilege—that have fallen to my lot during a term of office in which I have had the honour of welcoming more than the usual number of illustrious visitors."

"My Lord Mayor," said Horace, with absolute sincerity, "you really overwhelm me. I—I only wish I could feel that I had done anything to deserve this—this magnificent compliment!"

"Ah!" replied the Lord Mayor, in a paternally rallying tone. "Modest, my dear sir, I perceive. Like all truly great men! A most admirable trait! Permit me to present you to the Sheriffs."

The Sheriffs appeared highly delighted. Horace shook hands with both of them; indeed, in the flurry of the moment he very nearly offered to do so with the Sword and Mace bearers as well, but their hands were, as it happened, otherwise engaged.

"The actual presentation," said the Lord Mayor, "takes place in the Great Hall, as you are doubtless aware."

"I—I have been given to understand so," said Horace, with a sinking heart—for he had begun to hope that the worst was over.

"But before we adjourn," said his host, "you will let me tempt you to partake of some slight refreshment—just a snack?"

Horace was not hungry, but it occurred to him that he might get through the ceremony with more credit after a glass of champagne; so he accepted the invitation, and was conducted to an extemporised buffet at one end of the Library, where he fortified himself for the impending ordeal with a caviare sandwich and a bumper of the driest champagne in the Corporation cellars.

"They talk of abolishing us," said the Lord Mayor, as he took an anchovy on toast; "but I maintain, Mr. Ventimore—I maintain that we, with our ancient customs, our time-honoured traditions, form a link with the past, which a wise statesman will preserve, if I may employ a somewhat vulgar term, untinkered with."

Horace agreed, remembering a link with a far more ancient past with which he devoutly wished he had refrained from tinkering.

"Talking of ancient customs," the Lord Mayor continued, with an odd blend of pride and apology, "you will shortly have an illustration of our antiquated procedure, which may impress you as quaint."

Horace, feeling absolutely idiotic, murmured that he felt sure it would do that.

"Before presenting you for the freedom, the Prime Warden and five officials of the Candlestick-makers' Company will give their testimony as compurgators in your favour, making oath that you are 'a man of good name and fame,' and that (you will be amused at this, Mr. Ventimore)—that you 'do desire the freedom of this city, whereby to defraud the Queen or the City.' Ha, ha! Curious way of putting it, is it not?"

"Very," said Horace, guiltily, and not a little concerned on the official's account.

"A mere form!" said the Lord Mayor; "but I for one, Mr. Ventimore—I for one should be sorry to see the picturesque old practices die out. To my mind," he added, as he finished a pâté de foie gras sandwich, "the modern impatience to sweep away all the ancient landmarks (whether they be superannuated or not) is one of the most disquieting symptoms of the age. You won't have any more champagne? Then I think we had better be making our way to the Great Hall for the Event of the Day."

"I'm afraid," said Horace, with a sudden consciousness of his incongruously Oriental attire—"I'm afraid this is not quite the sort of dress for such a ceremony. If I had known—"

"Now, don't say another word!" said the Lord Mayor. "Your costume is very nice—very nice indeed, and—and most appropriate, I am sure. But I see the City Marshal is waiting for us to head the procession. Shall we lead the way?"

The band struck up the March of the Priests from Athalie, and Horace, his head in a whirl, walked with his host, followed by the City Lands Committee, the Sheriffs, and other dignitaries, through the Art Gallery and into the Great Hall, where their entrance was heralded by a flourish of trumpets.

The Hall was crowded, and Ventimore found himself the object of a popular demonstration which would have filled him with joy and pride if he could only have felt that he had done anything whatever to justify it, for it was ridiculous to suppose that he had rendered himself a public benefactor by restoring a convicted Jinnee to freedom and society generally.

His only consolation was that the English are a race not given to effusiveness without very good reason, and that before the ceremony was over he would be enabled to gather what were the particular services which had excited such unbounded enthusiasm.

Meanwhile he stood there on the crimson-draped and flower-bedecked dais, bowing repeatedly, and trusting that he did not look so forlornly foolish as he felt. A long shaft of sunlight struck down between the Gothic rafters, and dappled the brown stone walls with patches of gold; the electric lights in the big hooped chandeliers showed pale and feeble against the subdued glow of the stained glass; the air was heavy with the scent of flowers and essences. Then there was a rustle of expectation in the audience, and a pause, in which it seemed to Horace that everybody on the dais was almost as nervous and at a loss what to do next as he was himself. He wished with all his soul that they would hurry the ceremony through, anyhow, and let him go.

At length the proceedings began by a sort of solemn affectation of having merely met there for the ordinary business of the day, which to Horace just then seemed childish in the extreme; it was resolved that "items 1 to 4 on the agenda need not be discussed," which brought them to item 5.

Item 5 was a resolution, read by the Town Clerk, that "the freedom of the City should be presented to Horace Ventimore, Esq., Citizen and Candlestick-maker" (which last Horace was not aware of being, but supposed vaguely that it had been somehow managed while he was at the buffet in the Library), "in recognition of his services"—the resolution ran, and Horace listened with all his ears—"especially in connection with ..." It was most unfortunate—but at this precise point the official was seized with an attack of coughing, in which all was lost but the conclusion of the sentence, " ... that have justly entitled him to the gratitude and admiration of his fellow-countrymen."

Then the six compurgators came forward and vouched for Ventimore's fitness to receive the freedom. He had painful doubts whether they altogether understood what a responsibility they were undertaking—but it was too late to warn them and he could only trust that they knew more of their business than he did.

After this the City Chamberlain read him an address, to which Horace listened in resigned bewilderment. The Chamberlain referred to the unanimity and enthusiasm with which the resolution had been carried, and said that it was his pleasing and honourable duty, as the mouthpiece of that ancient City, to address what he described with some inadequacy as "a few words" to one by adding whose name to their roll of freemen the Corporation honoured rather themselves than the recipient of their homage.

It was flattering, but to Horace's ear the phrases sounded excessive, almost fulsome—though, of course, that depended very much on what he had done, which he had still to ascertain. The orator proceeded to read him the "Illustrious List of London's Roll of Fame," a recital which made Horace shiver with apprehension. For what names they were! What glorious deeds they had performed! How was it possible that he—plain Horace Ventimore, a struggling architect who had missed his one great chance—could have achieved (especially without even being aware of it) anything that would not seem ludicrously insignificant by comparison?

He had a morbid fancy that the marble goddesses, or whoever they were, at the base of Nelson's monument opposite, were regarding him with stony disdain and indignation; that the statue of Wellington knew him for an arrant impostor, and averted his head with cold contempt; and that the effigy of Lord Mayor Beckford on the right of the dais would come to life and denounce him in another moment.

"Turning now to your own distinguished services," he suddenly heard the City Chamberlain resuming, "you are probably aware, sir, that it is customary on these occasions to mention specifically the particular merit which had been deemed worthy of civic recognition."

Horace was greatly relieved to hear it, for it struck him as a most sensible and, in his own particular case, essential formality.

"But, on the present occasion, sir," proceeded the speaker, "I feel, as all present must feel, that it would be unnecessary—nay, almost impertinent—were I to weary the public ear by a halting recapitulation of deeds with which it is already so appreciatively familiar." At this he was interrupted by deafening and long-continued applause, at the end of which he continued: "I have only therefore, to greet you in the name of the Corporation, and to offer you the right hand of fellowship as a Freeman, and Citizen, and Candlestick-maker of London."

As he shook hands he presented Horace with a copy of the Oath of Allegiance, intimating that he was to read it aloud. Naturally, Ventimore had not the least objection to swear to be good and true to our Sovereign Lady Queen Victoria, or to be obedient to the Lord Mayor, and warn him of any conspiracies against the Queen's peace which might chance to come under his observation; so he took the oath cheerfully enough, and hoped that this was really the end of the ceremony.

However, to his great chagrin and apprehension, the Lord Mayor rose with the evident intention of making a speech. He said that the conclusion of the City to bestow the highest honour in their gift upon Mr. Horace Ventimore had been—here he hesitated—somewhat hastily arrived at. Personally, he would have liked a longer time to prepare, to make the display less inadequate to, and worthier of, this exceptional occasion. He thought that was the general feeling. (It evidently was, judging from the loud and unanimous cheering). However, for reasons which—for reasons with which they were as well acquainted as himself, the notice had been short. The Corporation had yielded (as they always did, as it would always be their pride and pleasure to yield) to popular pressure which was practically irresistible, and had done the best they could in the limited—he might almost say the unprecedentedly limited—period allowed them. The proudest leaf in Mr. Ventimore's chaplet of laurels to-day was, he would venture to assert, the sight of the extraordinary enthusiasm and assemblage, not only in that noble hall, but in the thoroughfares of this mighty Metropolis. Under the circumstances, this was a marvellous tribute to the admiration and affection which Mr. Ventimore had succeeded in inspiring in the great heart of the people, rich and poor, high and low. He would not detain his hearers any longer; all that remained for him to do was to ask Mr. Ventimore's acceptance of a golden casket containing the roll of freedom, and he felt sure that their distinguished guest, before proceeding to inscribe his name on the register, would oblige them all by some account from his own lips of—of the events in which he had figured so prominently and so creditably.

Horace received the casket mechanically; there was a universal cry of "Speech!" from the audience, to which he replied by shaking his head in helpless deprecation—but in vain; he found himself irresistibly pressed towards the rail in front of the dais, and the roar of applause which greeted him saved him from all necessity of attempting to speak for nearly two minutes.

During that interval he had time to clear his brain and think what he had better do or say in his present unenviable dilemma. For some time past a suspicion had been growing in his mind, until it had now almost swollen into certainty. He felt that, before he compromised himself, or allowed his too generous entertainers to compromise themselves irretrievably, it was absolutely necessary to ascertain his real position, and, to do that, he must make some sort of speech. With this resolve, all his nervousness and embarrassment and indecision melted away; he faced the assembly coolly and gallantly, convinced that his best alternative now lay in perfect candour.

"My Lord Mayor, my lords, ladies, and gentlemen," he began, in a clear voice which penetrated to the farthest gallery and commanded instant attention. "If you expect to hear from me any description of what I've done to be received like this, I'm afraid you will be disappointed. For my own belief is that I've done nothing whatever."

There was a general outcry of "No, no!" at this, and a fervid murmur of protest.

"It's all very well to say 'No, no,'" said Horace, "and I am extremely grateful to you all for the interruption. Still, I can only repeat that I am absolutely unaware of having ever rendered my Country, or this great City, a single service deserving of the slightest acknowledgment. I wish I could feel I had—but the truth is that, if I have, the fact has entirely slipped from my memory."

Again there were murmurs, this time with a certain under-current of irritation; and he could hear the Lord Mayor behind him remarking to the City Chamberlain that this was not at all the kind of speech for the occasion.

"I know what you're thinking," said Horace. "You're thinking this is mock modesty on my part. But it's nothing of the sort. I don't know what I've done—but I presume you are all better informed. Because the Corporation wouldn't have given me that very charming casket—you wouldn't all of you be here like this—unless you were under a strong impression that I'd done something to deserve it." At this there was a fresh outburst of applause. "Just so," said Horace, calmly. "Well, now, will any of you be kind enough to tell me, in a few words, what you suppose I've done?"

There was a dead silence, in which every one looked at his or her neighbour and smiled feebly.

"My Lord Mayor," continued Horace, "I appeal to you to tell me and this distinguished assembly why on earth we're all here!"

The Lord Mayor rose. "I think it sufficient to say," he announced with dignity, "that the Corporation and myself were unanimously of opinion that this distinction should be awarded—for reasons which it is unnecessary and—hum—ha—invidious to enter into here."

"I am sorry," persisted Horace, "but I must press your lordship for those reasons. I have an object.... Will the City Chamberlain oblige me, then?... No? Well, then, the Town Clerk?... No?—it's just as I suspected: none of you can give me your reasons, and shall I tell you why? Because there aren't any.... Now, do bear with me for a moment. I'm quite aware this is very embarrassing for all of you—but remember that it's infinitely more awkward for me! I really cannot accept the freedom of the City under any suspicion of false pretences. It would be a poor reward for your hospitality, and base and unpatriotic into the bargain, to depreciate the value of so great a distinction by permitting it to be conferred unworthily. If, after you've heard what I am going to tell you, you still insist on my accepting such an honour, of course I will not be so ungracious as to refuse it. But I really don't feel that it would be right to inscribe my name on your Roll of Fame without some sort of explanation. If I did, I might, for anything I know, involuntarily be signing the death-warrant of the Corporation!"

There was a breathless hush upon this; the silence grew so intense that to borrow a slightly involved metaphor from a distinguished friend of the writer's, you might have picked up a pin in it! Horace leaned sideways against the rail in an easy attitude, so as to face the Lord Mayor, as well as a portion of his audience.

"Before I go any farther," he said, "will your lordship pardon me if I suggest that it might be as well to direct that all reporters present should immediately withdraw?"

The reporters' table was instantly in a stir of anger, and many of the guests expressed some dissatisfaction. "We, at least," said the Lord Mayor, rising, flushed with annoyance, "have no reason to dread publicity. I decline to make a hole-and-corner affair of this. I shall give no such orders."

"Very well," said Horace, when the chorus of approval had subsided. "My suggestion was made quite as much in the Corporation's interests as mine. I merely thought that, when you all clearly understood how grossly you've been deluded, you might prefer to have the details kept out of the newspapers if possible. But if you particularly want them published over the whole world, why, of course—"

An uproar followed here, under cover of which the Lord Mayor contrived to give orders to have the doors fastened till further directions.

"Don't make this more difficult and disagreeable for me than it is already!" said Horace, as soon as he could obtain a hearing again. "You don't suppose that I should have come here in this Tom-fool's dress, imposing myself on the hospitality of this great City, if I could have helped it! If you've been brought here under false pretences, so have I. If you've been made to look rather foolish, what is your situation to mine? The fact is, I am the victim of a headstrong force which I am utterly unable to control...."

Upon this a fresh uproar arose, and prevented him from continuing for some time. "I only ask for fair play and a patient hearing!" he pleaded. "Give me that, and I will undertake to restore you all to good humour before I have done."

They calmed down at this appeal, and he was able to proceed. "My case is simply this," he said. "A little time ago I happened to go to an auction and buy a large brass bottle...."

For some inexplicable reason his last words roused the audience to absolute frenzy; they would not hear anything about the brass bottle. Every time he attempted to mention it they howled him down, they hissed, they groaned, they shook their fists; the din was positively deafening.

Nor was the demonstration confined to the male portion of the assembly. One lady, indeed, who is a prominent leader in society, but whose name shall not be divulged here, was so carried away by her feelings as to hurl a heavy cut-glass bottle of smelling-salts at Horace's offending head. Fortunately for him, it missed him and only caught one of the officials (Horace was not in a mood to notice details very accurately, but he had a notion that it was the City Remembrancer) somewhere about the region of the watch-pocket.

"Will you hear me out?" Ventimore shouted. "I'm not trifling. I haven't told you yet what was inside the bottle. When I opened it, I found ..."

He got no farther—for, as the words left his lips, he felt himself seized by the collar of his robe and lifted off his feet by an agency he was powerless to resist.

Up and up he was carried, past the great chandeliers, between the carved and gilded rafters, pursued by a universal shriek of dismay and horror. Down below he could see the throng of pale, upturned faces, and hear the wild screams and laughter of several ladies of great distinction in violent hysterics. And the next moment he was in the glass lantern, and the latticed panes gave way like tissue paper as he broke through into the open air, causing the pigeons on the roof to whirr up in a flutter of alarm.

Of course, he knew that it was the Jinnee who was abducting him in this sensational manner, and he was rather relieved than alarmed by Fakrash's summary proceeding, for he seemed, for once, to have hit upon the best way out of a situation that was rapidly becoming impossible.

CHAPTER XVII

HIGH WORDS

Once outside in the open air, the Jinnee "towered" like a pheasant shot through the breast, and Horace closed his eyes with a combined swing-switchback-and-Channel-passage sensation during a flight which apparently continued for hours, although in reality it probably did not occupy more than a very few seconds. His uneasiness was still further increased by his inability to guess where he was being taken to—for he felt instinctively that they were not travelling in the direction of home.

At last he felt himself set down on some hard, firm surface, and ventured to open his eyes once more. When he realised where he actually was, his knees gave way under him, and he was seized with a sudden giddiness that very nearly made him lose his balance. For he found himself standing on a sort of narrow ledge or cornice immediately under the ball at the top of St. Paul's.

Many feet beneath him spread the dull, leaden summit of the dome, its raised ridges stretching, like huge serpents over the curve, beyond which was a glimpse of the green roof of the nave and the two west towers, with their grey columns and urn-topped buttresses and gilded pineapples, which shone ruddily in the sun.

He had an impression of Ludgate Hill and Fleet Street as a deep, winding ravine, steeped in partial shadow; of long sierras of roofs and chimney-pots, showing their sharp outlines above mouse-coloured smoke-wreaths; of the broad, pearl-tinted river, with oily ripples and a golden glitter where the sunlight touched it; of the gleaming slope of mud under the wharves and warehouses on the Surrey side; of barges and steamers moored in black clusters; of a small tug fussing noisily down the river, leaving a broadening arrow-head in its wake.

Cautiously he moved round towards the east, where the houses formed a blurred mosaic of cream, slate, indigo, and dull reds and browns, above which slender rose-flushed spires and towers pierced the haze, stained in countless places by pillars of black, grey, and amber smoke, and lightened by plumes and jets of silvery steam, till all blended by imperceptible gradations into a sky of tenderest gold slashed with translucent blue.

It was a magnificent view, and none the less so because the indistinctness of all beyond a limited radius made the huge City seem not only mystical, but absolutely boundless in extent. But although Ventimore was distinctly conscious of all this, he was scarcely in a state to appreciate its grandeur just then. He was much too concerned with wondering why Fakrash had chosen to plant him up there in so insecure a position, and how he was ever to be rescued from it, since the Jinnee had apparently disappeared.

He was not far off, however, for presently Horace saw him stalk round the narrow cornice with an air of being perfectly at home on it.

"So there you are!" said Ventimore; "I thought you'd deserted me again. What have you brought me up here for?"

"Because I desired to have speech with thee in private," replied the Jinnee.

"We're not likely to be intruded on here, certainly," said Horace. "But isn't it rather exposed, rather public? If we're seen up here, you know, it will cause a decided sensation."

"I have laid a spell on all below that they should not raise their eyes. Be seated, therefore, and hear my words."

Horace lowered himself carefully to a sitting position, so that his legs dangled in space, and Fakrash took a seat by his side. "O, most indiscreet of mankind!" he began, in an aggrieved tone; "thou hast been near the committal of a great blunder, and doing ill to thyself and to me!"

"Well, I do like that!" retorted Horace; "when you let me in for all that freedom of the City business, and then sneaked off, leaving me to get out of it the best way I could, and only came back just as I was about to explain matters, and carried me up through the roof like a sack of flour. Do you consider that tactful on your part?"

"Thou hadst drunk wine and permitted it to creep as far as the place of secrets."

"Only one glass," said Horace; "and I wanted it, I can assure you. I was obliged to make a speech to them, and, thanks to you, I was in such a hole that I saw nothing for it but to tell the truth."

"Veracity, as thou wilt learn," answered the Jinnee, "is not invariably the Ship of Safety. Thou wert about to betray the benefactor who procured for thee such glory and honour as might well cause the gall-bladder of lions to burst with envy!"

"If any lion with the least sense of humour could have witnessed the proceedings," said Ventimore, "he might have burst with laughter—certainly not envy. Good Lord! Fakrash," he cried, in his indignation, "I've never felt such an absolute ass in my whole life! If nothing would satisfy you but my receiving the freedom of the City, you might at least have contrived some decent excuse for it! But you left out the only point there was in the whole thing—and all for what?"

"What doth it signify why the whole populace should come forth to acclaim thee and do thee honour, so long as they did so?" said Fakrash, sullenly. "For the report of thy fame would reach Bedeea-el-Jemal."

"That's just where you're mistaken," said Horace. "If you had not been in too desperate a hurry to make a few inquiries, you would have found out that you were taking all this trouble for nothing."

"How sayest thou?"

"Well, you would have discovered that the Princess is spared all temptation to marry beneath her by the fact that she became the bride of somebody else about thirty centuries ago. She married a mortal, one Seyf-el-Mulook, a King's son, and they've both been dead a considerable time—another obstacle to your plans."

"It is a lie," declared Fakrash.

"If you will take me back to Vincent Square, I shall be happy to show you the evidence in your national records," said Horace. "And you may be glad to know that your old enemy, Mr. Jarjarees, came to a violent end, after a very sporting encounter with a King's daughter, who, though proficient in advanced magic, unfortunately perished herself, poor lady, in the final round."

"I had intended thee to accomplish his downfall," said Fakrash.

"I know," said Horace. "It was most thoughtful of you. But I doubt if I should have done it half as well—and it would have probably cost me an eye, at the very least. It's better as it is."

"And how long hast thou known of these things?"

"Only since last night."

"Since last night? And thou didst not unfold them unto me till this instant?"

"I've had such a busy morning, you see," explained Horace. "There's been no time."

"Silly-bearded fool that I was to bring this misbegotten dog into the august presence of the great Lord Mayor himself (on whom be peace!)," cried the Jinnee.

"I object to being referred to as a misbegotten dog," said Horace, "but with the rest of your remark I entirely concur. I'm afraid the Lord Mayor is very far from being at peace just now." He pointed to the steep roof of the Guildhall, with its dormers and fretted pinnacles, and the slender lantern through which he had so lately made his inglorious exit. "There's the devil of a row going on under that lantern just now, Mr. Fakrash, you may depend upon that. They've locked the doors till they can decide what to do next—which will take them some time. And it's all your fault!"

"It was thy doing. Why didst thou dare to inform the Lord Mayor that he was deceived?"

"Why? Because I thought he ought to know. Because I was bound, particularly after my oath of allegiance, to warn him of any conspiracy against him. Because I was in such a hat. He'll understand all that—he won't blame me for this business."

"It is fortunate," observed the Jinnee, "that I flew away with thee before thou couldst pronounce my name."

"You gave yourself away," said Horace. "They all saw you, you know. You weren't flying so particularly fast. They'll recognise you again. If you will carry off a man from under the Lord Mayor's very nose, and shoot up through the roof like a rocket with him, you can't expect to escape some notice. You see, you happen to be the only unbottled Jinnee in this City."

Fakrash shifted his seat on the cornice. "I have committed no act of disrespect unto the Lord Mayor," he said, "therefore he can have no just cause of anger against me."

Horace perceived that the Jinnee was not altogether at ease, and pushed his advantage accordingly.

"My dear good old friend," he said, "you don't seem to realise yet what an awful thing you've done. For your own mistaken purposes, you have compelled the Chief Magistrate and the Corporation of the greatest City in the world to make themselves hopelessly ridiculous. They'll never hear the last of this affair. Just look at the crowds waiting patiently below there. Look at the flags. Think of that gorgeous conveyance of yours standing outside the Guildhall. Think of the assembly inside—all the most aristocratic, noble, and distinguished personages in the land," continued Horace, piling it on as he proceeded; "all collected for what? To be made fools of by a Jinnee out of a brass bottle!"

"For their own sakes they will preserve silence," said Fakrash, with a gleam of unwonted shrewdness.

"Probably they would hush it up, if they only could," conceded Horace. "But how can they? What are they to say? What plausible explanation can they give? Besides, there's the Press: you don't know what the Press is; but I assure you its power is tremendous—it's simply impossible to keep anything secret from it nowadays. It has eyes and ears everywhere, and a thousand tongues. Five minutes after the doors in that hall are unlocked (and they can't keep them locked much longer) the reporters will be handing in their special descriptions of you and your latest vagaries to their respective journals. Within half an hour bills will be carried through every quarter of London—bills with enormous letters: 'Extraordinary Scene at the Guildhall.' 'Strange End to a Civic Function.' 'Startling Appearance of an Oriental Genie in the City.' 'Abduction of a Guest of the Lord Mayor.' 'Intense Excitement.' 'Full Particulars!' And by that time the story will have flashed round the whole world. 'Keep silence,' indeed! Do you imagine for a moment that the Lord Mayor, or anybody else concerned, however remotely, will ever forget, or be allowed to forget, such an outrageous incident as this? If you do, believe me, you're mistaken."

"Truly, it would be a terrible thing to incur the wrath of the Lord Mayor," said the Jinnee, in troubled accents.

"Awful!" said Horace. "But you seem to have managed it."

"He weareth round his neck a magic jewel, which giveth him dominion over devils—is it not so?"

"You know best," said Horace.

"It was the splendour of that jewel and the majesty of his countenance that rendered me afraid to enter his presence, lest he should recognise me for what I am and command me to obey him, for verily his might is greater even than Suleyman's, and his hand heavier upon such of the Jinn as fall into his power!"

"If that's so," said Horace, "I should strongly advise you to find some way of putting things straight before it's too late—you've no time to lose."

"Thou sayest well," said Fakrash, springing to his feet, and turning his face towards Cheapside. Horace shuffled himself along the ledge in a seated position after the Jinnee, and, looking down between his feet, could just see the tops of the thin and rusty trees in the churchyard, the black and serried swarms of foreshortened people in the street, and the scarlet-rimmed mouths of chimney-pots on the tiled roofs below.

"There is but one remedy I know," said the Jinnee, "and it may be that I have lost power to perform it. Yet will I make the endeavour." And, stretching forth his right hand towards the east, he muttered some kind of command or invocation.

Horace almost fell off the cornice with apprehension of what might follow. Would it be a thunderbolt, a plague, some frightful convulsion of Nature? He felt sure that Fakrash would hesitate at no means, however violent, of burying all traces of his blunder in oblivion, and very little hope that, whatever he did, it would prove anything but some worse indiscretion than his previous performances.

Happily none of these extreme measures seemed to have occurred to the Jinnee, though what followed was strange and striking enough.

For presently, as if in obedience to the Jinnee's weird gesticulations, a lurid belt of fog came rolling up from the direction of the Royal Exchange, swallowing up building after building in its rapid course; one by one the Guildhall, Bow Church, Cheapside itself, and the churchyard disappeared, and Horace, turning his head to the left, saw the murky tide sweeping on westward, blotting out Ludgate Hill, the

Strand, Charing Cross, and Westminster—till at last he and Fakrash were alone above a limitless plain of bituminous cloud, the only living beings left, as it seemed, in a blank and silent universe.

"Look again!" said Fakrash, and Horace, looking eastward, saw the spire of Bow Church, rosy once more, the Guildhall standing clear and intact, and the streets and house-tops gradually reappearing. Only the flags, with their unrestful shiver and ripple of colour, had disappeared, and, with them, the waiting crowds and the mounted constables. The ordinary traffic of vans, omnibuses, and cabs was proceeding as though it had never been interrupted—the clank and jingle of harness chains, the cries and whip-crackings of drivers, rose with curious distinctness above the incessant trampling roar which is the ground-swell of the human ocean.

"That cloud which thou sawest," said Fakrash, "hath swept away with it all memory of this affair from the minds of every mortal assembled to do thee honour. See, they go about their several businesses, and all the past incidents are to them as though they had never been."

It was not often that Horace could honestly commend any performance of the Jinnee's, but at this he could not restrain his admiration. "By Jove!" he said, "that certainly gets the Lord Mayor and everybody else out of the mess as neatly as possible. I must say, Mr. Fakrash, it's much the best thing I've seen you do yet."

"Wait," said the Jinnee, "for presently thou shalt see me perform a yet more excellent thing."

There was a most unpleasant green glow in his eyes and a bristle in his thin beard as he spoke, which suddenly made Horace feel uncomfortable. He did not like the look of the Jinnee at all.

"I really think you've done enough for to-day," he said. "And this wind up here is rather searching. I shan't be sorry to find myself on the ground again."

"That," replied the Jinnee, "thou shalt assuredly do before long, O impudent and deceitful wretch!" And he laid a long, lean hand on Horace's shoulder.

"He is put out about something!" thought Ventimore. "But what?" "My dear sir," he said aloud, "I don't understand this tone of yours. What have I done to offend you?"

"Divinely gifted was he who said: 'Beware of losing hearts in consequence of injury, for the bringing them back after flight is difficult.'"

"Excellent!" said Horace. "But I don't quite see the application."

"The application," explained the Jinnee, "is that I am determined to cast thee down from here with my own hand!"

Horace turned faint and dizzy for a moment. Then, by a strong effort of will, he pulled himself together. "Oh, come now," he said, "you don't really mean that, you know. After all your kindness! You're much too good-natured to be capable of anything so atrocious."

"All pity hath been eradicated from my heart," returned Fakrash. "Therefore prepare to die, for thou art presently about to perish in the most unfortunate manner."

Ventimore could not repress a shudder. Hitherto he had never been able to take Fakrash quite seriously, in spite of all his supernatural powers; he had treated him with a half-kindly, half-contemptuous tolerance, as a well-meaning, but hopelessly incompetent, old foozle. That the Jinnee should ever become malevolent towards him had never entered his head till now—and yet he undoubtedly had. How was he to cajole and disarm this formidable being? He must keep cool and act promptly, or he would never see Sylvia again.

As he sat there on the narrow ledge, with a faint and not unpleasant smell of hops saluting his nostrils from some distant brewery, he tried hard to collect his thoughts, but could not. He found himself, instead, idly watching the busy, jostling crowd below, who were all unconscious of the impending drama so high above them. Just over the rim of the dome he could see the opaque white top of a lamp on a shelter, where a pigmy constable stood, directing the traffic.

Would he look up if Horace called for help? Even if he could, what help could he render? All he could do would be to keep the crowd back and send for a covered stretcher. No, he would not dwell on these horrors; he must fix his mind on some way of circumventing Fakrash.

How did the people in "The Arabian Nights" manage? The fisherman, for instance? He persuaded his Jinnee to return to the bottle by pretending to doubt whether he had ever really been inside it.

But Fakrash, though simple enough in some respects, was not quite such a fool as that. Sometimes the Jinn could be mollified and induced to grant a reprieve by being told stories, one inside the other, like a nest of Oriental boxes. Unfortunately Fakrash did not seem in the humour for listening to apologues, and, even if he were, Horace could not think of or improvise any just then. "Besides," he thought, "I can't sit up here telling him anecdotes for ever. I'd almost sooner die!" Still, he remembered that it was generally possible to draw an Arabian Efreet into discussion: they all loved argument, and had a rough conception of justice.

"I think, Mr. Fakrash," he said, "that, in common fairness, I have a right to know what offence I have committed."

"To recite thy misdeeds," replied the Jinnee, "would occupy much time."

"I don't mind that," said Horace, affably. "I can give you as long as you like. I'm in no sort of a hurry."

"With me it is otherwise," retorted Fakrash, making a stride towards him. "Therefore court not life, for thy death hath become unavoidable.'

"Before we part," said Horace, "you won't refuse to answer one or two questions?"

"Didst thou not undertake never to ask any further favour of me? Moreover, it will avail thee nought. For I am positively determined to slay thee."

"I demand it," said Horace, "in the most great name of the Lord Mayor (on whom be peace!)"

It was a desperate shot—but it took effect. The Jinnee quailed visibly.

"Ask, then," he said; "but briefly, for the time groweth short."

Horace determined to make one last appeal to Fakrash's sense of gratitude, since it had always seemed the dominant trait in his character.

"Well," he said, "but for me, wouldn't you be still in that brass bottle?"

"That," replied the Jinnee, "is the very reason why I purpose to destroy thee!"

"Oh!" was all Horace could find to say at this most unlooked-for answer. His sheet anchor, in which he had trusted implicitly, had suddenly dragged—and he was drifting fast to destruction.

"Are there any other questions which thou wouldst ask?" inquired the Jinnee, with grim indulgence; "or wilt thou encounter thy doom without further procrastination?"

Horace was determined not to give in just yet; he had a very bad hand, but he might as well play the game out and trust to luck to gain a stray trick.

"I haven't nearly done yet," he said. "And, remember, you've promised to answer me—in the name of the Lord Mayor!"

"I will answer one other question, and no more," said the Jinnee, in an inflexible tone; and Ventimore realised that his fate would depend upon what he said next.

CHAPTER XVIII

A GAME OF BLUFF

"Thy second question, O pertinacious one?" said the Jinnee, impatiently. He was standing with folded arms looking down on Horace, who was still seated on the narrow cornice, not daring to glance below again, lest he should lose his head altogether.

"I'm coming to it," said Ventimore; "I want to know why you should propose to dash me to pieces in this barbarous way as a return for letting you out of that bottle. Were you so comfortable in it as all that?"

"In the bottle I was at least suffered to rest, and none molested me. But in releasing me thou didst perfidiously conceal from me that Suleyman was dead and gone, and that there reigneth one in his stead mightier a thousand-fold, who afflicteth our race with labours and tortures exceeding all the punishments of Suleyman."

"What on earth have you got into your head now? You can't mean the Lord Mayor?"

"Whom else?" said the Jinnee, solemnly. "And though, for this once, by a device I have evaded his vengeance, yet do I know full well that either by virtue of the magic jewel upon his breast, or through that malignant monster with the myriad ears and eyes and tongues, which thou callest 'The Press,' I shall inevitably fall into his power before long."

For the life of him, in spite of his desperate plight, Horace could not help laughing. "I beg your pardon, Mr. Fakrash," he said, as soon as he could speak, "but—the Lord Mayor! It's really too absurd. Why, he wouldn't hurt a hair on a fly's head!"

"Seek not to deceive me further!" said Fakrash, furiously. "Didst thou not inform me with thy own mouth that the spirits of Earth, Air, Water, and Fire were subject to his will? Have I no eyes? Do I not behold from here the labours of my captive brethren? What are those on yonder bridges but enslaved Jinn, shrieking and groaning in clanking fetters, and snorting forth steam, as they drag their wheeled burdens behind them? Are there not others toiling, with panting efforts, through the sluggish waters; others again, imprisoned in lofty pillars, from which the smoke of their breath ascendeth even unto Heaven? Doth not the air throb and quiver with their restless struggles as they writhe below in darkness and torment? And thou hast the shamelessness to pretend that these things are done in the Lord Mayor's own realms without his knowledge! Verily thou must take me for a fool!"

"After all," reflected Ventimore, "if he chooses to consider that railway engines and steamers, and machinery generally, are inhabited by so many Jinn 'doing time,' it's not to my interest to undeceive him—indeed, it's quite the contrary!"

"I wasn't aware the Lord Mayor had so much power as all that," he said; "but very likely you're right. And if you're so anxious to keep in favour with him, it would be a great mistake to kill me. That would annoy him."

"Not so," said the Jinnee, "for I should declare that thou hadst spoken slightingly of him in my hearing, and that I had slain thee on that account."

"Your proper course," said Horace, "would be to hand me over to him, and let him deal with the case. Much more regular."

"That may be," said Fakrash; "but I have conceived so bitter a hatred to thee by reason of thy insolence and treachery, that I cannot forego the delight of slaying thee with my own hand."

"Can't you really?" said Horace, on the verge of despair. "And then, what will you do?"

"Then," replied the Jinnee, "I shall flee away to Arabia, where I shall be safe."

"Don't you be too sure of that!" said Horace. "You see all those wires stretched on poles down there? Those are the pathways of certain Jinn known as electric currents, and the Lord Mayor could send a message along them which would be at Baghdad before you had flown farther than Folkestone. And I may mention that Arabia is now more or less under British jurisdiction."

He was bluffing, of course, for he knew perfectly well that, even if any extradition treaty could be put in force, the arrest of a Jinnee would be no easy matter.

"Thou art of opinion, then, that I should be no safer in mine own country?" inquired Fakrash.

"I swear by the name of the Lord Mayor (to whom be all reverence!)" said Horace, "that there is no land you could fly to where you would be any safer than you are here."

"If I were but sealed up in my bottle once more," said the Jinnee, "would not even the Lord Mayor have respect unto the seal of Suleyman, and forbear to disturb me?"

"Why, of course he would!" cried Horace, hardly daring to believe his ears. "That's really a brilliant idea of yours, my dear Mr. Fakrash."

"And in the bottle I should not be compelled to work," continued the Jinnee. "For labour of all kinds hath ever been abhorrent unto me."

"I can quite understand that," said Horace, sympathetically. "Just imagine your having to drag an excursion train to the seaside on a Bank Holiday, or being condemned to print off a cheap comic paper, or even the War Cry, when you might be leading a snug and idle existence in your bottle. If I were you, I should go and get inside it at once. Suppose we go back to Vincent Square and find it?"

"I shall return to the bottle, since in that alone there is safety," said the Jinnee. "But I shall return alone."

"Alone!" cried Horace. "You're not going to leave me stuck up here all by myself?"

"By no means," said the Jinnee. "Have I not said that I am about to cast thee to perdition? Too long have I delayed in the accomplishment of this duty."

Once more Horace gave himself up for lost; which was doubly bitter, just when he had begun to consider that the danger was past. But even then, he was determined to fight to the last.

"One moment," he said. "Of course, if you've set your heart on pitching me over, you must. Only—I may be quite mistaken—but I don't quite see how you are going to manage the rest of your programme without me, that's all."

"O deficient in intelligence!" cried the Jinnee. "What assistance canst thou render me?"

"Well," said Horace, "of course, you can get into the bottle alone—that's simple enough. But the difficulty I see is this: Are you quite sure you can put the cap on yourself—from the inside, you know?" If he can, he thought, "I'm done for!"

"That," began the Jinnee, with his usual confidence "will be the easiest of—nay," he corrected himself, "there be things that not even the Jinn themselves can accomplish, and one of them is to seal a vessel while remaining in it. I am indebted to thee for reminding me thereof."

"Not at all," said Ventimore. "I shall be delighted to come and seal you up comfortably myself."

"Again thou speakest folly," exclaimed the Jinnee. "How canst thou seal me up after I have dashed thee into a thousand pieces?"

"That," said Horace, with all the urbanity he could command, "is precisely the difficulty I was trying to convey."

"There will be no difficulty, for as soon as I am in the bottle I shall summon certain inferior Efreets, and they will replace the seal."

"When you are once in the bottle," said Horace, at a venture, "you probably won't be in a position to summon anybody."

"Before I get into the bottle, then!" said the Jinnee, impatiently. "Thou dost but juggle with words!"

"But about those Efreets," persisted Horace. "You know what Efreets are! How can you be sure that, when they've got you in the bottle, they won't hand you over to the Lord Mayor? I shouldn't trust them myself—but, of course, you know best!"

"Whom shall I trust, then?" said Fakrash, frowning.

"I'm sure I don't know. It's rather a pity you're so determined to destroy me, because, as it happens, I'm just the one person living who could be depended on to seal you up and keep your secret. However, that's your affair. After all, why should I care what becomes of you? I shan't be there!"

"Even at this hour," said the Jinnee, undecidedly, "I might find it in my heart to spare thee, were I but sure that thou wouldst be faithful unto me!"

"I should have thought I was more to be trusted than one of your beastly Efreets!" said Horace, with well-assumed indifference. "But never mind, I don't know that I care, after all. I've nothing particular to live for now. You've ruined me pretty thoroughly, and you may as well finish your work. I've a good mind to jump over, and save you the trouble. Perhaps, when you see me bouncing down that dome, you'll be sorry!"

"Refrain from rashness!" said the Jinnee, hastily, without suspecting that Ventimore had no serious intention of carrying out his threat. "If thou wilt do as thou art bidden, I will not only pardon thee, but grant thee all that thou desirest."

"Take me back to Vincent Square first," said Horace. "This is not the place to discuss business."

"Thou sayest rightly," replied the Jinnee; "hold fast to my sleeve, and I will transport thee to thine abode."

"Not till you promise to play fair," said Horace, pausing on the brink of the ledge. "Remember, if you let me go now you drop the only friend you've got in the world!"

"May I be thy ransom!" replied Fakrash. "There shall not be harmed a hair of thy head!"

Even then Horace had his misgivings; but as there was no other way of getting off that cornice, he decided to take the risk. And, as it proved, he acted judiciously, for the Jinnee flew to Vincent Square with honourable precision, and dropped him neatly into the armchair in which he had little hoped ever to find himself again.

"I have brought thee hither," said Fakrash, "and yet I am persuaded that thou art even now devising treachery against me, and wilt betray me if thou canst."

Horace was about to assure him once more that no one could be more anxious than himself to see him safely back in his bottle, when he recollected that it was impolitic to appear too eager.

"After the way you've behaved," he said, "I'm not at all sure that I ought to help you. Still, I said I would, on certain conditions, and I'll keep my word."

"Conditions!" thundered the Jinnee. "Wilt thou bargain with me yet further?"

"My excellent friend," said Horace quietly, "you know perfectly well that you can't get yourself safely sealed up again in that bottle without my assistance. If you don't like my terms, and prefer to take your chance of finding an Efreet who is willing to brave the Lord Mayor, well, you've only to say so."

"I have loaded thee with all manner of riches and favours, and I will bestow no more upon thee," said the Jinnee, sullenly. "Nay, in token of my displeasure, I will deprive thee even of such gifts as thou hast retained." He pointed his grey forefinger at Ventimore, whose turban and jewelled robes instantly shrivelled into cobwebs and tinder, and fluttered to the carpet in filmy shreds, leaving him in nothing but his underclothing.

"That only shows what a nasty temper you're in," said Horace, blandly, "and doesn't annoy me in the least. If you'll excuse me, I'll go and put on some things I can feel more at home in; and perhaps by the time I return you'll have cooled down."

He slipped on some clothes hurriedly and re-entered the sitting-room. "Now, Mr. Fakrash," he said, "we'll have this out. You talk of having loaded me with benefits. You seem to consider I ought to be grateful to you. In Heaven's name, for what? I've been as forbearing as possible all this time, because I gave you credit for meaning well. Now, I'll speak plainly. I told you from the first, and I tell you now, that I want no riches nor honours from you. The one real good turn you did me was bringing me that client, and you spoilt that because you would insist on building the palace yourself, instead of leaving it to me! As for the rest—here am I, a ruined and discredited man, with a client who probably supposes I'm in league with the Devil; with the girl I love, and might have married, believing that I have left her to marry a Princess; and her father, unable ever to forgive me for having seen him as a one-eyed mule. In short, I'm in such a mess all round that I don't care two straws whether I live or die!"

"What is all this to me?" said the Jinnee.

"Only this—that unless you can see your way to putting things straight for me, I'm hanged if I take the trouble to seal you up in that bottle!"

"How am I to put things straight for thee?" cried Fakrash, peevishly.

"If you could make all those people entirely forget that affair in the Guildhall, you can make my friends forget the brass bottle and everything connected with it, can't you?"

"There would be no difficulty in that," Fakrash admitted.

"Well, do it—and I'll swear to seal you up in the bottle exactly as if you had never been out of it, and pitch you into the deepest part of the Thames, where no one will ever disturb you."

"First produce the bottle, then," said Fakrash, "for I cannot believe but that thou hast some lurking guile in thy heart."

"I'll ring for my landlady and have the bottle brought up," said Horace. "Perhaps that will satisfy you? Stay, you'd better not let her see you."

"I will render myself invisible," said the Jinnee, suiting the action to his words. "But beware lest thou play me false," his voice continued, "for I shall hear thee!"

"So you've come in, Mr. Ventimore?" said Mrs. Rapkin, as she entered. "And without the furrin gentleman? I was surprised, and so was Rapkin the same, to see you ridin' off this morning in the gorgious chariot and 'osses, and dressed up that lovely! 'Depend upon it,' I says to Rapkin, I says, 'depend upon it, Mr. Ventimore'll be sent for to Buckinham Pallis, if it ain't Windsor Castle!'"

"Never mind that now," said Horace, impatiently; "I want that brass bottle I bought the other day. Bring it up at once, please."

"I thought you said the other day you never wanted to set eyes on it again, and I was to do as I pleased with it, sir?"

"Well, I've changed my mind, so let me have it, quick."

"I'm sure I'm very sorry, sir, but that you can't, because Rapkin, not wishful to have the place lumbered up with rubbish, disposed of it on'y last night to a gentleman as keeps a rag and bone emporium off the Bridge Road, and 'alf-a-crown was the most he'd give for it, sir."

"Give me his name," said Horace.

"Dilger, sir—Emanuel Dilger. When Rapkin comes in I'm sure he'd go round with pleasure, and see about it, if required."

"I'll go round myself," said Horace. "It's all right, Mrs. Rapkin, quite a natural mistake on your part, but—but I happen to want the bottle again. You needn't stay."

"O thou smooth-faced and double-tongued one!" said the Jinnee, after she had gone, as he reappeared to view. "Did I not foresee that thou wouldst deal crookedly? Restore unto me my bottle!"

"I'll go and get it at once," said Horace; "I shan't be five minutes." And he prepared to go.

"Thou shalt not leave this house," cried Fakrash, "for I perceive plainly that this is but a device of thine to escape and betray me to the Press Devil!"

"If you can't see," said Horace, angrily, "that I'm quite as anxious to see you safely back in that confounded bottle as ever you can be to get there, you must be pretty dense! Can't you understand? The bottle's sold, and I can't buy it back without going out. Don't be so infernally unreasonable!"

"Go, then," said the Jinnee, "and I will await thy return here. But know this: that if thou delayest long or returnest without my bottle, I shall know that thou art a traitor, and will visit thee and those who are dear to thee with the most unpleasant punishments!"

"I'll be back in half an hour, at most," said Horace, feeling that this would allow him ample margin, and thankful that it did not occur to Fakrash to go in person.

He put on his hat, and hurried off in the gathering dusk. He had some little trouble in finding Mr. Dilger's establishment, which was a dirty, dusty little place in a back street, with a few deplorable old chairs, rickety washstands, and rusty fenders outside, and the interior almost completely blocked by piles of dingy mattresses, empty clock-cases, tarnished and cracked mirrors, broken lamps, damaged picture-frames, and everything else which one would imagine could have no possible value for any human being. But in all this collection of worthless curios the brass bottle was nowhere to be seen.

Ventimore went in and found a youth of about thirteen straining his eyes in the fading light over one of those halfpenny humorous journals which, thanks to an improved system of education, at least eighty per cent. of our juvenile population are now enabled to appreciate.

"I want to see Mr. Dilger," he began.

"You can't," said the youth. "'Cause he ain't in. He's attending of an auction."

"When will he be in, do you know?"

"Might be back to his tea—but I wasn't to expect him not before supper."

"You don't happen to have any old metal bottles—copper or—or brass would do—for sale?"

"You don't git at me like that! Bottles is made o' glorss."

"Well, a jar, then—a big brass pot—anything of that kind?"

"Don't keep 'em," said the boy, and buried himself once more in his copy of "Spicy Sniggers."

"I'll just look round," said Horace, and began to poke about with a sinking heart, and a horrid dread that he might have come to the wrong shop, for the big pot-bellied vessel certainly did not seem to be there. At last, to his unspeakable joy, he discovered it under a piece of tattered drugget. "Why, this is the sort of thing I meant," he said, feeling in his pocket and discovering that he had exactly a sovereign. "How much do you want for it?"

"I dunno," said the boy.

"I don't mind three shillings," said Horace, who did not wish to appear too keen at first.

"I'll tell the guv'nor when he comes in," was the reply, "and you can look in later."

"I want it at once," insisted Horace. "Come, I'll give you three-and-six for it."

"It's more than it's wurf," replied the candid youth.

"Perhaps," said Horace, "but I'm rather pressed for time. If you'll change this sovereign, I'll take the bottle away with me."

"You seem uncommon anxious to get 'old on it, mister!" said the boy, with sudden suspicion.

"Nonsense!" said Horace. "I live close by, and I thought I might as well take it, that's all."

"Oh, if that's all, you can wait till the guv'nor's in."

"I—I mayn't be passing this way again for some time," said Horace.

"Bound to be, if you live close by," and the provoking youth returned to his "Sniggers."

"Do you call this attending to your master's business?" said Horace. "Listen to me, you young rascal. I'll give you five shillings for it. You're not going to be fool enough to refuse an offer like that?"

"I ain't goin' to be fool enough to refuse it—nor yet I ain't goin' to be fool enough to take it, 'cause I'm only 'ere to see as nobody don't come in and sneak fings. I ain't got no authority to sell anyfink, and I don't know the proice o' nuffink, so there you 'ave it."

"Take the five shillings," said Horace, "and if it's too little I'll come round and settle with your master later."

"I thought you said you wasn't likely to be porsin' again? No, mister, you don't kid me that way!"

Horace had a mad impulse to snatch up the precious bottle then and there and make off with it, and might have yielded to the temptation, with disastrous consequences, had not an elderly man entered the shop at that moment. He was bent, and wore rather more fluff and flue upon his person than most well-dressed people would consider necessary, but he came in with a certain air of authority, nevertheless.

"Mr. Dilger, sir," piped the youth, "'ere's a gent took a fancy to this 'ere brass pot o' yours. Says he must 'ave it. Five shillings he'd got to, but I told him he'd 'ave to wait till you come in."

"Quite right, my lad!" said Mr. Dilger, cocking a watery but sharp old eye at Horace. "Five shillings! Ah, sir, you can't know much about these hold brass antiquities to make an orfer like that."

"I know as much as most people," said Horace. "But let us say six shillings."

"Couldn't be done, sir; couldn't indeed. Why, I give a pound for it myself at Christie's, as sure as I'm standin' 'ere in the presence o' my Maker, and you a sinner!" he declared impressively, if rather ambiguously.

"Your memory is not quite accurate," said Horace. "You bought it last night from a man of the name of Rapkin, who lets lodgings in Vincent Square, and you paid exactly half a crown for it."

"If you say so I dare say it's correct, sir," said Mr. Dilger, without exhibiting the least confusion. "And if I did buy it off Mr. Rapkin, he's a respectable party, and ain't likely to have come by it dishonest."

"I never said he did. What will you take for the thing?"

"Well, just look at the work in it. They don't turn out the like o' that nowadays. Dutch, that is; what they used for to put their milk and such-like in."

"Damn it!" said Horace, completely losing his temper. "I know what it was used for. Will you tell me what you want for it?"

"I couldn't let a curiosity like that go a penny under thirty shillings," said Mr. Dilger, affectionately. "It would be robbin' myself."

"I'll give you a sovereign for it—there," said Horace. "You know best what profit that represents. That's my last word."

"My last word to that, sir, is good hevenin'," said the worthy man.

"Good evening, then," said Horace, and walked out of the shop; rather to bring Mr. Dilger to terms than because he really meant to abandon the bottle, for he dared not go back without it, and he had nothing about him just then on which he could raise the extra ten shillings, supposing the dealer refused to trust him for the balance—and the time was growing dangerously short.

Fortunately the well-worn ruse succeeded, for Mr. Dilger ran out after him and laid an unwashed claw upon his coat-sleeve. "Don't go, mister," he said; "I like to do business if I can; though, 'pon my word and honour, a sovereign for a work o' art like that! Well, just for luck and bein' my birthday, we'll call it a deal."

Horace handed over the coin, which left him with a few pence. "There ought to be a lid or stopper of some sort," he said suddenly. "What have you done with that?"

"No, sir, there you're mistook, you are, indeed. I do assure you you never see a pot of this partickler pattern with a lid to it. Never!"

"Oh, don't you, though?" said Horace. "I know better. Never mind," he said, as he recollected that the seal was in Fakrash's possession. "I'll take it as it is. Don't trouble to wrap it up. I'm in rather a hurry."

It was almost dark when he got back to his rooms, where he found the Jinnee shaking with mingled rage and apprehension.

"No welcome to thee!" he cried. "Dilatory dog that thou art! Hadst thou delayed another minute, I would have called down some calamity upon thee."

"Well, you need not trouble yourself to do that now," returned Ventimore. "Here's your bottle, and you can creep into it as soon as you please."

"But the seal!" shrieked the Jinnee. "What hast thou done with the seal which was upon the bottle?"

"Why, you've got it yourself, of course," said Horace, "in one of your pockets."

"O thou of base antecedents!" howled Fakrash, shaking out his flowing draperies. "How should I have the seal? This is but a fresh device of thine to undo me!"

"Don't talk rubbish!" retorted Horace. "You made the Professor give it up to you yesterday. You must have lost it somewhere or other. Never mind! I'll get a large cork or bung, which will do just as well. And I've lots of sealing-wax."

"I will have no seal but the seal of Suleyman!" declared the Jinnee. "For with no other will there be security. Verily I believe that that accursed sage, thy friend, hath contrived by some cunning to get the seal once more into his hands. I will go at once to his abode and compel him to restore it."

"I wouldn't," said Horace, feeling extremely uneasy, for it was evidently a much simpler thing to let a Jinnee out of a bottle than to get him in again. "He's quite incapable of taking it. And if you go out now you'll only make a fuss and attract the attention of the Press, which I thought you rather wanted to avoid."

"I shall attire myself in the garments of a mortal—even those I assumed on a former occasion," said Fakrash, and as he spoke his outer robes modernised into a frock-coat. "Thus shall I escape attention."

"Wait one moment," said Horace. "What is that bulge in your breast-pocket?"

"Of a truth," said the Jinnee, looking relieved but not a little foolish as he extracted the object, "it is indeed the seal."

"You're in such a hurry to think the worst of everybody, you see!" said Horace. "Now, do try to carry away with you into your seclusion a better opinion of human nature."

"Perdition to all the people of this age!" cried Fakrash, re-assuming his green robe and turban, "for I now put no faith in human beings and would afflict them all, were not the Lord Mayor (on whom be peace!) mightier than I. Therefore, while it is yet time, take thou the stopper, and swear that, after I am in this bottle, thou wilt seal it as before and cast it into deep waters, where no eye will look upon it more!"

"With all the pleasure in the world!" said Horace; "only you must keep your part of the bargain first. You will kindly obliterate all recollection of yourself and the brass bottle from the minds of every human being who has had anything to do with you or it."

"Not so," objected the Jinnee, "for thus wouldst thou forget thy compact."

"Oh, very well, leave me out, then," said Horace. "Not that anything could make me forget you!"

Fakrash swept his right hand round in a half circle. "It is accomplished," he said. "All recollection of myself and yonder bottle is now erased from the memories of every one but thyself."

"But how about my client?" said Horace. "I can't afford to lose him, you know."

"He shall return unto thee," said the Jinnee, trembling with impatience. "Now perform thy share."

Horace had triumphed. It had been a long and desperate duel with this singular being, who was at once so crafty and so childlike, so credulous and so suspicious, so benevolent and so malign. Again and again he had despaired of victory, but he had won at last. In another minute or so this formidable Jinnee would be safely bottled once more, and powerless to intermeddle and plague him for the future.

And yet, in the very moment of triumph, quixotic as such scruples may seem to some, Ventimore's conscience smote him. He could not help a certain pity for the old creature, who was shaking there convulsively prepared to re-enter his bottle-prison rather than incur a wholly imaginary doom. Fakrash had aged visibly within the last hour; now he looked even older than his three thousand and odd years. True, he had led Horace a fearful life of late, but at first, at least, his intentions had been good. His gratitude, if mistaken in its form, was the sign of a generous disposition. Not every Jinnee, surely, would have endeavoured to press untold millions and honours and dignities of all kinds upon him, in return for a service which most mortals would have considered amply repaid by a brace of birds and an invitation to an evening party.

And how was Horace treating him? He was taking what, in his heart, he felt to be a rather mean advantage of the Jinnee's ignorance of modern life to cajole him into returning to his captivity. Why not suffer him to live out the brief remainder of his years (for he could hardly last more than another century or two at most) in freedom? Fakrash had learnt his lesson: he was not likely to interfere again in human affairs; he might find his way back to the Palace of the Mountain of the Clouds and end his days there, in peaceful enjoyment of the society of such of the Jinn as might still survive unbottled.

So, obeying—against his own interests—some kindlier impulse, Horace made an effort to deter the Jinnee, who was already hovering in air above the neck of the bottle in a swirl of revolving draperies, like some blundering old bee vainly endeavouring to hit the opening into his hive.

"Mr. Fakrash," he cried, "before you go any farther, listen to me. There's no real necessity, after all, for you to go back to your bottle. If you'll only wait a little—"

But the Jinnee, who had now swelled to gigantic proportions, and whose form and features were only dimly recognisable through the wreaths of black vapour in which he was involved, answered him from his pillar of smoke in a terrible voice. "Wouldst thou still persuade me to linger?" he cried. "Hold thy peace and be ready to fulfil thine undertaking."

"But, look here," persisted Horace. "I should feel such a brute if I sealed you up without telling you—" The whirling and roaring column, in shape like an inverted cone, was being fast sucked down into the vessel, till only a semi-materialised but highly infuriated head was left above the neck of the bottle.

"Must I tarry," it cried, "till the Lord Mayor arrive with his Memlooks, and the hour of safety is expired? By my head, if thou delayest another instant, I will put no more faith in thee! And I will come forth once more, and afflict thee and thy friends—ay, and all the dwellers in this accursed city—with the most painful and unheard-of calamities."

And, with these words, the head sank into the bottle with a loud clap resembling thunder.

Horace hesitated no longer. The Jinnee himself had absolved him from all further scruples; to imperil Sylvia and her parents—not to mention all London—out of consideration for one obstinate and obnoxious old demon, would clearly be carrying sentiment much too far.

Accordingly, he made a rush for the jar and slipped the metal cover over the mouth of the neck, which was so hot that it blistered his fingers, and, seizing the poker, he hammered down the secret catch until the lid fitted as closely as Suleyman himself could have required.

Then he stuffed the bottle into a kit-bag, adding a few coals to give it extra weight, and toiled off with it to the nearest steamboat pier, where he spent his remaining pence in purchasing a ticket to the Temple.

Next day the following paragraph appeared in one of the evening papers, which probably had more space than usual at its disposal:

"SINGULAR OCCURRENCE ON A PENNY STEAMER

"A gentleman on board one of the Thames steamboats (so we are informed by an eye-witness) met with a somewhat ludicrous mishap yesterday evening. It appears that he had with him a small portmanteau, or large hand-bag, which he was supporting on the rail of the stern bulwark. Just as the vessel was opposite the Savoy Hotel he incautiously raised his hand to the brim of his hat, thereby releasing hold of the bag, which overbalanced itself and fell into the deepest part of the river, where it instantly sank. The owner (whose carelessness occasioned considerable amusement to passengers in his immediate vicinity) appeared no little disconcerted by the oversight, and was not unnaturally reticent as to the amount of his loss, though he was understood to state that the bag contained nothing of any great value. However this may be, he has probably learnt a lesson which will render him more careful in future."

THE EPILOGUE

On a certain evening in May Horace Ventimore dined in a private room at the Savoy, as one of the guests of Mr. Samuel Wackerbath. In fact, he might almost be said to be the guest of the evening, as the dinner was given by way of celebrating the completion of the host's new country house at Lipsfield, of which Horace was the architect, and also to congratulate him on his approaching marriage (which was fixed to take place early in the following month) with Miss Sylvia Futvoye.

"Quite a small and friendly party!" said Mr. Wackerbath, looking round on his numerous sons and daughters, as he greeted Horace in the reception-room. "Only ourselves, you see, Miss Futvoye, a young lady with whom you are fairly well acquainted, and her people, and an old schoolfellow of mine and his wife, who are not yet arrived. He's a man of considerable eminence," he added, with a roll of reflected importance in his voice; "quite worth your cultivating. Sir Lawrence Pountney, his name is. I don't know if you remember him, but he discharged the onerous duties of Lord Mayor of London the year before last, and acquitted himself very creditably—in fact, he got a baronetcy for it."

As the year before last was the year in which Horace had paid his involuntary visit to the Guildhall, he was able to reply with truth that he did remember Sir Lawrence.

He was not altogether comfortable when the ex-Lord-Mayor was announced, for it would have been more than awkward if Sir Lawrence had chanced to remember him. Fortunately, he gave no sign that he did so, though his manner was graciousness itself. "Delighted, my dear Mr. Ventimore," he said pressing Horace's hand almost as warmly as he had done that October day of the dais, "most delighted to make your acquaintance! I am always glad to meet a rising young man, and I hear that the house you have designed for my old friend here is a perfect palace—a marvel, sir!"

"I knew he was my man," declared Mr. Wackerbath, as Horace modestly disclaimed Sir Lawrence's compliment. "You remember, Pountney, my dear fellow, that day when we were crossing Westminster Bridge together, and I was telling you I thought of building? 'Go to one of the leading men—an R.A. and all that sort of thing,' you said, 'then you'll be sure of getting your money's worth.' But I said, 'No, I like to choose for myself; to—ah—exercise my own judgment in these matters. And there's a young fellow I have in my eye who'll beat 'em all, if he's given the chance. I'm off to see him now.' And off I went to Great Cloister Street (for he hadn't those palatial offices of his in Victoria Street at that time) without losing another instant, and dropped in on him with my little commission. Didn't I, Ventimore?"

"You did indeed," said Horace, wondering how far these reminiscences would go.

"And," continued Mr. Wackerbath, patting Horace on the shoulder, "from that day to this I've never had a moment's reason to regret it. We've worked in perfect sympathy. His ideas coincided with mine. I think he found that I met him, so to speak, on all fours."

Ventimore assented, though it struck him that a happier expression might, and would, have been employed if his client had remembered one particular interview in which he had not figured to advantage.

They went in to dinner, in a room sumptuously decorated with panels of grey-green brocade and softly shaded lamps, and screens of gilded leather; through the centre of the table rose a tall palm, its boughs hung with small electric globes like magic fruits.

"This palm," said the Professor, who was in high good humour, "really gives quite an Oriental look to the table. Personally, I think we might reproduce the Arabian style of decoration and arrangement generally in our homes with great advantage. I often wonder it never occurred to my future son-in-law there to turn his talents in that direction and design an Oriental interior for himself. Nothing more comfortable and luxurious—for a bachelor's purposes."

"I'm sure," said his wife, "Horace managed to make himself quite comfortable enough as it was. He has the most delightful rooms in Vincent Square." Ventimore heard her remark to Sir Lawrence: "I shall never forget the first time we dined there, just after my daughter and he were engaged. I was quite astonished: everything was so perfect—quite simple, you know, but so ingeniously arranged, and his landlady such an excellent cook, too! Still, of course, in many ways, it will be nicer for him to have a home of his own."

"With such a beautiful and charming companion to share it with," said Sir Lawrence, in his most florid manner, "the—ah—poorest home would prove a Paradise indeed! And I suppose now, my dear young lady," he added, raising his voice to address Sylvia, "you are busy making your future abode as exquisite as taste and research can render it, ransacking all the furniture shops in London for treasures, and going about to auctions—or do you—ah—delegate that department to Mr. Ventimore?"

"I do go about to old furniture shops, Sir Lawrence," she said, "but not auctions. I'm afraid I should only get just the thing I didn't want if I tried to bid.... And," she added, in a lower voice, turning to Horace, "I don't believe you would be a bit more successful, Horace!"

"What makes you say that, Sylvia?" he asked, with a start.

"Why, do you mean to say you've forgotten how you went to that auction for papa, and came away without having managed to get a single thing?" she said. "What a short memory you must have!"

There was only tender mockery in her eyes; absolutely no recollection of the sinister purchase he had made at that sale, or how nearly it had separated them for ever. So he hastened to admit that perhaps he had not been particularly successful at the auction in question.

Sir Lawrence next addressed him across the table. "I was just telling Mrs. Futvoye," he said, "how much I regretted that I had not the privilege of your acquaintance during my year of office. A Lord Mayor, as you doubtless know, has exceptional facilities for exercising hospitality, and it would have afforded me real pleasure if your first visit to the Guildhall could have been paid under my—hm—ha—auspices."

"You are very kind," said Horace, very much on his guard; "I could not wish to pay it under better."

"I flatter myself," said the ex-Lord Mayor, "that, while in office, I did my humble best to maintain the traditions of the City, and I was fortunate enough to have the honour of receiving more than the average number of celebrities as guests. But I had one great disappointment, I must tell you. It had always been a dream of mine that it might fall to my lot to present some distinguished fellow-countryman with the freedom of the City. By some curious chance, when the opportunity seemed about to occur, the thing was put off and I missed it—missed it by the nearest hair-breadth!"

"Ah, well, Sir Lawrence," said Ventimore, "one can't have everything!"

"For my part," put in Lady Pountney, who had only caught a word or two of her husband's remarks, "what I miss most is having the sentinels present arms whenever I went out for a drive. They did it so nicely and respectfully. I confess I enjoyed that. My husband never cared much for it. Indeed, he wouldn't even use the State coach unless he was absolutely obliged. He was as obstinate as a mule about it!"

"I see, Lady Pountney," the Professor put in, "that you share the common prejudice against mules. It's quite a mistaken one. The mule has never been properly appreciated in this country. He is really the gentlest and most docile of creatures!"

"I can't say I like them myself," said Lady Pountney; "such a mongrel sort of animal—neither one thing nor the other!"

"And they're hideous too, Anthony," added his wife. "And not at all clever!"

"There you're mistaken, my dear," said the Professor; "they are capable of almost human intelligence. I have had considerable personal experience of what a mule can do," he informed Lady Pountney, who seemed still incredulous. "More than most people indeed, and I can assure you, my dear Lady Pountney, that they readily adapt themselves to almost any environment, and will endure the greatest hardships without exhibiting any signs of distress. I see by your expression, Ventimore, that you don't agree with me, eh?"

Horace had to set his teeth hard for a moment, lest he should disgrace himself by a peal of untimely mirth—but by a strong effort of will he managed to command his muscles.

"Well, sir," he said, "I've only chanced to come into close contact with one mule in my life, and, frankly, I've no desire to repeat the experience."

"You happened to come upon an unfavourable specimen, that's all," said the Professor. "There are exceptions to every rule."

"This animal," Horace said, "was certainly exceptional enough in every way."

"Do tell us all about it," pleaded one of the Miss Wackerbaths, and all the ladies joined in the entreaty until Horace found himself under the necessity of improvising a story, which, it must be confessed, fell exceedingly flat.

This final ordeal past, he grew silent and thoughtful, as he sat there by Sylvia's side, looking out through the glazed gallery outside upon the spring foliage along the Embankment, the opaline river, and the shot towers and buildings on the opposite bank glowing warm brown against an evening sky of silvery blue.

Not for the first time did it seem strange, incredible almost, to him that all these people should be so utterly without any recollection of events which surely might have been expected to leave some trace upon the least retentive memory—and yet it only proved once more how thoroughly and honourably the old Jinnee, now slumbering placidly in his bottle deep down in unfathomable mud, opposite the very spot where they were dining, had fulfilled his last undertaking.

Fakrash, the brass bottle, and all the fantastic and embarrassing performances were indeed as totally forgotten as though they had never been.

And it is but too probable that even this modest and veracious account of them will prove to have been included in the general act of oblivion—though the author will trust as long as possible that Fakrash-el-Aamash may have neglected to provide for this particular case, and that the history of the Brass Bottle may thus be permitted to linger awhile in the memories of some at least of its readers.

F. Anstey – A Concise Bibliography

Vice Versa (1882)
The Black Poodle And Other Tales (1884)
The Giant's Robe (1884)
The Tinted Venus (1885)

A Fallen Idol (1886)
Burglar Bill And Other Pieces (1888)
The Pariah (1889)
Voces Populi (1890)
Tourmalin's Time Cheques (1891)
Mr. Punch's Model Music-Hall Songs And Dramas (1892)
The Talking Horse And Other Tales (1892)
The Travelling Companions (1892)
The Man From Blankley's And Other Sketches (1893)
Mr. Punch's Pocket Ibsen (1893)
Under the Rose (1894)
Lyre and Lancet (1895)
The Statement of Stella Maberly, Written By Herself (1896)
Baboo Jabberjee, B. A. (1897)
Puppets At Large (1897)
Love Among The Lions (1898)
Paleface And Redskin (1898)
The Brass Bottle (1900)
A Bayard From Bengal (1902)
Only Toys! (1903)
Salted Almonds (1906)
Winnie, An Everyday Story (1909)
In Brief Authority (1915)
Percy and Others (1915)
The Last Load (1925)
The Would-Be Gentleman (Adapted From Molière's Le Bourgeois gentilhomme) (1927)
The Imaginary Invalid (Adapted From Molière's Le Malade imaginaire) (1929)
Humour and Fantasy (1931)
A Long Retrospect (1936)